Praise for PAULA QUINN
and her novels

Lord of Temptation

"Will enchant and entertain . . . Passion, danger, treachery, and heartbreak fill the pages of this splendid novel . . . don't miss *Lord of Temptation*."
—RomRevToday.com

"Quinn's lively romance . . . offers two spirited protagonists as well as engaging minor characters . . . The sharp repartee and dramatic finale make this a pleasant read."
—*Publishers Weekly*

"Quinn wins readers' hearts with a light touch, even as she invokes strong themes of slavery, freedom, and the need for independence."
—*Romantic Times BOOKclub Magazine*

"A truly magnificent tale . . . Dante is a perfect hero and lover and Gianelle is special—perfect for each other. The passion is fantastic—unbeatable!"
—RomanceReviewsMag.com

Lord of Desire

"Four stars! . . . Fast-paced and brimming with biting, sexy repartee, and a sensual cat-and-mouse game."
—*Romantic Times BOOKclub Magazine*

more . . .

LORD
of
SEDUCTION

Also by Paula Quinn

Lord of Desire
Lord of Temptation

LORD
of
SEDUCTION

Paula Quinn

NEW YORK   BOSTON

Copyright © 2006 by Paula Quinn
Excerpt from *Laird of the Mist* copyright © 2006 by Paula Quinn

Cover design by Diane Luger
Cover illustration by Jon Paul Ferrara
Typography by David Gatti
Book design by Stratford Publishing Services

Warner Books
Hachette Book Group USA
1271 Avenue of the Americas
New York, NY 10020
Visit our Web site at www.HachetteBookGroup.USA.com.

Printed in the United States of America

First Printing: December 2006

10 9 8 7 6 5 4 3 2 1

To my mom and dad,
You've both been through so much this year.
I admire your strength.
I hope I've inherited your courage.
I'm forever grateful for your love and support.
I will be there for you always,
as you have been for me.

Acknowledgments

MY SINCEREST THANKS to my wonderful editor, Devi Pillai, for always believing there's a perfect sculpture within the clay, and for helping me create it. Every good review I get, I have you to thank.

To Andrea Somberg, not only are you a fantastic agent, but you're an incredible person. Your honor is rare and more appreciated than this writer can find the words to express.

To Grier Horstmann, Emiley Poelker, and Lisa Googe, thank you for the endless encouragement you've given me even before I was published. I will value your friendship forever.

To Terra Codack, Janalee Ruschhaupt, and to all the wonderful ladies (and gentleman) at The Mystic Castle, thank you for your wonderful words and support. You've made me feel like a best-selling author already. I cannot thank you enough.

To Nora Harris, thank you for taking such wonderful care of my dad. Your kind smiles and tender touches helped him heal. I will never forget.

To my husband and my children, I love you.

And, most importantly, I thank God for giving me the desires of my heart.

Prologue

LADY TANON RISANDE gathered all her breath for a scream she hoped would alert her father to her peril. But a rock struck her in the shoulder, and she yelped instead. For a moment, she teetered on the thick branch in the tree she was sitting in, her huge green eyes opened wide with terror. She flailed her arms to grab hold of something and plummeted to the ground.

If it weren't for the lights swimming around her head, Tanon would have thrown up. Oh, and wouldn't it have been wonderful to do the like all over Roger deCourtenay. She thought about it while she spat a few blades of summer grass and a small pebble from her mouth.

Tanon heard Roger laughing before she lifted her face to glare at him. That is, she wanted to glare at him. *Oui*, just the way her father glowered down at Cook when he almost broke his tooth on a stone in the bread. She tried to flare her nostrils and squint her eyes all mean and dark as William had taught her, but her bottom lip began to tremble against her chin. Her eyes filled with huge tears instead.

Roger laughed harder. In fact, he laughed so hard he couldn't breathe. Bending at the middle, he held his belly with one hand and covered his mouth with the other. He must have feared some passerby wouldn't know what he was laughing at, so he released his gaping mouth to point at her and squeal afresh. It would have been mortifying enough if he didn't have an audience, but to his good fortune, he did. Most of the children living at Winchester Castle were there. Tanon could forgive Hilary and Janie Pendleton for laughing at her, as they were a bit younger than she was and didn't realize how rude they were. Henry and Thomas Drake had made nervous faces while Roger hurled his rocks at her. But like all the other children, they said nothing. Better Tanon than them. They were all afraid of Roger. Tanon was afraid of him, too. But that wasn't why she didn't pick up a rock and hurl it right back at him. She didn't want him to tell his father, the Earl of Blackburn, because his father would tell the king. And Tanon didn't ever want to make William angry with her. She wasn't afraid of William. Oh, *non,* she loved the king almost as much as she loved her own papa. He made the best faces of all. Even better than the mean scowls her mama's lady maid, Elsbeth, made.

Tanon knew Roger didn't like her. She not only refused to go along with his cruel pranks, like putting ants in the goat's milk and rubbing tree sap on Chloe the cat's paws, but she had the audacity to admonish him for being such a bully. It didn't stop him from being mean, though. When she cried at seeing poor Chloe's failed attempts to walk, Roger and the others teased her for a full se'nnight.

Right now, though, Tanon didn't care why he disliked her. Fueled by his coaxing, the other children laughed at her, called her Twiggy Tanon, and snorted like pigs when she crossed their paths, because her best friend was Petunia the pig. There was one small consolation; none of the children had ever struck her, until today. Tanon was Lord Brand the Passionate's daughter, after all. And when it came to Tanon, her papa could be even meaner than Roger.

"Twiggy Tanon dropped outta that tree like a scrawny chicken!" Roger howled with glee. When he saw Tanon ball her hands into little fists, he sobered quickly and stomped toward her. When he was satisfied that his looming presence over her was frightening enough to make her wet her skirts, he clenched his teeth and shook his fist in her face. His blond hair fell into his eyes and over the spray of freckles across his nose. "If you tell your father, I'll skin your pig and then eat her for supper."

Tanon gasped; two tears spilled over the rims of her long black lashes. Roger took one look at her and doubled over again, pointing to her mouth.

"Toothless Tanon!" he shouted and did a little dance in the grass, still holding his belly.

Tanon snapped her mouth shut, but inside she flicked her tongue across her teeth. She looked around the tall summer-green blades, spotted her tooth, and then took off running before Roger could see her sobbing.

She ran straight into the arms of her beloved William.

"Here, now, where are you running off to, little one?" William put his enormous hands on her shoulders and stopped her in her tracks. When Tanon wiped her eyes, keeping her head bent, he squatted in front of her to get a look at her face. He was scowling when Tanon peeked up at him. She wished she could look that mean. "Would you like to tell me who made you cry?" he asked.

Tanon shook her head no but caught his suspicious frown aimed at Roger and the others down the hill. An instant later, William plucked her gently from the ground. Tanon was sure her William was taller than the tree she just fell out of, but he would never drop her, and she settled into his brawny chest, safe at last. He was, after all, the king.

"Ma précieuse," he cooed after she offered him her most grateful dimple-inducing smile. "Did you know you're missing a tooth?" he asked, and then he stroked her long raven curls when she buried her face in his neck and cried for all she was worth.

Her papa was even less pleased by her appearance than she was after she peered in her mother's tiny looking glass. Tanon didn't like it, but she had to lie to her papa. She had no choice. She was sure God would forgive her. Petunia's life was at stake, after all.

"I tell you I fell out of a tree, Papa," she insisted after a long time of being questioned in William's private solar.

"And no one caused you to fall from this tree, Tanon?" Lord Brand Risande paced before his daughter with his hands folded behind his back.

Though his gaze was wonderfully warm when he looked at her, Tanon swallowed, praying he couldn't tell she was lying. She shook her head, afraid to speak lest he had some secret fatherly way of knowing her deceit by the quavering pitch of her voice.

"William told me he saw Roger deCourtenay and the

Drake boys. They had naught to do with your lost tooth or falling from the tree?"

Tanon kept a clear vision of Petunia's big brown eyes and her chubby little body in her mind to strengthen her. She would never put someone she loved, even if that some*one* was a some*thing,* in jeopardy. Still, she couldn't look her papa in the eyes when she spoke. She fingered the colorful stitching in her gown instead. "*Non,* Papa. They had naught to do with it."

Brand glanced at William, who sat casually in a huge chair beside the hearth. Brand knew his daughter often tripped over her own feet and could have easily fallen out of the tree without any help, but the way she was fidgeting in her chair told him she was lying. Whom was she trying to protect? William shrugged his massive shoulders, offering no answers to the unspoken question.

"Tanon." Her papa's voice was so soft and soothing it somehow, magically, made her look at him, and he smiled. "You're the oldest, daughter. You must remember to always set a good example for your brothers and tell the truth. I should like to know if anyone is making you unhappy. King William invited us to his home for the summer in the hopes that you would enjoy yourself and mayhap make some friends."

"Oh, but I have made a friend, Papa." Tanon grinned at him, exposing the little gaping hole where her front tooth used to be. "Petunia is my friend."

"Petunia is a pig," her father gently reminded her. William couldn't help but smile at her.

Tanon chose to ignore her father's low opinion of her closest friend. She loved Petunia, and she was certain Petunia loved her in return.

"Your mother is quite upset that you fell out of a tree," her papa told her, making her feel terrible all over again. "You could have broken your neck instead of just your tooth. Now tell me what happened." He folded his arms across his chest and stared at her, waiting.

Tanon fidgeted in her seat. She looked at William, and he winked at her. "Papa?"

"Oui?"

"Have you ever had a best friend?"

"William is my best friend."

Tanon gave William her widest smile, pleased that her papa loved him almost as much as she did. "Wouldn't you do anything to make certain no mean boys ever hurt him?"

Her papa nodded his head and then went to her chair and knelt in front of her. "Did mean boys tell you they were going to hurt Petunia?"

Tanon gasped. *"Non!"* She simply could not believe how clever her papa was! How did he know she was talking about Petunia? Oh, she lamented, now her dear sweet Petunia would surely end up on Roger deCourtenay's supper table. Huge tears welled up in her eyes, and her lower lip began to tremble. She looked at William because he had such a nice face, and she needed to stop herself from crying so that her papa wouldn't get angry and beat Roger deCourtenay's hide.

"Your papa would do anything to keep me safe, my little love," William told her, rising to his feet. That was all he did, but it brought an end to her papa's questions. "Why, I would even call it a noble thing to tell a few untruths to protect someone, or something, you love." He leaned over and kissed the top of Tanon's head. "*Oui*, noble indeed. Don't you agree, Brand?"

"I do." Her papa smiled at her, and Tanon blew out an explosive breath. "Go find your mother and let her tidy your hair. And Tanon," he called when she bolted out of her chair and skipped toward the door. "No more climbing trees."

She nodded, clearly disappointed, but didn't argue as she left.

"She lied to me to protect a pig." Brand poured two cups of ale and handed one to William before he sat down.

"*Oui*." William grinned. He couldn't have been more pleased if Hereward the Wake were found hanged in the courtyard outside. "'Tis rare to find such bravery and devotion in one so young, Brand. Brynna has done well raising her."

Brand laughed softly, leaning back in his chair. "You're a married man, William. When will you cease pining for my wife?"

"Never," the king replied. He downed his drink and let out a long sigh.

"Wales?" Brand asked, knowing what prompted his longtime friend to begin pacing.

"*Oui*, Wales. They're resilient bastards, the Welsh. *Merde*, Brand, they're savage."

"So I've heard."

"I understand why the Mercian king, Offa, sought so forcefully to keep them out of England centuries ago. Their princes fight among themselves as fervently as they fight us. Fortunately for us, all their internal wars have left them weak. My marcher lords have been able to hold them off along the borders. Still, there is resistance to our occupancy. Herefordshire has sustained particularly high losses."

"I know," Brand said. "Hugh La Morte lost his entire garrison there last spring."

"Oui." William nodded and turned to stare into the flames of the crackling hearth. "Brand, I've recently met with a Welsh prince, a descendent of King Rhodri and the son of Tewdwr Mawr, who many years ago was king of Deheubarth in the south. Rival princes have challenged his inherited territorial rights, but I've no doubt he will someday rule all of southern Wales. I've yet to see any man fight as he does. He moves at the touch of a breeze."

"Do you plan on helping him accomplish becoming king of the south, William?"

The king shrugged his shoulders. "Perhaps. He's an intelligent man. I believe that if he is able to take the throne in Deheubarth, we may be able to secure peace between our people. The marches along central Wales are almost secured. The fighting there against us has all but ceased. I wish the same for the south."

Brand nodded, listening. He knew there was something more pressing on William's mind.

"I've invited him to Winchester to meet you. He arrives in two days with his nephews."

"To meet me?" Brand laughed softly. "Why?"

William's charcoal eyes met Brand's, and the regret in them caused Brand's smile to fade. "Why, William?" he asked again, more serious this time.

"Because, *mon ami,* I've promised Tanon to Rhys's nephew Cedric."

Brand bolted to his feet, his eyes wide with disbelief,

then anger. "You would sacrifice my daughter to buy allegiance from savages?"

William looked away. Now was not the time to think about how much he loved Tanon and her parents. Now was time to be a king and make decisions for the good of England. "*Non,* I would secure the loyalty of a family with the power to end a resistance that could last another hundred years and cost more lives than you or I can comprehend. The marcher lords rule the land they inhabit by my own decree. What goes on there is almost completely out of my hands. But I must show my support for peace."

"By pledging my daughter?"

"My goddaughter," William reminded him in a somber tone. "Forgive me." He placed his hand on Brand's shoulder as he moved to pass him. "I am surrounded by enemies."

~

Tanon was curious about the news when she overheard her nurse, Rebecca, discussing the arrival of "the savage Welsh" at Winchester. Tanon had no idea who the savage Welsh was, but she decided that he must be someone of great importance when she heard her papa telling her mama that William had promised him something very precious. It must have been something precious indeed, because Mama wept for hours after that.

Tanon wanted to look pretty on the day of the savage Welsh's arrival, as she was William's friend. She even let Rebecca and Alysia tug on her curls without so much as a peep of complaint. What kind of example would she set if their guest thought William's friends were as dirty as the pigpen? Of course, Tanon didn't mind playing in the pigpen, even though it meant having to take a bath; it was fun to play in the mud with Petunia.

She wished she was allowed to play with the horses, especially Uncle Dante's white one. Ayla was so pretty with her snowy white mane and wild eyes. Everyone else was afraid of her, but not Tanon. She even hoped to ride her one day.

"Don't you look lovely this morn," William said after she entered the throne room with her parents and stopped before the king's special chair.

"Thank you, William." She flashed him a toothless grin and then moved closer to him and whispered, "You might think of telling the same to Mama. She has been crying all morn. I think it's because she is getting fatter than Clara the cow. I do hope this time she has a girl, because I am sick of brothers."

It was only after a man chuckled softly beside the king that Tanon noticed him and the group of boys staring at her. These must be William's guests, though she hadn't thought there would be so many of them. She hoped her mama never had that many boys.

They looked strange. Who ever heard of boys wearing braids? Their breeches were fashioned from hide, their patterned tunics belted with rope. And even the smallest boy carried a dagger tucked at his waist. His wildness appealed to her. She smiled at him, remembering her lessons in good manners, and because he was smiling at her. One of the taller boys behind him scowled at her. Tanon decided she didn't like that one. He had mean eyes like Roger's. The younger one had eyes of pretty blue.

Tanon curtsied to the youngest guest. "Well met."

"*Cyfarchion*," the boy replied.

She crinkled her nose and giggled. "What does that mean?"

" 'Tis *Cymraeg*. Welsh," the oldest man corrected himself with a low chuckle. He had a nice smile, like the boy. "It means 'greetings.' My nephews haven't learned all of your words yet."

Tanon hoped that when they did their voices would sound as musical as his.

"Lady Risande," William said. Tanon straightened her shoulders, knowing by his use of her title that she needed to be especially polite now. "This is Prince Rhys ap Tewdwr, and these are his nephews." He called out eight names in all, but Tanon took notice of only two. Cedric, the mean-looking one, whom William gestured to first, and Gareth, the younger boy.

"Are you all princes?" Tanon asked, spreading her wide gaze over the brothers.

"I haven't any children of my own. When I become king of Deheubarth"—Prince Rhys bent to her and winked, and she giggled at the way the last word rolled off his lips—"I will make my nephews princes."

While Tanon laughed, Gareth lifted his finger to her dimple and poked it gently. Cedric murmured something. Tanon couldn't understand it, but she knew it was rude by the way he clenched his jaw and by the way Gareth glared at him over his shoulder.

Tanon decided not to smile at Cedric anymore, since he was being so ill-mannered, but on Gareth she bestowed her friendliest grin. She hoped he would speak to her more, because the guests' peculiar words made her belly tickle.

Tanon couldn't really say whether Gareth was someone she might want to make friends with. He was proving to be as ill-mannered as his brother. He hadn't spoken a single word to her since their introduction two days ago. He ignored her when she tried to speak to him. William kept asking her to be more polite to Cedric. But he refused to use his Anglo words with her, so she didn't understand him. Also, William had told her that Cedric was ten and seven. Tanon was certain that he wouldn't want to play with her, so she gave up trying to be nice to him.

"You're very quiet, aren't you?" she asked Gareth one day, appearing beside him while he made his way toward the stables.

He didn't speak or even look at her but picked up his pace to walk ahead. Tanon clenched her hands at her sides. "I think you're a very rude mute."

That was when she noticed how soft his hair looked. His loose braid draped down his back. Two stray locks of gold dangled at his shoulders. He pivoted to look at her. He didn't say anything. He simply stood there looking too old for a boy of only ten summers. His face was pensive, his blue eyes narrowed on hers.

"My brothers speak . . ." he began and then shook his head. "My brothers said you are *gelyn*—my enemy."

The hard expression Tanon tried to maintain faded into a look of heartrending disbelief. "Your enemy? But why? What have I done?"

He looked at her as if he wanted to say something else. A breeze drifted across his face, and without another word he turned and strode away.

The next few days passed in much the same manner, but Tanon had stopped trying to talk to Gareth. Instead, she followed him. She watched him ride his horse around William's land with his uncle and his brothers. His brothers seemed to enjoy thrashing him, or at least trying to thrash him. Most of the time they failed. Even on a steed as large as her papa's, Gareth avoided being struck, either by ducking low over his saddle or arching his back.

In the great hall, Tanon covertly watched him eat his food. She even giggled when he stuck his finger in Cook Charlie's tarts to check what was inside before shoving them into his mouth.

Gareth finally did speak to Tanon at the end of his first week at Winchester. It was a lovely summer afternoon, and she was thoroughly enjoying it with Petunia. She skipped in a field of yellow daisies behind the barn, singing a song she'd heard some of the men singing in the great hall after they'd drunk all of William's wine. It wasn't a ditty fit for a young girl, but Tanon didn't know that, and she was barely mindful of her voice anyway, what with picking daisies and all.

She didn't hear Roger and the Drake brothers sneaking up on her until their scratchy voices shattered her reverie.

"Twiggy Tanon goes snort, snort, snort!" A round of laughter followed that insult before another voice rang out.

"Mayhap she sleeps with the swine, too. She certainly sings like one."

The three boys circled her and her pig. And then Roger began to chase Petunia. Tanon shouted at him to stop, but he snorted at her and laughed again. Luckily, Petunia was too quick for Roger, but he almost struck her with his foot when he tried to kick her. Tanon screamed and shook her fist at him.

"You leave her alone this instant, Roger deCourtenay, or I'll—"

"You'll what?" he challenged, his eyes gleaming with anger as he stopped chasing Petunia and took a step closer to Tanon. "What will you do?"

He lifted his hand to strike her, and Tanon squeezed her eyes shut. The Drake boys looked around to make certain no one was watching.

But someone was.

Tanon opened her eyes just in time to see Gareth reach Roger, yank him around so that they faced each other, and then shove him backward with such force Roger landed hard on his rump.

"Gwna mo chyffwrdd 'i!" Gareth shouted at him. And oh, did he look mean!

"What?" Roger deCourtenay's lip actually trembled. He wasn't laughing now.

"Bod cerddedig," her new champion growled, motioning with his hand for Roger to run away.

Tanon wanted to clap her hands before Roger and the others even had time to flee. She sprang forward, tripped over her skirts, and then righted herself again. "You did it! You frightened Roger deCourtenay!" Tanon had never been so happy in her life. She would have leaped right into Gareth's arms if he weren't already turning away.

"Please, wait," she pleaded, barely able to stop herself. She touched his hand before he moved to leave her. "You saved Petunia." She didn't know if he understood her or not, so she smiled at him.

He just stood there staring at her for a moment. Then

he did what she'd been waiting for. He smiled back. And this time it was even better than the first.

~

They hardly left each other after that. Roger was sent to Normandy a few days later. With their leader gone and a new champion watching over her, the other children left Tanon alone. She spent the remainder of her summer days playing with Gareth.

Unfortunately, just when Tanon decided she liked Gareth even better than Petunia, the summer was over and she had to go home.

Chapter One

TWELVE YEARS LATER . . .

HE ARRIVED AT WINCHESTER CASTLE with the beginning of a storm. Tanon should have known when he entered the great castle doors that he had come to Winchester to change someone's life. When his men entered behind him, a gust of wind blew into the long corridor, swirling his long silken mane around his face. Garbed in a sleeveless doeskin tunic embroidered with a border of indigo, he looked like some fierce Celtic hero who had just stepped out of a bard's tale. Golden armbands wreathed the sleek sinew in his arms, and a matching golden torc ringed his neck. Something feral sparked his eyes, making them gleam like polished sapphires.

He swept those breathtaking eyes over Tanon as she descended the long staircase. His gaze softened and touched her like a curious caress. Then his lips slanted upward into a slow, decadently sensual smile.

Tanon stumbled on the last two stairs. He moved instantly to catch her, his broad, sure fingers closing around her waist.

"I have you."

His voice was deep, smoky velvet with an edge of steel. He captured her brief, mortified glance with his and held it just long enough to set her heart pounding.

"You're most kind," Tanon offered. She swept a non-existent wrinkle out of her burgundy gown and hurried away.

She stopped at the entrance of Winchester Castle's great hall and pushed the stranger from her mind. Ladies did not gush like mewling kittens over men—especially men who were clearly pagan. She drew out a quick breath and forged a pleasant smile before stepping inside.

It wasn't that she didn't like being here. King William's lavish castle was as familiar as her own dear home at Avarloch. But her father's high place at the king's table demanded courtly etiquette. She smiled at stuffy nobles and was polite to lords and ladies, even those she wasn't fond of. She would never bring shame to her family or give William cause for disappointment by behaving oddly. She was no longer a child.

She looked around, letting her gaze absorb the vast expanse of tapestry-lined walls gilded in firelight. Laughter permeated the air as knights lifted their goblets in salute to one another. Ladies giggled coyly or scolded children running around the tables like buzzing flies. A troubadour sat beside one of the great hearths singing a forlorn love song while calculating the tinkle of coin as it was deposited into the wide-brimmed hat at his feet.

Tanon swept a lone midnight curl off her shoulders before straightening them. She would need all the fortitude she possessed to face this night. Among the guests who had traveled to Winchester for the summer tourney was Lord Roger deCourtenay, Earl of Blackburn, the man she was promised to wed.

The union was not made through any choice of her own, of course. She was a noble's daughter, and if that wasn't enough to ensure her a proper marriage to a noble of no lesser title, then being treasured by the king of England was.

Roger was no longer the hellion who bullied her when she was six. He'd been sent to Normandy shortly after the summer he made her fall out of a tree. It was whispered that his time spent under the tutelage of the king's son Robert was punishment for his treatment of her, but Tanon had never told William of it, so she doubted the whispers were true.

He'd returned a changed man, or so the court believed. His time in Normandy had fashioned him into a man of great skill and had earned him the respect of the other nobles. But Tanon still didn't like him. She would marry him if she must, but she resented having to endure endless hours of her handmaidens tugging on her unruly curls, just to pin them up, and being fitted into layers of her finest wool to look pleasing for a man who preferred the more voluptuous, more scantily clad ladies of the court. She didn't care if Roger never looked at her, but she hated enduring such tedium for naught.

Still, she was more fortunate than most earls' daughters, who were doomed to marry men three times their age, or worse—Prince Cedric of Wales. She had tried not to look too relieved when her father informed her that Cedric had been exiled from his land after making an attempt on his uncle's life and their betrothal was canceled.

She remembered from her childhood the quiet warning in Cedric's eyes. She hadn't known it then, but the Welsh held little affection for the Normans who kept them out of England.

She never saw her brave champion Gareth again after that summer in Winchester, but she had thought of him often, every winter, anticipating each coming spring. Then, as the years wore on and he never returned, she put away her childish daydreams. When she had heard that Gareth was killed in the northern regions of Wales last year, she said a prayer for his soul.

Tanon spotted her mother sitting with her uncle Dante at the far end of the hall. Lady Brynna Risande inclined her head, moving her ear closer to Dante's lips to hear him over the cheers coming from the table beside them. Standing a few feet away, Tanon's father, Lord Brand the Passionate, lifted two of his fingers to his lips and then held them aloft to her mother. As if he couldn't bear to be away from her for more than a few moments, he went to her. After exchanging a quiet word with his brother, Brand tossed his arm around his wife and drew her into his close embrace.

Tanon watched her parents, her heart clenching at the love that exuded from every glance they shared, every touch, every smile. Her mother never had to sit through hours of combing and dressing for Tanon's father to lose his breath at the sight of her. Here was what she had hoped for as a child, what she'd always envisioned for herself when she took a husband: love, friendship, passion, tenderness. She let go of that hope when she learned of her betrothal to Roger. She could survive a loveless marriage. Her gaze drifted to her nursemaid, Rebecca, sitting at her father's table. It was far better than one of the alternatives.

She looked to the dais where King William sat. Tanon smiled at the king. Oh, how she loved him, almost as much as she loved her father. She knew William had only her best interests in mind when he'd promised her to Roger. Lord Blackburn's family was wealthy, with lands in England and Normandy. Her king wanted to secure her comfort and safety. She couldn't fault him for that.

Poor William. He looked weary, but that was to be expected, what with the Danes always threatening invasion, not to mention the unrest with the border Welsh. She'd been taught a little about the politics of Wales, as it had been believed she would live there.

After years of raids by the Welsh along the borders separating England and Wales, William had appointed some of his noble vassals to guard the marches, or borderlands, giving his marcher lords free rein to subdue the savages in any way they saw fit. Some of these lords had pushed their armies farther into Wales, occupying much of the east and some of the south, and causing the people to revolt. Among Wales's warriors many rebels arose, but one in particular, called Wyfyrn, had caused considerable distress to the marcher lords over the years. Wyfyrn had slaughtered four of the Norman overlords and their entire garrisons.

Tanon shivered at the thought of such bloodthirsty barbarians and thanked the saints that her king had kept peace in England. Dear William, he'd even made amends with Hereward the Wake. The king needed another friend at his side. He spent much of his time in Normandy without her father, who often was away on the king's business or managing his own lands.

Tanon found her betrothed laughing with Lady Eleanor Fitzdrummond, a beauty whose mammoth breasts matched her enormous ego. Tanon didn't like her, and she didn't care for any man who did.

"A friend of yours?" A voice spoke behind her.

Tanon sighed without turning. "My betrothed."

"Fool."

Tanon finally turned to him, insult lifting her brow. "Pardon?"

A beguiling smirk quirked one corner of his mouth. "Him. Not you."

"Oh." Her thoughts scattered, taking Roger with them. Saints, it was the man who'd nearly caused her to break her neck on the stairs. Unfortunately, his effect on her hadn't changed. Her breath halted as she stared up into his captivating eyes. His smirk deepened into a smile so warm and familiar, it tempted her to smile back.

His face was bare save for a slight tuft of deep gold just beneath a full, sulky lower lip. A darker shadow along his jaw implied a hint of arrogance. His long hair fell like liquid over his shoulders and reflected the flickering light of the hearth fire. He exuded confidence and virility in waves. Tanon felt as if she were looking at a different species. This one was mesmerizing and wild like a magnificent, untameable horse. Scottish, she guessed, fighting back the heat threatening to color her cheeks. He'd probably arrived with one of the many clans to compete in the tourney. He hadn't said enough for her to place his lyrical accent, but she didn't need to hear it to know that he was foreign.

"Are you here to compete?" She knew she should excuse herself and hurry toward her father, but the spark of intelligence in his eyes piqued her curiosity.

"Aye." He glanced at her betrothed and then slid his gaze back to her. "I imagine I am. I was unaware of your betrothal, Lady Risande."

"No one is aware of it," Tanon told him, glancing toward Roger again. "My marriage was arranged to Lord deCourtenay just a few months ago. It is to be announced this night."

"Lord deCourtenay?" the stranger asked. He cut his gaze to William and dipped his brow.

"Is something the matter?" Tanon asked.

"Nay." He tilted his head back to her. "You care for him, then?"

Tanon would have laughed if there was an ounce of happiness in her. She shook her head. *"Non,"* she answered honestly.

The stranger seemed to find some relief in that. His gaze on her softened.

Tanon angled her head at him. She felt as if she had seen him somewhere before, but she couldn't place him. "You have the advantage, my lord." She offered him a candid look. "You know who I am."

"Aye." The way his eyes searched her felt familiar, but when he lifted his finger to the crease in her cheek, she drew back from his touch, her heart pounding madly. *Non,* it couldn't be him. She felt a pang of disappointment. Gareth was dead.

"You were described to me in great detail by a mutual acquaintance a number of years ago. He said your eyes rival the verdant moors of Cymru." While the stranger spoke, he took Tanon's hand and lifted it to his mouth. "And that your nose crinkles when you laugh." He turned her hand over and pressed his lips to the inside of her wrist. His gaze brushed her face from beneath thick, dark lashes.

"Allow me to escort you to your father." His fingers caressed hers as he fit her hand into the crook of his arm.

Unable to breathe, Tanon took a moment to blink and slow her thudding heart. She had mastered keeping her emotions in check, especially here in the king's court. But her skin felt flush, her mouth dry.

Her betrothed was sitting a few feet away. It would be unseemly for another man to escort her on his arm to her father. She began to move her hand away from him.

"Thank you for your kind offer, my lord. But—"

"Come," he offered quietly, stilling her with his probing gaze and warm fingers atop hers. "Your father's table is but a few feet away. Grant me a moment to speak to you."

Although he looked feral, Tanon couldn't deny his courtly manners. She nodded, giving in with the first genuine smile she had offered anyone since arriving at Winchester. Another curl came loose from the maze of pins poking her head and fell over her brow. She blew it away. "Are you going to tell me your name?" she asked, oblivious to the amusement that made his eyes grow warm, while she frowned at the springy coil that defiantly found its way back over her eye. "Or shall I call you 'stranger' for the rest of the evening?"

"If you promise to spend the rest of the evening with me, then aye, I shall tell you my name."

She liked his boldness and the self-assurance that slowed his steps to a leisurely pace. He was in no rush to end their encounter, and despite her better judgment, neither was she. "I'm afraid I'm not permitted to bargain, my lord."

"Pity, then." He suddenly frowned, looking even more striking than before. "I shall have to concede." He turned to look behind him and nodded to one of the men who had entered the castle with his small entourage. The burly-looking brute slammed the end of a pole into the rushes and yanked on a small strip of leather. A banner unfurled, revealing the ruby image of a four-legged dragon.

Tanon's father and uncle were among the first to spring from their seats.

"What is the meaning of this?" King William bellowed over the sound of benches being pushed away from tables as the rest of his men, including Roger, stood up, ready for a fight.

Tanon looked up at the banner. Her eyes opened wide, recognizing the ruby dragon. Wales! When she met the stranger's rueful glance, she stumbled backward. Dear God, what were Welshmen doing in Winchester? She felt fingers shackle her wrist. Her father pulled her farther away and moved in front of her.

From her vantage point behind her father, Tanon lowered her gaze to the daggers protruding from the cuffs of the Welshman's boots, the thick belt around his slim waist. He stood arrow straight. His tightly honed legs were encased in tan leather trousers. The snug fit revealed more of his considerable male attributes than Tanon cared to think about. His trim body coiled taut with leashed energy. He looked as fierce as his countrymen were reported to be.

The man carrying the banner stepped forward and

cleared his throat. "His Highness, Lord Gareth of De-heubarth, Prince Regent of Ystrad Towi."

Tanon's heart lurched. Gareth? She took an involuntary step forward as an old longing to reunite with her friend returned to her. *Non,* this couldn't be the little boy who had gallantly rescued her from Roger so many years ago. And Gareth died while fighting in northern Wales. She groped for her father's hand to steady her.

"Your Majesty." The prince turned to face the king. "Forgive my uncle for not sending word of my arrival."

"Gareth?" the king ventured as if he could not believe his own eyes. "I was told you were killed over a year ago." The king fell back into his seat. "This is quite a shock."

"Aye, it was for my uncle as well when he finally saw me," Gareth said, his voice calm despite the hundreds of well-trained knights standing ready to kill him if he made one move toward the king. "One of my men betrayed me in battle, and I was imprisoned in Prince Dafydd's holding in the north for near a dozen months." A grin crept over his lips. "I have his daughter to thank for my life."

Tanon stared at him. Could this be the same soft-cheeked boy who had become her best friend that summer so long ago? *Oui,* it was him. His silky hair had darkened a shade or two with the years, and his face was no longer soft but carved to rugged perfection. But his eyes were still as vividly blue as she remembered. Why hadn't he told her who he was earlier? Her eyes slid to the small group of men who had entered the castle with him and who now stood at the doors of the hall. All were armed, and each one looked more deadly than the next.

"How did you and your men cross the marches?" William cast Gareth a pointed look. Like Offa's Dyke, built centuries before to keep the warring Celts from entering England, so were the marches guarded by overlords.

"With careful planning, my lord." When William raised an eyebrow, Gareth said what the king wanted to hear. "Without bloodshed on either side."

William scowled, knowing there wasn't a Welshman alive who wasn't thirsty for Norman blood. He had made alliances with Rhys ap Tewdwr before the prince became king of Deheubarth, but their treaty for peace had never been sealed. "Your uncle should have sent a missive regarding your arrival. My writ would have assured you safe entrance into England. In any case, I'm pleased that you live, Gareth." William offered him a scant smile before his smoky gray gaze fell on Tanon, and then on her father.

"Brand, you remember King Rhys's nephew."

Gareth offered Brand a casual nod, glancing only briefly at the possessive hold he had on his daughter. "My lord, I'm happy to find you in good health. It has been many years since I last saw you."

"*Oui*." The Lord of Avarloch's hand closed even tighter around Tanon.

"Your family has grown," Gareth said, smiling at the five smaller faces gaping at him from around the lord's table. He turned his bold gaze on Tanon. "But you have not changed. You are as beautiful as I remember, though I did find your missing tooth quite enchanting."

Flashes of his boyish smile raced across Tanon's memory and warmed her blood. She had dreamed of Gareth the entire winter of her sixth year. In her dreams they had played together as they had that summer when she told him stories of damsels and the knights who rescued them from mean dragons named Roger.

She looked at Roger now. He swayed on his feet from drinking, and his glassy gaze fixed hard on Gareth.

"Tell me, Gareth." King William's commanding voice interrupted her thoughts. "What brings you back to Winchester? Is your uncle well? His family?"

"Aye, they are well. His son, Gruffydd, passed his third year in the spring. Fatherhood has strengthened my uncle's resolve to bring peace to Cymru."

"Ah, good news, good news." William held his cup aloft for a moment, toasting the peace Gareth spoke of.

Gareth smiled and folded his hands behind his back. "I'm glad you still desire peace as well, Your Majesty."

"Of course I do. We have lost many on both sides."

"My people prefer not to be subjugated by yours, Sire," Gareth answered in a nonthreatening tone to match his stance. Still, Roger stepped forward. William held up his hand and gestured for him to take his seat.

"I have no desire to conquer Wales, Gareth."

"And yet your noble barons have built castles along our borders—"

"For England's protection against Welsh attacks," William said without anger. He wasn't opposed to any man who had the courage to stand up to him.

"They move farther into Cymru each month, claiming more of our land without your disapproval."

Finally, William's gaze hardened on him. "And what does your uncle do to stop men like Wyfyrn from massacring England's vassals along the entire length of Wales, from the southern marches to the north?"

"The Serpent Dragon eludes even us," Gareth argued.

"But why should my uncle hunt a man for defending his land against overlords who burn down our villages and defile our women?"

The king leaned forward in his chair, looking like he might leap from it at Gareth's charges. "Are you telling me that the men Wyfyrn killed all did these things?"

"I am, Your Majesty," Gareth confirmed quietly.

William cut his gaze to Brand and then ran his hand over his jaw. "I was unaware."

"With respect"—Gareth bowed slightly—"you were unaware because after you gave your marcher lords free rein, you turned your back on what became of us."

"You err, Gareth. I traveled to Wales not three years past to seek counsel with your uncle on the issue of peace between our people."

"Then I beg you, my lord, let us speak of it now again," Gareth said. "It is for peace that I have come to claim what is now rightfully mine." He didn't blink or flinch when William's powerful gaze penetrated his.

Somewhere behind Brand, Tanon's mother slammed her palm down on the table. "You're mad if you think—"

"My lady." Gareth's voice was quiet, almost soothing, but the raw force radiating from him shook Tanon to her core. "I am not here to fight—or to argue." He turned to the king again. "I'm simply here to seal the treaty you agreed to twelve years ago when you put your writ on parchment and swore with my uncle on the holy relics. It was done for peace between our people," he said earnestly. "But I fear peace is slipping through our hands. There is already famine in some parts of the land. I have come to put an end to it once and for all."

"William—" Brand began.

The king raised his palm to quiet him, admiring the depth of the young prince's desire to save his people from the ravages of war and the courage it took to stand before England's king and declare it.

"You were with King William when he met with my uncle." Gareth addressed Brand again. "You agreed this was the only way to stop the bloodshed. I ask you not to refuse." He spoke with authority, and Tanon doubted many people had ever refused his commands.

"He will not refuse," William said with stern assurance mixed with a hint of regret. "King Rhys and I want peace. Had I known you were alive, I would have sealed our treaty sooner."

Expelling a breath, Gareth bowed. When he straightened, he tossed back his head, sweeping his deep tawny hair off his shoulders. "I will be traveling to my uncle's fortress in Llandeilo in a few weeks. I will relay your words to the king of the South. He will advise the people of your continued goodwill."

"Do so." William leaned back in his chair, his eyes narrowed with deadly conviction. "But know this. If any harm comes to her, it will cost you your head. Peace be damned."

Gareth smiled easily. "Her value to you is noted, Sire."

William sighed and pinched the bridge of his nose in his fingers. "*Enfer,* she is betrothed."

"So I have recently learned." Gareth looked over his shoulder and met Roger's scalding gaze. His lips curled into a wry grin as his eyes met Tanon's once again. "It seems I have arrived just in time."

Chapter Two

Tanon sat in a carved chair in the king's private solar, her hands folded neatly in her lap, her chin dipped to her chest. She could hear her mother weeping softly, but she didn't look up, afraid that if she saw her mother's tears, she would be unable to hold back her own. Her father paced behind her chair. Tanon could almost hear his teeth grinding with frustration and anguish while William spoke to her.

"*Ma précieuse,* you understand this must be done."

"Of course," Tanon replied quietly, her eyes veiled beneath the inky darkness of her lashes.

"There is no greater vow between people than one made for peace."

Tanon nodded but said nothing. She refused to voice the nagging whisper that had tormented her every day since she had first learned of her betrothal to Cedric, and then to Roger.

What about love?

Her father rushed to his wife's side when Brynna stifled a sob. Tanon lifted her gaze briefly to watch them.

She had accepted her fate to live in a loveless marriage. Twice! It had taken every ounce of fortitude she possessed to lock away her hopes of ever being loved by a man the way her father loved her mother.

"Naught has changed, really," William gently reminded her and her parents. "This course was set many years ago."

Oui, Tanon thought. She'd never been happy about it, and that was *before* she'd learned what a barbaric place Wales was. She glanced at Gareth leaning against the large alcoved window, his boots crossed at his ankles, his arms folded across his chest. He'd been her friend once. He had cared about her. She'd spent years wishing she could marry him rather than his brother. But that was long ago, before so much destruction and death had separated their people. She knew as little about him now as she knew about the wild lands he came from.

"We thought," Brynna said, swiping the tears from her eyes, "after Cedric was exiled, Tanon could remain in England. William, Wales is too far off."

Tanon squeezed her eyes shut. Dear God, it was. And where in blazes was this Ystrad Towi? In Deheubarth, no doubt, which could have been at the other end of the world as far as she was concerned. If she had to marry for something other than love, then Roger was the best choice for her. His castle in Blackburn was only a day's ride from Avarloch.

"What about Roger?" Tanon asked the king softly.

"What about him?" Gareth said. Tanon angled her head

to look at him. And then wished she hadn't. The Gareth she remembered was gone. In his place stood a man whose arresting stare demanded her full attention.

Silently defying him, she dipped her gaze away from his. "Lord deCourtenay will take offense to having our vow of marriage broken just a few weeks before our wedding. Perhaps it would be more prudent to wait—"

"Something tells me he'll get over you quickly enough."

Tanon snapped her eyes up at Gareth. "That was an extremely unkind thing to say."

He didn't look repentant. In fact, his gaze on her darkened.

"Forgive me," he said, his mocking tone a stark contradiction to his apology. "I thought you would be relieved to find yourself free of him."

"In exchange for living in Wales?" Tanon expelled a tight little snort.

Gareth pushed himself off the window and took a step toward her. A tinge of fear quickened her pulse as he came closer, his expression warrior hard. "How can you hold contempt for a country you have never even seen?"

"I don't need to see it to know it is a country fraught with war," she said, keeping her voice steady, her challenge soft. She hadn't meant to insult him, but she wasn't about to back down from the anger flashing across his eyes. "I know that it is a country divided by kingdoms and kings, one whose own nephew could not be trusted and had to be banished."

Tanon's father moved toward her with a look that warned Gareth to move away. But Gareth had one more thing to say.

"Tanon." The familiar tenderness in his voice drew her eyes to his. "You speak as if you are my enemy."

"Gareth," William interjected, his tone signaling that he'd heard enough, but Gareth had already swung away from her on his way back to the window.

"He is right." Tanon stopped the king before he said anything else. Gareth turned back to her, but she lowered her gaze. "I will do what is required of me."

What was required of her.

Hell, that wasn't the response he had been hoping for. Gareth set his hips back against the window. He didn't know what he expected, but it wasn't this. He understood that his appearance at Winchester had been a shock to the king and to the Risandes. He'd even concede that Tanon had a right to be a little reluctant about marrying him, but the way she had just accepted her fate, as if she was about to be bound to a horned demon from her worst nightmares, pricked him in the heart. He was a fool to have thought she would rejoice at seeing him again. Why should she? They had spent one summer together. She hadn't recognized him earlier. She probably didn't even remember him. But he remembered her. The girl who had stood apart from the rest. The one whose complete lack of guile made him smile, at the risk of being thrashed by his brothers. She was direct and inquisitive, thriving on her *own* happiness—he glanced at the king and her family— not everyone else's. He'd thought of her often, imagining the girl he'd left had grown into a spirited beauty. He'd returned to find a Norman lady, refined and obedient. He attributed her prejudiced opinion of Cymru to being brought up in Norman courts. The stars only knew what she'd been taught about his people. She was probably scared out of her wits by him, yet she'd just agreed to marry him without quarrel or complaint. It had angered him to hear her concern over deCourtenay, but she'd told him that they had been betrothed only for a short time and she didn't care for him. Christ, she'd accepted *that* fate, it would seem, without complaint as well.

There was barely a trace of the winsome abandon he'd once found so irresistible in her glade-green eyes. Her face hadn't changed, though. Looking at her still seized his breath. He recalled the way she had stared up at him earlier in quiet fascination, the silent gasp that parted her lips when he kissed her hand, as if no man had ever done the like before. He had been tempted to lean down and cover that sweet coral mouth with his own.

"Now, what are we to do about deCourtenay?" William thought out loud, jarring Gareth's concentration away from Tanon's lips. "Tanon's right. He might take offense and ask to fight for her hand."

"Then allow them to fight," Brand suggested, grazing Gareth with a cool look. "I'd like an opportunity to see if the prince has the skills required to protect my daughter."

Gareth took up the challenge with a respectful bow. "The tourney begins tomorrow. Allow me to prove my skill against deCourtenay there. If I win, your daughter will return to Cymru with me, as my wife, without doubt that I will do all that is necessary to secure her safety, just as I do for my people. If I lose, I will wish her happiness with"—a withering smirk touched his lips—"her doting husband and bid her farewell."

William eyed the Welsh prince narrowly. He'd heard many things about this man's great skill, but deCourtenay also knew how to wield a sword well. Perhaps the prince's arrogance would work in the Risandes' favor. If deCourtenay won, Tanon could remain in England without him having broken his agreement with King Rhys. If he refused Gareth's bargain, they would always wonder what fate would have chosen for Tanon this day. "I will allow it." He sighed with the weight of decisions he already regretted having to make.

"You may leave us now." The king waved his hand in Gareth's direction. "See my steward, Rupert, for chambers for you and your men while you're here."

Tanon stood and tugged on Gareth's wrist after he bowed and turned to leave. Suspicion creased her brow. She dragged her lower lip between her teeth, drawing Gareth's gaze back to her mouth. "I thought I was vital to the peace of your country. Why would you risk the lives you claim are in danger by returning without me?"

Gareth stared into the shifting facets of her eyes, feeling his pulse quake. God help him, she still made his chest feel like he'd been kicked in it. "I risk nothing, my lady." His voice was a honeyed murmur while he lifted the edge of his mouth in a confident half grin. "I will not lose."

Tanon watched him leave. Somehow, his back was just as masculine as the front. Everything about him was sensual. He had no doubt in the outcome. He intended to win. Her heart rebelled at the idea of living in Wales, but her blood rushed through her veins. Gareth's bold smiles lured a part of her that craved excitement. The kind that had been denied her by her noble upbringing. His gaze stirred feelings that made her want to run into the safe, uninterested arms of Roger deCourtenay, sealing the fate she'd prepared herself for. But a buried part of her was curious to find out if the champion of her youth had become as dangerous as he looked.

"Tanon." The voice of her king drew her attention back to her family. "I would not ask this of you if it were not so vital to so many."

Tanon nodded. She had been raised as a child to obey her king. She had always been protected by the gentlest of men, and she would always do her best to please them, especially when a request was fraught with such need.

Swallowing her emotions, she met William's tender gaze. "I will not disappoint you."

An hour after Brand left the solar with Brynna, he returned alone, finding the king where he'd left him, sprawled in a chair facing the hearth fire. Brand acknowledged the man sitting beside William with a brief glance as he crossed the room to pour himself a drink. Though almost fourteen years had passed since Hereward the Wake had led a mighty rebellion against the Normans in Peterborough, Brand still found it inconceivable that the beefy Saxon had laid down his sword and had not only sworn fealty to William, but had become one of the king's emissaries and his good friend.

"I fear your wife will never forgive me." William stared into the cup clutched within his thick fingers. With one swift motion, he guzzled its contents and then tossed the cup into the crackling flames. *"Je suis désolé, mon ami."*

Brand closed his eyes for a moment. The king should not be sorry for doing what was needed to bring peace to his land. Brand had had a part in this decision that they all hoped would end the fighting between the Normans and the Welsh. At William's request, he had agreed to let his eldest daughter be taken away from him, to live among England's enemy as a symbol, a gesture that the Normans desired peace. Brand clenched his jaw, regretting his decision for the thousandth time since he'd made it. Many daughters were given over for land, title, or peace. His own wife had been forced to marry him to avoid bloodshed between the Saxons and the Normans. But this was his daughter, William's goddaughter, and Brand was glad that his best friend shared his grief.

"Brynna understands the sacrifices required for peace. Tanon will come to understand them as well." Brand clenched his teeth as he carried his cup to the hearth and leaned his shoulder against the arched mantel. "What do we know about Prince Gareth? I remember Cedric, but I've never given his younger brother much thought."

"We know a fair amount," William told him, looking up. "Remember, Hereward spent a full winter with King Rhys and Gareth a number of years ago."

Brand flicked his gaze to the red-haired Saxon. "Tell me."

Crossing his booted ankle over his thigh, Hereward settled more comfortably in his seat. "Prince Gareth rules part of the northern region of Ystrad Towi in regent for King Rhys's son."

"I know." Brand exhaled a frustrated sigh. "And he fought against one of the princes of the north and was believed to be dead. Hereward, tell me about him, this man who is to be my daughter's husband. Is he even-tempered? Fair to his people?"

"From what I observed of him during my visit with

him, he is even-tempered and compassionate. His prior rebellion against the Normans was to protect his people. His people respect him and obey his word as law. He earned their esteem by holding back a regiment of Lord Fitzgerald's army when the Normans tried to move farther into the west, not once, but three times. As a leader, he possesses great finesse and charm that have won him the hearts of even some of King Gruffydd's people in the Gwynedd, but he won't hesitate to slice the head from anyone who tries to bring harm to his people. I've seen him do it." The glint in Hereward's pale green eyes reminded Brand that this softly spoken Saxon had once impaled the heads of fifty Normans in the courtyard of his father's castle. "The twenty men he arrived with are part of his *Teulu,* or personal guardsmen, elite in their skill," Hereward continued. "Four of those men are his closest friends, sworn to give their lives in defense of his, though he does not require their protection. He is a confident warrior. He wields a sword as if he were born with one."

Brand ran his hand over his jaw, trying desperately to accept the inevitable; he'd given up his daughter to the Welsh.

"He will keep her safe," Hereward said, as if reading Brand's thoughts. He liked the Risandes, had respected them even during the years the brothers had hunted him for the killing of their sister, which he had naught to do with. He harbored no ill will toward Brand, even though the woman he loved was in love with the earl. Hereward doubted Brand was even aware of Tanon's nurse, Rebecca. His eyes were on his wife and family.

"Prince Gareth is not a barbarian, Brand," Hereward said. "He's intelligent, and his first choice is always diplomacy, not force. In truth, your daughter will do far better with him than she would have done with his brother."

"I don't know that," Brand told him, the worry in his eyes remaining, despite Hereward's assurances. "I want to travel to Wales with her." Brand turned back to the king. "I need to see for myself that she will be accepted in her new home."

"You cannot," William answered, a sharp barb of regret jabbing deep into his heart as he watched Brand ready himself for a fight. The king stopped him before it began. "You are my highest commander, *mon ami*. Everyone in Scotland, Wales, and France knows who you are. The moment you step foot on Welsh land, they will suspect you are there for war. Your life, and our agreement for peace, will mean naught. Give Gareth and his uncle some time to convince their people of our sincerity. Then you may visit her. In the meantime, Gareth will secure her well-being."

"The prince barely knows her!" Brand's voice erupted into a roar. "All you have convinced me of tonight is that the people come first to the prince. Who will protect Tanon if his people turn on her?"

"I will."

Brand turned to point his stare at Hereward as the Saxon, who had once been William's most powerful enemy, offered him a faint smile and repeated his vow.

"I will travel with her and guard her with my sword and with my life."

Brand didn't want to send Tanon off with Hereward any more than he wanted to send her off with Gareth. This was the man whose followers had killed his sister Katherine thirteen years ago. It had taken almost that many years before Brand believed Hereward had nothing to do with her death. But that didn't mean he trusted the Saxon with his daughter.

Hereward stood and placed a large hand on Brand's shoulder. "I will let no harm come to her. You have my word."

Brand gritted his teeth and left the solar.

Chapter Three

GARETH FOLLOWED THE KING'S STEWARD down the long, dimly lit corridor. It had taken him over a quarter of an hour to find out who the hell Hubert was. But, Gareth considered, since there had to be more than three hundred guests roaming the castle, a hundred of them bastard Normans named Hubert, a quarter of an hour wasn't really all that long to locate the right one. What really irked him was that when he finally found the steward, he discovered that Hubert spoke only French. Gareth tried to remain patient while he repeated his request for rooms, and the steward shook his head and repeated a string of words Gareth didn't understand. Finally, Gareth had to haul the man to a door, give it a hard whack with his fist, and shout, "Rooms for us! Now!" before Hubert began moving.

Hell, he was tired, Gareth thought as he followed Hubert along the maze of cavernous corridors that made up Winchester's third landing. He and his men had traveled on horseback for over a fortnight, sleeping on pallets on the hard ground. His body ached for a soft bed. He guessed his weariness was the reason he'd allowed Brand Risande to rattle his resolve when they'd met in the great hall just before Gareth found the steward. Whatever the reason, Gareth now understood fully why his uncle had warned him on several occasions to use caution around the earl's daughter. He remembered Tanon's father from his childhood, though they had barely spoken.

Every warrior in Cymru knew of Lord Brand and Dante Risande. They were King William's best, most lethal commanders, but Gareth had no idea that facing the Lord of Avarloch off the battlefield might be as deadly as facing him on it. Gareth had trained hard under King Rhys's stringent instruction since he was a boy. Ofttimes, he'd been so exhausted after a lesson that he fell into bed without supper. He'd grown up fighting merciless princes, and Normans armed with sword, ax, and spear. But no one had ever threatened to gut him wide open while smiling at him like an angel. Gareth had to spend another ten long breaths assuring Tanon's father that he would see to her happiness and protection. God's fury, the man still growled at him. Madoc, Gareth's first in command, insisted on having a go with the Norman earl, but Gareth refused his request. It wouldn't do to kill his betrothed's father or lose his best friend two days before the wedding.

His wedding! Christ, he thought as he turned left behind Hubert. He was truly going through with it. Tomorrow he would fight to be bound forever to a Norman in order to give his countrymen along the borders the promise of a better life. Of course, Cymru would still suffer the sorrows of war brought about by the other rival princes who ruled in Gwynedd and Powys, but that was another matter to be dealt with in another way.

What the hell did he know of marriage, anyway? He was a warrior with no time to coddle such demanding beings as wives. He had villages to oversee, men to train, and people who depended on him to keep them safe. He had enough to keep his mind occupied without worrying about the comfort of a woman.

Even if that woman was Tanon.

Odd, he hadn't thought about one of those things since she smiled at him. He couldn't think of anything but the alluring flash of her dimple, those lush black curls falling over her eyes. The sweet mixture of honey and huskiness of her voice. She was as delicate a beauty as she was when she was six. He remembered when she shouted at him that day on his way to the barn. "A rude mute," she had called him. He had turned to look at her and every thought escaped him, save one. She was breathtaking. Like her, he hadn't understood why they were supposed to be enemies. Up until then, he'd fought only his brothers. He wanted to tell her that day that he would make things right.

But that was long ago. At twelve summers he had faced his first enemy on the battlefield and left his childhood behind. He hadn't stopped fighting since.

Hubert paused at an oak door to his left and stared at it. *"Peut-être celle-ci est vide."*

"This one?" Gareth asked, pointing to the door.

Hubert bobbed his head up and down and then stepped around him and fled the way he had come.

The first thing to hit Gareth when he opened the door was the soft scent of lavender. His eyes assessed the chamber and stopped at the pearl white screen nestled between an enormous canopied bed and a slightly smaller wardrobe of polished wood. The silhouette of a delicately formed female moved behind the thin partition.

"Rebecca?" the woman said.

Gareth smiled, recognizing Tanon's dulcet voice. He knew he should leave before she saw him and her screams brought the entire castle running to her rescue. He should, but he wasn't about to. He leaned against the bedpost and crossed his arms over his chest.

"Have you heard the terrible news? I'm to marry a *Welshman!*" The way she said the word was akin to saying a savage.

Gareth's smile faded into a scowl. He thought about flinging the screen aside and showing her just what a savage he could be, but he was determined to prove to her that what she'd been told about him and his people was untrue. Did savages give up their freedom and bind themselves forever to their enemy for peace?

"I've already undressed," she called out, and, as if to drive that torturous fact home, she tossed a pair of gossamer hose over the top of the screen. "My gown was so heavy, I couldn't wait to tear it off."

Gareth willed himself not to move toward the screen as a wickedly hot jolt scalded his spine and went directly between his legs.

"I will be done in a moment. If you're not too tired, I just need you to brush my hair. I'm afraid I've tangled it trying to remove all the pins Lorette and Eloise used to tie it up." She stepped out from behind the flimsy barrier, the gauzy nightdress she'd slipped over her head falling over her bare, creamy hips to her ankles. The crown of her head slipped through the top of the nightdress, followed by a nimbus of wild blue-black curls. "I really prefer to wear it loose. I—" Her mouth opened as wide as her eyes. Her stunned gaze fell to his hand cupped against the fullness of his groin. The embodiment of pure male insolence, he adjusted himself, leaned his shoulder against her bedpost, and smiled.

Tanon stepped back and hit into the screen, knocking it to the floor. "What—what are you doing in my room?"

Her room? He would have to remember to thank Hubert in the morn for his error. He took his time letting his gaze traverse every delectable contour defined against her thin nightdress. "Allowing the view to convince me that I'm not making the biggest mistake of my life by marrying you."

"Marrying *me*? Why . . . Oh, I never—" Tanon bit her bottom lip to stop herself from saying something unladylike. She grabbed the edge of the sheet and pulled it to cover herself. "Please leave."

He dragged his gaze to her face. "In a moment."

His boldness coaxed a flutter from her belly. "Knave," she flung at him, then backed away when he took a step toward her.

"If I was a knave"—his deep voice simmered with checked desire as he came closer, and his eyes seared beneath his tawny brows—"you'd be flat on your back in this bed, *my lady*." He spoke her courtly title with mocking sweetness.

Tanon thought about bolting for the door. But she'd have to get around him first. The problem was, he seemed to take up every inch of the room. Every movement that brought him nearer to her snatched more air from her body. His eyes were scalding blue flames, devouring her.

No man had ever gazed at her so boldly. "If you come any closer, I will be forced to strike you," she said.

His smile softened as if he considered her threat nothing short of adorable. When he stood close enough to her to feel her short gasps of breath on his chin, he lifted his fingers to her face and caressed her cheek with the back of his knuckles, then smoothed her heavy, coal black waves off her shoulder. "It was worth it."

She should scream, or kick him, or push him away. Anything would be better than simply standing there gaping up into his eyes. She'd been afraid that he was going to try to force himself on her. But the intimacy of his tender touch nearly buckled her knees. His nearness, and the dark, exhilarating hint of forest mingled with the scent of leather, bathed her in warmth. It was a scent that had clung to her memory even after she had forgotten him. Looking at him, she had the odd sensation of waking from sleep. Every nerve ending blazed, every sense was shockingly aware of his virility. She had grown up surrounded by men, but not one of them ever made her so aware of her femininity. She wrenched her gaze from his, though a traitorous part of her wanted to examine him thoroughly. He was the most rugged, sensuously beautiful man she'd ever seen. If that wasn't bad enough, the promise of sinful corruption in his eyes excited her.

"You must leave now," she said, needing to convince herself that she hadn't gone completely mad. "You shouldn't be here. It's indecent."

He moved away from her and picked up the robe draped over a small chair beside the bed. He turned and handed it to her. "Indecent? Were my intentions that obvious, then? I thought I demonstrated incredible control."

The sexual catch in his voice made her hurry with her robe.

"My, but you've certainly become crude since you've . . ." Against her will her eyes scanned his broad shoulders. " . . . grown up. If my father finds you in here, he will kill you."

A cool smirk curled his pagan mouth. "Your concern for my well-being is most touching."

She considered telling him that she didn't care one whit about his well-being when the door to her chambers opened.

Of all the fearsome men in Tanon's life, none of them sported a temper as lethal as her mother's or her aunt Gianelle's. For the moment though, both women looked too stunned to say a word as they stood in the doorway.

"Katherine, go get your father," Tanon's aunt finally said to a small child hovering around her skirts. "Make haste," she added without taking her eyes off the feral-looking man standing in the center of the room.

Gareth eyed the petite golden beauty. "The child's father wouldn't be the big one with . . ." He held his hand to his bare bicep and extended it outward. When the woman nodded, he exhaled heavily.

"You have exactly ten breaths to explain what you're doing in my daughter's room." Dressed in a gown of spun golden silk, Lady Brynna Risande stood as regal as any queen with her slender arms folded beneath her heaving bosom. Her face was only a few shades lighter than the luxurious crown of russet plaited on her head.

"I didn't know it was her room when I entered it."

The other woman crossed his path on her way to Tanon. The delicate string of tiny bluebells wreathing her amber brow only added to her fey beauty, but what she lacked in height, she more than made up for in courage, for as she passed him, she slapped his arm and muttered something venomous in French.

Never having been slapped by a woman before, Gareth didn't know whether to laugh or admonish her. He turned to aim his incredulous stare at Tanon's mother but confronted a scowling, silver-eyed giant instead.

Lord Dante Risande, Gareth thought, looking up. Christ, the man was all muscle. He hoped that what he'd heard of him was true—that this was the brother who queried first and diced later.

"What are you doing in my niece's chamber?"

Gareth breathed a slight sigh of relief. "It's the room I was given by Hubert, the king's steward."

Dante's raven brows dipped over his eyes, making him look a little more dangerous than Gareth was comfortable with at present. Fighting the Norman king's favored earls would not be in the best interest of his people.

"The king's steward is Rupert," Dante corrected him. "Did he bring you to this room?"

"Rupert?" Gareth echoed and then laughed softly at himself. "That explains why Hubert brought me *here.*"

"Who is this Hubert?" Brynna demanded, not trusting the foreign prince.

"I've certainly no idea," Gareth said benignly. "I demanded a room, and he led me to this one."

Dante stared at him in silence, his steely gaze as unnerving as his brother's ruthless smile had been. And then he grinned, realizing what had happened. "You frightened one of William's guests enough to make him play chatelain? You must be quite a fearsome warrior when you're not getting slapped around by women."

Dante laughed when Gareth cut his disapproving gaze to Dante's wife. "Come." The brawny Norman earl tossed his arm around Gareth's shoulder. "Best you leave this room before my brother finds you in it. He is not as even-tempered as I."

"So I've heard," Gareth told him.

"Oui?" Dante asked as he led Gareth out of the room. "Tell me, what else have you heard about me?"

Chapter Four

TANON SWATTED A BEE away from her face and adjusted the powder blue wimple beneath her chin. She forced herself to smile at the woman walking beside her, deciding that the bee's confounded buzzing in her ear wasn't half as irritating as Hilary Pendleton's constant chattering. It wasn't that she didn't like Hilary, but was her friend going to go on all morn about Winchester's royal guest?

"'Tis said his countryman, Wyfyrn, breached the stronghold of Lord Hamilton's castle on the marches and killed the mighty lord in his bed." Hilary flicked her dark braid off her shoulder and scooped her arm through Tanon's. "This Wyfyrn is said to wear a helm fashioned in the likeness of a dragon. I heard Phillip the gardener telling the king's steward that Wyfyrn and his men killed Lord Hamilton's entire garrison, not with one attack, but with a series of methodical ambushes performed with great stealth. When Hamilton tried to send a missive to King William for reinforcements, Wyfyrn killed every messenger sent from the castle before they reached Offa's

Dyke. The same was done to the guardsman who subsequently escorted the messengers. After that, Lord Hamilton himself tried to leave Wales, but Wyfyrn toyed with him. With hardly anyone left to guard the castle," Hilary said, finalizing her tale with a satisfied smile, "Wyfyrn waited until the evening and killed Lord Hamilton in his bed."

"A horrible tale." Tanon shivered.

"They are an uncivilized people, for certain." Hilary sounded a bit breathless. "Still, your prince has quite a disarming smile for one who comes from such a primitive land."

"Hmm." Tanon would have rolled her eyes if she didn't think it would hurt Hilary's feelings.

"His commander, Madoc, is positively terrifying," Hilary mercilessly continued.

Tanon gaped at her, stunned at the dreamy smile her friend wore. "Are you telling me that the prince's right-hand man is named Mad Dog?" Tanon felt a bit faint.

"*Non,* silly. You are pronouncing it incorrectly. It's *Mah-dug.* But now that you mention it, he does have a look about him like he might sport fangs."

Tanon sighed. What was the point in being angry with Hilary when the entire castle was abuzz with whispers of the notorious Welsh prince and his rowdy entourage? Tanon was amazed at how quickly word had spread as to why he had arrived. Even before she'd stepped out of her chambers this morn, the whispers were echoing throughout the corridors.

"But she's already betrothed to Lord Blackburn."

"I heard the prince demanded her hand at the threat of war."

"Nay, I heard that the prince values peace above all else."

Tanon valued peace as well, but she disliked being traded for it twice.

She had tried to tell herself last eve that marrying Gareth was better than marrying Roger. It was a noble thing to sacrifice oneself for such a worthy cause. But that was before the bold brute sauntered into her room and pretended to be Rebecca! And, oh, the way he'd looked at her! God help her, just his presence in her room had made her breathless. He'd stood there so arrogantly by her bed, like he had every right to feast his eyes on her. When he had touched her, she nearly sighed aloud. She didn't like how he had stormed back into her life and reawakened all her girlish fantasies. At least he hadn't tried to kiss her. Thinking about it now, she chewed her lower lip. Was she so unappealing that even a Welshman refused to lay his mouth on her? She saw how he had looked at her body. Why hadn't he tried to kiss her? Mayhap he wasn't pleased at what he saw. She should be relieved, though, that the prince didn't find her to his liking. She certainly didn't want to kiss him. Ever.

Determined not to let him spoil the last shred of good humor she possessed, Tanon turned her attention to the colorful pavilions strewn across the magnificent lawns of Winchester Castle. Nobles and knights were still arriving from as far away as Normandy to pay their yearly homage to the king and to compete in the many tournaments that would last for up to a se'nnight. Ladies dressed in their finest gowns strolled the lawns, giggling at jesters who somersaulted in their paths. Children squealed with laughter at the antics of little wooden marionettes staged upon piled haystacks dotting the fields. Stalls lined the western wall, alive with singing minstrels and vendors raucously shouting their wares. It was a time to celebrate the peace brought to England by its conqueror, as fragile as that peace was. And although the jousting and sword-fighting competitions were brutal indeed, the men sported smiles and good cheer. The generous purses awarded to the victors, along with endless vats of ale, added to the merry mood.

"Come," Hilary said, tugging on Tanon's arm. "Your prince and his men have been practicing all morn. Their skill is causing quite a stir."

It took Tanon a moment to realize where Hilary was leading her. When she saw the lists a few yards away, she dug her heels into the ground. "*Non,* I don't want to see the certainty of my demise as it comes upon me." She pulled Hilary back, her eyes wide with dread. "You know if he defeats Lord deCourtenay, I am his."

Hilary narrowed her hazel eyes on her, casting Tanon an indignant look. "You could do worse, Tanon. Remember old Lord Edwin DeValance, who requested your hand last summer? Be grateful that your father didn't agree to *that* union."

Heavens, she'd almost forgotten Lord DeValance, the one-eyed Earl of Gloucester who'd accidentally killed his wife while he practiced his swordplay.

Tanon squared her shoulders. "It matters not, Hilary. I would rather marry the Earl of Blackburn than live in Wales."

"Good God." Hilary pointed past Tanon. "You don't honestly want to marry that rascal. He cares only for your dowry."

Tanon looked over her shoulder. Appearing quite convalesced from his soused condition of the previous night, Lord Blackburn strolled with Lady Fitzdrummond, smiling as though he hadn't a care in the world.

"He doesn't seem very concerned about losing you," Hilary mumbled.

Why would he be? Tanon thought. He had always hated her. Even so, where was the man's pride? Was he going to simply sit back and hand her over to the prince without even lifting an eyebrow? Vaguely, she felt Hilary moving her along while she stared at Roger. What was the point in fighting? Anyone had to be better than that scandalous worm.

"I've had other offers, you know," she said, her pride pricking her shoulders.

"But none from the likes of him."

They stood just outside the low-circled wall of the lists. All around them, men, and even some women, cheered, tossing coins into the circle. Others swore and stormed away, shaking their heads in disbelief.

None like him. Damnez-le, Hilary was right. Tanon's breath stalled in her chest at the sight of her future husband within the ringed wall. For there was no longer any doubt in her mind that Prince Gareth was going to pound Roger into a bloody pulp. She was going to Wales. But even while her hopes that she might remain close to her family faded, her skin tingled at the sight of Gareth.

With a dagger clutched in each fist, he moved with the sinuous agility of a great cat. A glistening sheen of sweat accentuated the bronzed sinew in his bare arms. Thin strips of corded leather were wound tightly around his biceps. His tight legs, encased in buff-colored doeskin, crouched, and then, in one fluid move, he sprang forward to deliver a blow to his opponent that sent the knight's sword flying. He landed perfectly balanced on the pads of his bare feet and tossed back his locks of glimmering gold.

He looked elemental and terribly barbaric. The power in his sapphire eyes quickened Tanon's pulse when his gaze caught hers. He offered her a sudden, arresting smile. Heat licked down her spine and went straight to her belly.

"And look there." Hilary gestured subtly with her veiled chin. Tanon severed her gaze from Gareth's and brought it to a man watching the practice with eyes of deep sable, hooded beneath a brooding brow, a mop of mink curls spilling over his forehead. "That's Madoc. You cannot see it from here, but he sports a small scar along his jaw." Hilary breathed with a lusty sigh just as Madoc turned his dark gaze on them. She smiled, but he slid his eyes to Tanon briefly before turning back to Gareth. "Isn't he the most dangerous-looking man you've ever seen?"

Madoc definitely had a forbidding look to him, but Gareth was a lethal menace. Before she was tempted to look at him again, she excused herself to Hilary and left the wall. She tripped over the hem of her gown and muttered a tight oath while she righted herself.

Gareth excited and frightened her. And, by God, she loathed the idea of being afraid of anything. She was a Risande, for goodness' sake! Her mother would never have run away as she just had. Her father would be ashamed if he knew how her heart was threatening to pump right out of her chest, even now, halfway across the lawn. And that was exactly what frightened her, not Gareth's effect on her, but the fact that he affected her at all. How could one look from him make her skin feel so tingly all over?

Witnessing her parents' love had made her ache for love. Passion certainly wasn't a stranger to Tanon. Her parents often kissed in front of their children. Their glances were full of meaning, and their tender touches and secret whispers that ended in the privacy of their bedchamber had taught Tanon that passion was not only acceptable, but something to be sought.

But with whom? Cedric? Roger? She didn't want to let herself feel with men like those. What purpose would it serve? Why hope for something she would never have? She couldn't deny Gareth was attractive. But she would not allow him to stir that hope.

Mumbling to herself, she made her way toward the many vendors' stalls set up along the western wall of the castle. Why did he have to come back? She was perfectly content in her predictable little world.

She stopped short in front of a row of colorful stalls. Heavens. She hadn't thought about what being married to Gareth would entail. Roger reminded her of a dog, sniffing in whatever direction the scent came from. She preferred not to think of his bed. She'd been a child last time she saw Cedric, but she knew she would have been unhappy with him. She was curious about Gareth, though, intimidated a little by his innate sensuality and intrigued by it as well.

She'd been taught about the Welsh along the marches. They were men and women willing to fight their enemies to the death. But a few times, when her father's soldiers were lost in their cups, they spoke of the people who lived in the deeper parts of Wales, called the Wild Lands, where the princes still ruled. It was said that the natives dressed scantily, and Tanon believed it now, seeing Gareth garbed

in his sleeveless tunics. They danced around great bonfires to music that could tempt angels into committing
wanton acts. They prayed to heathen gods and swore on
ancient relics. They celebrated pagan feast days whose
names Father Anveley forbade to be spoken at court.

Tanon patted her flushed cheeks at the thought of
Gareth running half-naked through some ancient forest,
hunting down a virgin. Namely, her. When her skin began
to feel clammy beneath her gown, she decided to stop
thinking of Gareth altogether, at least until they stood before the priest, exchanging vows. Her brow creased with
worry. Would her new betrothed insist they be wed by a
high priest donning war paint and holding a pike with a
head on the end of it?

"Goodness, Tanon, you're working yourself up into an
unnecessary fluster," she murmured to herself before offering the vendor a graceful smile. "One tart, if you
please, kind sir."

The vendor handed her a steaming apple tart and
waited while she dug her free fingers into the small hanging pouch at her side in search of a coin.

A large, callused hand suddenly covered hers and
lifted the tart, her fingers still attached, to a set of decadently carved lips.

"Hell, that's good."

Tanon looked up and stared into the face that had been
plaguing her thoughts. How was it possible that he looked
so fit and charged with vitality after practicing all morn?
"Your Highness, do you mind?" she gently scolded.
Gareth shook his head no and took another bite while she
watched. "I haven't even paid for it yet, and it's almost
gone."

He tossed the vendor two coins and demanded two more tarts. While he waited, he stepped around her and plucked what was left of her pastry from her sticky fingers and then leaned his back against the stall.

Resting her fists on her hips, Tanon stared at him while he consumed the last morsel.

"You're very ill-mannered," she declared a bit shakily when he began to lick his fingers.

"I need to keep up my strength if I'm to chase you about these grounds." He crossed his ankles and let his blue eyes glide over her, slowly, relishing every detail from her foot to her crown.

"I would prefer it if you didn't chase me. It's unbecoming," Tanon said stiffly while Gareth received the tarts from the vendor. Surely that would sting his pride some.

He shrugged, causing the muscles in his shoulders to roll and pulse. "Then don't run away from me."

Forest. Naked. Virgin.

Tanon drew her lower lip between her teeth and bit down, hard. "I wasn't running away," she finally managed with a proud tilt of her chin. "I was merely hungry."

"Well, then, allow me to satisfy your craving." The husky timbre of his voice unraveled her thoughts and her nerves.

He offered her a tart and a courtly bow that surprised her—unlike the rakish grin that followed. She was certain he had just offered her something other than a sweet pastry. Unable to stop them, her eyes settled on his mouth. The full suppleness of his lips intoxicated her. Why, she was certain he could tempt a nun into kissing him with that mouth.

She accepted the tart from his hand but didn't eat it, determined to show him that she had control over her appetite, or whatever it was that he offered to satisfy.

Gareth took a hearty bite of his. Tanon covertly watched the strong angles of his jaw while he chewed, then turned away when she realized that she was staring at his lips again.

"Don't you have to prepare for the competition?"

"Nay, I'm ready."

She cast his bare feet a quick glance. Another wave of unwanted heat knotted her belly. She never thought a man's feet could be so sensual, but there was something completely feral about his lack of footwear. Like he belonged in the woods instead of a castle. *Untamed.* She spotted her aunt talking with Hereward by the gardens and set off in their direction, eager to get away from Gareth and the unwanted effect he was having on her.

"Nothing so fine has ever pleased my tongue in Cymru."

Unbidden heat coursed through Tanon's veins at his words, his lilting voice so close to her ear behind her. She stumbled, but his hands closed around her waist. He held her still for a moment, her rump intimately close to his thighs. She closed her eyes, willing herself to breathe as she brought her hands up to cover his. "Let me go," she demanded quietly. What a bold cad he was for speaking to her so, for touching her so. Surely he wasn't going to try to kiss her right here in the open. And did he truly believe she could please his tongue? Heavens! But how would she accomplish that?

"I'm a lady, and I don't—"

Obeying her command, he stepped beside her and groaned, finishing off his tart.

His tart? He'd been speaking of his food? Tanon's face

burned before she quickened her pace away from him. What in the world had come over her? Why was she even thinking about kissing him?

"Pity you don't cook," he said, catching up and casting his sunlit gaze over the many faces strolling the lawns.

"Who says I don't?" When he looked at her, she arched her brow.

He smiled, coaxing another flip from her heart. "You're a noble's daughter. I presumed—"

"You presumed incorrectly, sir. I've spent many hours in the kitchens with my mother and our cook. I can prepare delicacies that would make your mouth water."

With a mere slant of his lips he made a spring of warmth rush across her cheeks. "That's good to know, Tanon."

Her name coming so leisurely from his mouth had a peculiar effect on her. It was a liberty he should not have taken unless he knew her well.

He folded his hands behind his back and took up his steps with her once again. "What else are you proficient at?"

"Sewing." She took a bite of her tart, grateful to be talking about her domestic skills. It kept her thoughts off the melting warmth his closeness caused. "And I can read."

"Truly?" His gaze flickered to hers again, interested.

She found herself wanting to smile at him. "I've also studied the lute."

He stopped walking and turned to face her fully. "Mayhap you could play for me one day."

"Mayhap," she replied breathily.

Sensuality deepened the color of his eyes when his gaze strayed to her mouth. "You're skilled at many things,

Tanon." He lifted his broad fingers and rubbed the pad of his thumb along the corner of her lower lip. "Is there nothing I could teach you?"

His touch sparked a fire through her blood. Her eyes opened wide at his audacity, but she couldn't form a coherent thought.

He gave her a slow, lingering smile and then held up the small crumb he'd just plucked from her lips and placed it on his tongue. "Forgive me, such a sweet delight tempts me beyond reason."

Forgive him? Forgive him for making her feel like an uncivilized wench? She gave a quick look around, feeling like she stood naked on the lawns.

"This veil." He lifted his fingers to her wimple and swept the back of his knuckles across her cheek ever so slightly. "It is an adornment, aye?"

She nodded.

"It's useless compared to your laughter. When might I hear it again?"

She took a step back, breaking contact with him as memories of their summer together flooded her thoughts. *Stop it,* she chided herself. He'd returned for peace, nothing more. Hadn't he made that clear enough to the king? And she was glad. He was taking Cedric's place. They would marry for peace and care nothing for each other. It was exactly what she had readied herself for all these years.

"You're quite bold, my lord." She eyed him while she patted the long veil covering her neck. "You take liberties by touching me so freely."

"I'm your betrothed." He couldn't keep his smile from

widening at the soft blush in her cheeks, the sweet, indignant curl of her mouth.

His eyes traced the contours of her face. The warmth in their golden-fringed depths made her feel bare, open. She folded her arms across her chest as if to shield herself from him. "I daresay you are not. Not until you have—"

"You've never been kissed, have you?"

Tanon gaped at him, willing herself not to look at his lips. "Why do you ask me that kind of question?"

"Because I want an answer."

She frowned at his logical, albeit arrogant, reply. His question put her in a bit of a quandary. Roger rejected her. Must she suffer the humiliation of admitting that no man had ever tried to kiss her?

"I don't make a habit out of kissing my suitors," she answered haughtily. It wasn't really a lie.

"You've always been the perfect lady, haven't you, Tanon." His smile turned so tender it made her legs wobble. "Save when you were climbing trees."

Tanon suddenly missed laughing with him. Being with Gareth again made her remember a time when she didn't worry about what others thought of her. But she was a noble's daughter, bound by expectations that ofttimes felt too heavy to bear. She cleared her throat and squared her chin. She would never shame her family by behaving with anything less than the decorum she'd been taught. Her days of climbing trees and chasing pigs were long over.

"A civilized man would expect nothing less than a lady in his wife." She offered him a practiced smile and forbade herself to stumble as she left him.

Watching the soft sway of her hips, Gareth inhaled

deeply, thinking of the challenge before him. Mayhap she was right about him. Would a civilized man find himself tempted to haul her into his arms and kiss her with such scandalous passion they'd set every tongue in Winchester wagging? Yet somewhere beneath all those layers of linen and polished refinement was the spirited, carefree girl he remembered. He was determined to find her.

Chapter Five

WINCHESTER'S TOURNAMENT FIELD spread across ten acres with separate sections partitioned off for jousting, archery, sword fighting, and the *melee a cheval,* in which over a hundred knights would fight on horseback in a writhing mass of dulled swords and wooden axes.

Seated with her family in a stand just above the western perimeter of the field, Tanon enjoyed a clear view of practicing acrobats, jugglers, and dancing bears and their handlers. Dozens of knights were preparing for the day's activities, their squires hurrying to and fro to arm their lords with spear and sword, and to make certain the knights' thick wool padding and chain mail were securely in place. Excitement and energy charged the air and made Tanon's heart accelerate. The rumbling of so many voices became deafening to her ears. She looked around at the enormous stands encircling her, the hundreds of faces watching with anticipation, sharing laughter and shouts of approval or disapproval when a certain knight rode across the field.

Unwittingly, her eyes searched for Gareth among the competitors, but they found Roger instead. He stood with a group of his knights, polishing their swords beneath the sun. The metal flashed in Tanon's eyes. She thought of one of those blades piercing Gareth's flesh, his lifeblood soaking the grass. She'd seen Gareth at practice, heard the confidence in his voice in the king's solar when he promised her that he would not lose. She had believed it was enough to grant him victory, but now, seeing Roger dressed in chain mail and clutching a sword as long as her leg, she wasn't so sure. Roger wasn't a boy anymore. He'd spent many years learning from William's own son how to wield that sword.

Dear God, she didn't want to marry Roger. She didn't care if Normandy did him any good or not. She didn't care about his nobility, or his manners, or his land. The thought of spending the rest of her life with him turned her stomach. Especially now that Gareth had returned.

When she saw the company of mounted Welshmen entering the field, her anxieties faded into new ones. Her heart thudded faster as the lead rider made his way around the circumference of the field, cantering toward her on a massive warhorse cloaked in trappings of red and gold. She knew it was Gareth, for no other man on the field possessed the arrogance to forgo the protective padding beneath his chain mail and tabard of rich scarlet. Rebecca had told her that most Welshmen didn't fight on horseback, but Tanon remembered Gareth riding so skillfully when he was ten. His posture was arrow straight, his rugged face angled slightly toward the sun. When he tugged his stallion's reins to slow his pace as he drew near, he moved with a leisure that was almost predatory. Mesmerized by his grace and confidence, Tanon couldn't turn away when his stunning blue eyes fastened directly on her.

He was going to win, and then he was going to claim her. She knew that with one look.

Tanon licked her lips, which had gone dry, and broke her gaze from his. She wasn't used to the way her body reacted to him. He tempted her to tear away her mantle of propriety. The sensual candor of his smiles teased and promised delights that made her feel reckless. The warmth in his eyes roused desires she thought she had vanquished.

"Sweeting, you're flushed." Her mother, sitting beside her, pressed her palm against Tanon's veiled cheek. "Are you ill?"

"Non." Tanon forced a smile and returned her gaze to Gareth to watch him ride away.

"I know how hard this is for you," her mother said in a quiet voice. "I, too, was forced to marry a man I didn't know."

Tanon had known Gareth once. "But you came to love him, and he, you."

"Look at me, my love," her mother said, hearing the unhappiness deep in her daughter's voice. "Hereward has assured us that Prince Gareth and his people are not the savages we've been told of by the marcher lords. We know you do not want to marry Lord deCourtenay. We were opposed to that union as well. But your father would have you looked after, protected by an army. And the deCourtenays could provide that." She set her emerald gaze on Gareth on the field. "He is rumored to be unbeaten in battle. But if he proves today that he cannot protect you, your father will go to William, even defy him if he must." She returned her gaze to her daughter. "Pray the prince does not lose, for you will never be happy with Lord de-Courtenay. You have a chance at happiness with the Welshman. I saw the way he looked at you a moment ago. I recognize it. Though I wasn't pleased to find him in your room last eve, 'tis the same place your grandfather, may the Lord keep his beloved soul, found your father the night before our wedding."

Tanon chewed her lower lip, quirking her brow as a thought occurred to her. "Did Father kiss you when he went to your room?"

Brynna smiled, remembering. "*Oui,* he kissed me." The blush spreading across her cheeks convinced Tanon that he'd done more than that.

"Gareth didn't kiss me," Tanon confirmed, sounding neither pleased nor disheartened.

"Of course he didn't. He didn't want to risk having his lips sliced off." Brynna smiled and squeezed her daughter's hand. "There will be trying times ahead for you both. I will not be there to help you through them—nay, Tanon, you must accept this," she interrupted when Tanon tried to protest. "When you were younger, you were so much like your father. This will be an adventure for you. Let yourself enjoy it."

"I will be fine, Mother." Tanon patted Brynna's hand and gave her a reassuring smile, not wanting to upset her any further in her condition. "I will miss you, that is all."

The heralds trumpeted the beginning of the festivities. Soon more jugglers, acrobats, and mummers lined the field. Tanon was drawn into the excitement, and her mood lightened. She smiled when Randalf the bard sang about a beautiful red-haired lady whose smile was like the gossamer wings of a butterfly beating against his heart. Her clear alabaster skin, he crooned, and eyes as green as a summer glade, tempted him to steal a kiss before his dying day. Alas, the fair lady's heart belonged to a ruthless rogue with hair as black as his temper. Tanon playfully chided her father when he mumbled about Randalf finding out just how damned black his heart could be. Her uncle, on the other hand, cheered from his seat, where he reclined lazily with his boots propped atop the short wall when the bard sang next about his wife.

Soon the parade of mounted knights began. A majestic assemblage of horses adorned in cloth of gold and silver, green, red, and purple moved slowly around the perimeter of the field. The men were led in groups by their captains, who carried their banners.

Tanon spotted Gareth carrying the ruby dragon rampant, his men's magnificent horses keeping a measured gait behind him. Lord deCourtenay was announced, and the crowd cheered. Tanon yawned as he rode his destrier around the field.

A few minutes later, Gareth pranced his mount before the king's raised stall, then bowed in his saddle when he turned to face her.

After the rest of the knights were announced, the trumpeter sounded the last call, and squires raced to their tasks. The jousting competition began. Two of Roger's men unseated their opponents without incident, although Madoc nearly impaled his adversary with his blunt-tipped pike.

Finally Gareth and Roger faced off. Both men looked equally sized in the saddle, but Tanon could tell by the stiffness of his movements that Roger was overly padded. Gareth's brawn was pure muscle. He would not lose.

When the earl's lance shattered above a foot, and Gareth's only six inches, Blackburn earned two points. The riders repositioned, received new lances, and thundered toward each other again. The crowd rose to their feet as the riders grew closer. The silence was complete but for the pounding of the hooves of the two frothing steeds about to meet, it seemed, head-on. At the very last instant before impact, Gareth bent low in the saddle and flipped his pike in his gloved hand for a better grip. Lance met shield. Wood cracked and splintered into hundreds of shards, and Roger deCourtenay catapulted out of his saddle.

Tanon finally remembered to breathe when the crowd erupted into shouts of "Huzzah!" Even William gave Gareth a nod of approval as the Welshman rode past him.

Gareth tipped his head back and reveled in the afternoon breeze that cooled his damp face.

Tanon couldn't take her eyes off him. He might be a pagan, but he was the most breathtaking pagan she'd ever seen. Not that she'd seen many. She found herself thinking of him in ways that made her muscles quiver.

She watched him slip from his mount. When he pulled his tabard over his head and unhooked his chain mail, stepping over it where it fell to the ground, a collective gasp rang through the stands, followed by utter silence.

Roger threw him a mocking smile, and Tanon could only guess that he did so believing that Gareth had just made a very foolish error. Tanon had to agree. This was no practice. Even though his opponent did not fight for blood, points were gained by connecting sword to mail. Without the protection of his heavy metal armor, Gareth's flesh could possibly be torn to shreds with each point Roger earned.

The trumpet sounded. The crowd cheered. Tanon squeezed her eyes shut. It wasn't until she heard her father voice his disbelief that she found the courage to peek through her fingers.

Gareth wasn't bloody at all. In fact, he didn't sport a single welt on his bare arms or on any other exposed flesh that she could see. Roger had yet to touch him, and it was clear why. Gareth moved like a breeze, striking before Roger even saw him coming, and then retreating again. He parried every blow with an ease that made Roger's clambering movements almost comical. When Roger swung left, Gareth leaped to the right with such perfect grace that even Normans began to cheer for him.

Tanon looked on, awestruck, her blood fired by his energy, his skill that whispered to her someplace too deep to comprehend, that this man was capable of protecting her in the face of any danger. In the space of ten breaths, he delivered seven blows that would have ended Roger's life had they been inflicted on the battlefield. The clash of his sword echoed throughout the stands as it smashed against Roger's armor.

But the competition was not ended so easily. One of Roger's guardsmen, Sir Albert FitzSimmons, took offense to his lord's swift defeat and called out to Gareth to take him on if he was able.

With one final swing, Gareth sent the flat of his blade crashing into the side of Roger's helmet. An instant later, his weapon pointed at FitzSimmons.

"Points?" Gareth shouted.

"Eight," the new competitor replied with a grin as he advanced. Two other knights belonging to the earl's garrison stepped onto the field, and another three followed on their heels. When two more appeared at Gareth's right, wielding an ax and mace, Madoc, watching from the edge of the field, unsheathed the two long swords dangling from either side of his hips. He took a step forward, resting both blades over his shoulders, but Gareth motioned him to go back to the others.

Watching, Tanon clutched her mother's hand. "He refuses aid! Is he mad?"

"Non," her uncle answered softly, his voice stilled on a breath of anticipation. "He is sure."

On the field, Gareth's golden armbands glinted beneath the afternoon sun as he slowly looped his sword over his head. In position, he beckoned FitzSimmons with a slight jerk of his blade.

Tanon's nerves coiled into springs about to launch her to her feet when FitzSimmons swung. The man was huge. She could almost feel the thundering vibration in her own arm when blade smashed into blade.

Gareth spun, bringing his sword around in a wide arc. He feigned a blow to the right, and then gained the first point when his blade struck FitzSimmons's shoulder. Another man leaped forward and lunged at Gareth's belly. The prince sidestepped, and as the knight passed him, Gareth swiped his blade across his opponent's mailed back with enough grinding pressure to fire sparks. He strode toward the next competitor with all the unbridled arrogance of a king, his long tawny hair swaying off his shoulders, his sharp eyes gleaming like blue steel, taking in every movement around him.

Watching him, Tanon's breath quickened as his every move became a sensual feast for her eyes. Forgetting the fear that he might be injured fighting so many men, her gaze drank in the tight slabs of muscle that gave power to his thighs as he lunged and leaped. He did not need to brace those legs, for he was perfectly balanced. Here was a man. Not the boys her uncle Dante laughed at, teasing that they couldn't woo a sheep to their chambers on a cold winter's night.

Gareth grew more deadly, more brutal with each new man who challenged him, delivering chopping wounds his opponents would be nursing for the next se'nnight. He ducked, parried, and swung, all in the time it took to blink. A point was earned with a loud cry as his opponent sank to his knees, blood spurting from his calves.

There was one man left, one point to be won. Gareth tossed his head back as he cut a direct path to where the knight stood waiting for him, looking a bit uneasy.

"He draws blood. He's enjoying this, brother," Tanon heard her uncle say.

"*Oui,*" her father agreed, his cerulean gaze narrowed on the Welsh warrior. "He is fighting his country's enemy with the king's permission. And *merde,* he is doing it well."

Tanon inhaled sharply as Gareth leaned left to avoid a clean swipe to his arm. He whirled around, dropped to one knee, and drove his sword backward into the knight's armored belly without injury.

The stands went wild. But the sounds of their cheers went unnoticed by Tanon as Gareth, still on one knee, looked up and smiled at her.

Tanon was grateful that she hadn't stood up, for every bone and muscle went weak. Saints, but he still had the most wondrous smile. For one maddening moment, when his mouth curved, it no longer mattered that he was going to take her away. She wanted to touch him, to feel his heart pounding hard in his chest. She wanted to run her fingers down the sinuous, sweaty contours of his arms and revel in his supreme strength and skill. Just looking at him gave birth to images so perversely sexual, she nearly choked on the shame of it when her mother squeezed her fingers.

"He comes."

Gareth paused only to wipe his blade before he sheathed it. He looked determined. Unstoppable. When he reached her, he turned only for a moment to her father.

"My lord," he said, his breath short with exertion, "with your blessing." He reached over the wall and took Tanon's hand, bringing her to her feet. "I claim your daughter."

Chapter Six

IT WAS BEYOND ARROGANT. It was downright barbaric the way Gareth had "claimed" her. Was she some prize to be won like chattel at the whims of men? Why, he behaved like a victorious warlord from a less civilized time. Tanon had almost expected him to haul her over his shoulder and carry her away.

She quivered while two of her personal handmaidens hastened to dress her. At her shoulder, her dearest friend and nursemaid, Rebecca, wove her long tresses into a heavy plait.

Swabbing her clammy cheeks with the backs of her knuckles, Tanon wished her body would decide if it was hot or cold. She wouldn't burden her mother with her troubles, but if she didn't speak to someone, she would go mad.

"Rebecca," she asked softly. "I would speak with you about this power Prince Gareth has over my thoughts."

"Nay, Eloise." Rebecca stopped braiding and called out to one of the handmaidens laying out Tanon's gown on her bed. "Not the dark blue. Tanon will wear the amber tonight."

"Tomorrow," Tanon went on, almost oblivious to Lorette fitting a clean linen shift over her head, "I will be his wife." Gripping Eloise's shoulders, Tanon lifted one foot into her hose, and then the other.

Lowering her eyes to conceal the shame of her thoughts, Tanon pressed on. "He makes me feel quite . . . odd. And not at all like a lady."

Rebecca smiled, her gaze softened with understanding. "He's awakening your womanhood."

Tanon's blood rushed to her face so swiftly she nearly passed out. "Well, what if I don't want . . . That is, I cannot seem to control my own thoughts. He makes my stomach feel as if it's on fire. What if I cannot . . ." She floundered for the right words. Heavens, she had never worried about sharing Roger's bed. With him, she would have done what was required of her and hoped he left her alone the remainder of the time. But she worried over it with Gareth. She slapped her palms against her thighs. "I've never even been kissed!"

"Your body will know what to do when the time comes," Rebecca assured her with a gentle pat on the arm. "If he has a tender hand, your body will react. Simply let it."

"And if his hand is hurtful?"

"Then your father will deliver him into an early grave."

"My father will not be there! He is leaving me at the mercy of—"

"Mind your tongue when you speak of your father." The nurse wagged her finger at Tanon. "You know as well as I that he would be with you if he could."

Tanon looked away and sighed. Dear Rebecca, she'd

been Brynna's handmaiden before Tanon's mother even met her father. She'd helped deliver Tanon and her siblings into the world, then doted on them like a mother. Tanon loved her dearly and knew that Rebecca favored her above her brothers and sisters. And she knew the reason for it. Tanon resembled her father. Rebecca, Tanon was certain, harbored a secret, forbidden love for Brand Risande. It was obvious to everyone who lived at Avarloch, though Rebecca believed she concealed her feelings well. The woman could hardly look at Tanon's father without her fair complexion turning bright pink. But despite stories of a much younger Brynna chasing Rebecca from her chambers after finding the handmaiden bathing Brynna's new husband, Tanon's mother didn't seem to mind the way Rebecca grew flustered around him. Tanon didn't mind, either. She knew her father's heart belonged to no one but his wife. It was what her father's unreturned affection had cost Rebecca that tore at Tanon's heart. She had become the children's nurse and remained with the Risandes for the last score of years. She never married, and it was a pity, because she was such a giving, beautiful woman. Her wheaten hair was still untouched by silver, her eyes as blue as Tanon remembered from her childhood. But her gaze had become vacant, her spine more staunch. She would have been better off marrying a man she didn't love than sacrificing her heart to a man who could never love her back.

She breathed out a long sigh while her handmaidens dressed her in a gown of warm amber linen with emerald silk embroidered into the long cuffs and neckline. Rebecca covered Tanon's head with a cascading wimple of matching fabric and secured the veil with a thin band of gold over her brow.

Tanon clutched her nurse's hand and held it to her heart. "I don't want to leave you alone."

Rebecca smiled tenderly. "I won't be alone, sweeting. I will—" Her words were caught up in Tanon's tight embrace.

"Come to Wales with me, Rebecca, I beg you. Oh, I beg you. Leave my father's service and come with me. Mother has Elsbeth, and I could not bear the thought of not knowing how you fare."

Though it would nearly shatter Rebecca's heart to leave the Risandes, she could not refuse Tanon. The girl had never been away from her father's care. How could they send her off to Wales with no one but Hereward the Wake? What did he know of comforting a woman? He'd never been married, had no daughters. What would that oaf do when her Tanon needed her hair combed or had need to speak of womanly things?

The nurse withdrew and plucked a napkin from her girdle and wiped her nose. The poor dear was about to be carted off to what Rebecca's Saxon ancestors called the Wild Territories, and she was worried about her nurse! "Of course I will come with you if your husband allows it," Rebecca promised. "Though I think you've naught to fret about. The prince will fall deeply in love with you once he comes to know your kind heart. You are so much like your father."

Tanon smiled softly, knowing the sooner she got Rebecca away from her father, the better.

Gareth swiped the drying cloth over his belly and reached for a fresh pair of black leather breeches. He was alone, mayhap for the last time in his life. He wondered if other husbands were this nervous the night before they were bound in matrimony. Every woman he'd ever been with, and all those he might ever have been with in the future, flashed through his thoughts, teasing, pouting, sashaying away from him forever. He exhaled and pulled a black woolen shirt over his head. He was certain of two things. One, he was willing to watch all those women leave—if it would bring peace with the Normans. And two, his wife-to-be was lovelier than all the others combined. Her eyes were so vividly green, until the sunlight hit them at a certain angle and sparked tiny flecks of blue in the center. The way she looked when she veiled those eyes beneath her sweep of feathery lashes, the shape of her face, the delicate way she moved her arms, the way she breathed, all worked at usurping his attention, his every waking thought. Exactly the way she had consumed his thoughts until he was ten and two, and facing his first enemy on a battlefield.

He never could forget her completely, for her name was known throughout Cymru. He'd heard it spoken many times during Celebration in Deheubarth with his uncle. Tanon Risande, the Norman who would unite their countries. That union was to take place between her and Cedric, and hell, Gareth hated his brother for years over it. Yet when his uncle had offered her to him, Gareth had almost refused. He'd wanted peace with her people from the first time he met her. But no matter how much he had wanted to glory in her toothless smiles as a boy, as a man, he wanted nothing to do with her people. Until he saw her again.

Even though she pretended to be someone else, he knew her. He'd left a playful, happy little girl and returned to a pillar of flawless manners. But there was something deeply provocative about her. It made her plump lips part with short, scant breaths when he smiled at her. A hunger smoldered beneath that fragile shell of innocence and etiquette. He wanted to peel that shell away and expose the woman beneath.

He wasn't unfeeling to how difficult it was going to be for her to leave her family. He would do his best to help her adjust. An easy task. It was the time he was going to have to take with her that made him doubt his control. He wanted to touch her and watch her come undone. He wanted to kiss her, taste her breath, take her like a beast in heat. But she was marrying a prince, not an animal. He'd prove it to her if it killed him.

A light smile creased his mouth at the thought of how oblivious she was to her beauty. He'd been with enough women to know when they were aware of their power over men. Tanon hadn't used her lovely dimple to try to beguile him. All the more reason that it had. He was certain now, after his encounter with her father, that the reason she had never been kissed was not for lack of men wanting to brand that mouth, but because every man in Winchester and Avarloch feared her father. Gareth was glad he would be the first to kiss her. The first to—

There came a knock at his door.

"Come," he called.

Three men plunged into his room, followed by Madoc, who sauntered in and then kicked the door closed with the back of his boot.

"Why the hell do we have to bathe before we eat?" the

first complained, scratching a square jaw blanketed beneath thick chestnut whiskers. "I just bathed a fortnight past."

"Aye, Alwyn, and you smell like a boar who's been lying in shit for that long," Madoc snarled. He crossed the room and flung himself on Gareth's bed. "Tomas, toss me an apple."

Tomas, a tall, lanky man with light brown waves tied at his nape, looked around the room for the bowl of fruit. "There are no apples here."

"Try below stairs." Madoc closed his eyes and settled deeper into the pillow. "In the kitchens, mayhap."

Tomas gaped at him. "I'm not going all the way to the kitchen to get you an apple."

"Very well." Madoc swung his legs off the mattress and stood up in one swift movement. "I'll fetch it myself." He patted his brother on the shoulder. His grin would have been pleasant if not for the promise of retribution cooling his dark eyes.

"I'll get the damned apple, you bastard," Tomas ground out between clenched teeth, hating the fact that he always surrendered to his brother's unspoken threats. Madoc had never lifted a finger to him, but he had a way of staring into a man's eyes that made many an enemy soil their breeches before they fled the way they'd come.

"You're probably afraid of wandering around the castle alone," Tomas muttered under his breath, trying to salvage his pride as he strode out of the room.

Madoc turned back to Gareth, unfazed by his brother's insult. "I found Bleddyn roaming around in the cellars."

"Aye?" Gareth sat at the edge of the bed and looked up vaguely from tying his boots. "Was he lost?"

" 'Tis his claim." Madoc pulled a dagger out of his boot and slid the tip under his fingernail. "I don't like him."

"You don't like anyone," Gareth replied succinctly.

"He was your brother Cedric's man."

Gareth paused to shrug. "So were you."

"My loyalty has always been to you," Madoc answered, his voice clipped with offense.

Gareth looked up from his boot and smiled. "Aye, it has. I trust your instincts. Keep an eye on Bleddyn."

"We must discuss the issue of bathing. I'm not using their soap," Alwyn avowed. "I won't smell like a Norman."

"You'll smell like a lily flower if it's required," Gareth said flatly, rising from the bed. "You must learn to adapt to whatever circumstance you're in, in order to gain control over it." It was this wise advice given to him by his uncle that had saved his hide on more than one occasion. He'd been trained to battle his way to victory, but he preferred using his wits. Fewer people died that way. "We're breaking bread with the Risandes tonight," he reminded them. "I don't want any of you intentionally bumping shoulders with anyone like you did last eve. No looking for fights. Remember why we're here."

"To get the girl," Cian, Madoc's youngest brother, confirmed, his dark gold eyes eclipsed by a wild tumble of matching curls.

"To secure peace for our people," Gareth corrected him patiently. "Whatever the cost. If it requires that we eat, drink, and smile with Normans, then we will do so."

"Or sleep with them," Alwyn grumbled with disgust. He looked around the room for something to spit into.

"Alwyn." Gareth's voice deepened with command. "Whatever your feelings toward the Normans, I share them. But Lady Risande is to be my wife. You will honor and respect her, the same way you do me. Is that clear?"

"Aye, Gareth." Alwyn scowled at him. "Just don't forget what she is."

"She is one of us, and we shall treat her with kindness," Gareth said firmly. When Alwyn nodded, Gareth said in a lighter tone, "No killing anyone." He looked directly at Madoc. "Understand? I know it's been difficult for you."

Madoc shrugged his shoulders, but he didn't look happy about it. "You're not even married yet and you've gone soft."

Passing him to leave the room, Gareth laughed quietly. "Meet me in the lists later and I'll show you how soft I am."

As Gareth descended the stairs, his thoughts returned to Tanon. He mulled over the best course of action to take with her. This marriage had a purpose, and he would see it fulfilled. He would not forget she was a Norman, but he would try to make her happy and strengthen a Norman–Cymry alliance. That meant devoting time to her, helping her adjust to her new way of life. Take his time showing her that he wasn't an uncivilized barbarian. Strip her slowly and tenderly of fear, her innocence, and finally her clothes. Make love to her in every way imaginable.

All feats he could accomplish. Adapt. Be in control of the circumstances. Forget that once, long ago, she had turned his world upside down. Christ, he thought as he reached the bottom of the stairs and grew anxious at the prospect of seeing her. This wasn't going to be easy.

~

Tanon left her chambers shortly after Gareth and his men left his. Rebecca had disappeared down the long hall, on her way to Lady Brynna's chambers, so Tanon was alone when she began to descend the stairs and saw Gareth standing at the bottom with Eleanor Fitzdrummond. For a moment, Tanon simply remained in her spot, watching them. So, the prince found full heaving bosoms as enticing as Roger found them. She should have guessed he would. No man could smile the way that Welsh snake did unless his thoughts were preoccupied with fleshly desires . . . or apple tarts. Well, she didn't care if he kissed Eleanor right there in front of her. Perhaps he might even decide to drag Lady Fitzdrummond off to Wales instead of her. *Oui,* then she could marry Roger as planned.

She took another step down, ready to walk right past them, when Gareth smiled at something the wench said. Oh, it wasn't just any smile, such that Tanon might be able to forget while she lived out the remainder of her miserable days with the drunken Earl of Blackburn. It was a knee-melting smirk alit with amusement and riddled with male arrogance.

Goodness, but seeing him with Eleanor stirred her temper. How could he so blatantly disregard her feelings by flirting with the same woman who had tried to steal her previous husband-to-be? Why did she even care? She didn't, she decided, descending the stairs and stabbing at Gareth and Eleanor with a venomous glare as she passed them.

A figure appeared from out of the shadows to her right and stepped into her path. Tanon looked up into a set of wide, dark eyes and a starkly chiseled jaw, marred by a thin scar. His jaw twitched before he spoke.

"Your betrothed is that way and will escort you into the great hall." Without taking his eyes off her, he pointed over her shoulder toward Gareth.

Tanon would have stepped around him and proceeded on her way if she could convince her feet to move. This was Madoc, and up close he looked infinitely more deadly than he did out of doors and halfway across the lists.

"My, but you're an ogre," she scolded him gently before turning her back to him to face Gareth again.

Madoc stared at her braced shoulders with a faint smile softening his features.

Tanon said nothing, offered no greeting to Gareth while he sauntered toward her. Eleanor was gone, but the sting she caused Tanon remained.

"Madoc, you may go." Gareth looked over her shoulder and waited until his first in command disappeared into the great hall before he addressed Tanon. "You really must stop running away from me." His voice was a compelling blend of silk and steel.

Tanon did her best not to let that voice, those eyes, glittering in the torchlit hall, affect her. She was angry with herself for even caring about what he did with Eleanor. She hadn't with Roger. Still, Gareth had once been her champion. Pity he had changed into such a lout. "I'm surprised you took notice," she replied, trying to keep her voice blasé.

An amused smile softened his lips before he feigned a pout. "You think I can be lured as easily as deCourtenay? Tanon, I'm insulted."

She gaped at him. "Oh, please do forgive me, then, for being as insensitive as you."

Gareth looked a bit surprised at the flash of temper lighting her eyes. When he spoke, his voice was tender. "Lady Fitzdrummond's offer to throw herself into my bed was refused. Do you really think I would toss away gold in exchange for clay?"

Tanon bristled. Eleanor offered to throw herself into his bed? Oh, if she wasn't a la—"Gold?"

"Aye." He nodded, taking in the exact way confusion quirked her brow.

Tanon wasn't fully certain, but for the space of a breath he looked as if he were fighting not an armed opponent, but her effect on him.

Silly, she chastised herself, remembering all too clearly how she'd thought he meant to kiss her today, when in truth he'd been thinking of his sweet pastry. She wouldn't be so naïve again.

Her value to you is noted. He had said those words to the king. William loved her, and the Welsh obviously knew it. That's why Gareth needed her. She was the perfect peace offering, Wales's security that the Normans would not attack and risk killing her while she lived among them.

"Gold is a precious asset to your people right now, is it not?"

Gareth stared at her, looking like he wanted to say something. Before he could, Tanon averted her gaze from his. "I've already resigned myself to this marriage. You've no need to—"

He closed the distance between them in one stride. His scent of leather and forest hovered over her. She looked up into his eyes gleaming with heat beneath his long lashes.

". . . pretend that you . . ." Her words caught in her throat when he lifted his hand to her face. Her eyes opened wider. "What do you think you're doing?" She could barely breathe as he angled his head, bringing his mouth closer to hers. This time there was no mistake. He was going to kiss her! Tanon knew she should move away, but his smile was so captivating, so familiar before his lips brushed across hers. He didn't stop there, that she might be able to gain some control over her limbs and push him away, calling him a scoundrel for kissing her right here in the corridor, but caressed her mouth with beguiling tenderness and lingering hunger that pulled a low moan from her.

Gareth withdrew slowly and spread his gaze over her hooded eyes, her parted lips. Christ, he almost groaned aloud, this was going to be infinitely more difficult than he thought.

Chapter Seven

TANON SAT AT HER FATHER'S TABLE watching Gareth share his drink with Hereward the Wake beside the great hearth. Supper had already been served, and her newly betrothed still hadn't come to her table. He knew where her family's table was, for he'd looked to it a dozen times already.

Her mouth still tingled from his kiss. Saints, she'd been kissed! She almost lifted her fingers to her lips, remembering how wonderful it felt. Wonderful—and terrifying. For it tore away at her defenses and left her weak and willing.

Eleanor Fitzdrummond had the audacity to saunter by Gareth on three separate occasions, but to Tanon's relief, he didn't so much as blink in the wench's direction. Had he truly refused Eleanor? The thought of it made him even more attractive, blast him. It would be tragic if she allowed herself to care for a man who valued her only for the safety she could provide for his people.

She wished she didn't find him so compelling to look at.

Every time she noticed something about him that she hadn't noticed before, like the way his thumb stroked the side of his cup while he listened to Hereward, or the way the soft black wool of his shirt caressed the molded angles of his chest, she forced herself to look away. But before she could help herself, she was staring again. Just when she decided to turn her attention somewhere else for good, he caught her eye and winked at her.

"Who's the man hovering around the prince?" Dante asked Brand. "His jousting skills were a bit unconventional at the tourney today, but most impressive."

"He's Gareth's first in command," her father answered, sparing Madoc a brief glance. "His name is Madoc ap . . ." Brand rolled the word around in his mouth for a moment, then gave up. "*Enfer,* they have a strange language. I cannot pronounce the name. A simple word like 'greetings' is transformed into *cyfarchion.* Try saying that while keeping your tongue in the right place."

Rebecca, who always sat at the Risandes' table, lifted her serviette to her mouth and began to cough. Tanon patted her back and held a cup to the nurse's lips.

"Well, whatever his name is, he's already given you three"—Dante narrowed his shimmering gaze on Madoc—"*non,* four black glares, brother."

"I think he took offense to something I said to his lord on the way to his room last eve."

Tanon turned to her father. "What did you say to him?"

"Just a little advice from his betrothed's father about keeping you safe," Brand told her with a soft smile.

Dante laughed, knowing exactly what kind of advice Brand had offered Prince Gareth. He turned to his wife, flashing his dimple at her. "Brand makes enemies wherever he goes. Aren't you happy you married the charming brother?"

"I think she would have preferred the handsome one. *Oui, ma belle soeur?"* Brand favored Gianelle with a smile so breathtaking that when she saw it, one of the serving women dropped a mushroom into Tanon's cup.

Sighing, Gianelle popped a small slice of heron into her mouth. "I have learned to make do with what I have, *mon frère plus beau.*"

Dante laughed and swooped down on her, burying his face into her neck. She giggled at something he whispered to her and swatted him with her serviette.

Tanon watched them with a longing gaze and then smiled at Robert, their oldest son, and their daughters, Katherine and Cassandra. She was glad her mother was still above stairs with her maid Elsbeth, tending to Tanon's twin sisters, Ellie and Anne, for she didn't think she could bear watching the affection between her parents tonight.

"Good eve, my lords," Gareth interrupted Tanon's solemn thoughts while Hereward dragged out a chair opposite Rebecca's. "Ladies," the prince added, his voice velvet as he looked at Tanon.

The way he stared was bold considering who was sitting at the table. But, Tanon reasoned, he'd already taken a liberty with her in the hall. She belonged to him, and he made no attempt to hide that fact. Still, she glanced at her father from beneath her lashes just to make certain he wasn't about to slay Gareth with his sword.

"Gareth, welcome to the table." Brand offered him a pleasant though somewhat stiff smile. After introducing everyone, including Tanon's siblings, Brand leaned back in his chair and waited for Gareth to be seated. "Excuse my wife's absence. She is still above stairs tending to our daughters. They ate too many honey cakes today." He patted his flat stomach to indicate their malady.

"And your wife is caring for them?" Gareth asked, sincerely surprised as he settled in beside Tanon.

"Of course." Brand brought a flagon of ale to his lips. "Why do you ask?"

Gareth shrugged his shoulders. "I was told that Norman noblewomen have no inclination to tend to their children. That's why their sons grow to be—"

"You've been terribly misinformed." Tanon cut him off, offended that he would think such a thing about her mother.

Turning to her, Gareth slanted his mouth. "Forgive me for making such a rash judgment of people I don't know."

She caught the irony and conceded him the point. Her toes curled when he offered her a smile of truce.

Dante used his foot beneath the table to push away the empty chair across from him. "Have a seat," he invited the man standing behind Gareth's chair. His friendly smile deepened into a challenging smirk. "Madoc, *oui?*"

"Nay," Madoc answered with a sardonic sneer of his own. "I prefer to stand."

"I understand." Dante's eyes glimmered over the rim of his goblet when he lifted it to his mouth. "Standing makes you look bigger."

Beside him, Gianelle covered her mouth with her hand to conceal her amusement.

"So do petite wives," Madoc countered, and bowed slightly to her.

Dante laughed and lifted his cup to Madoc. "Ah, finally, someone who can match words with me besides my beautiful wife. Sit and share a drink with me, and perhaps in the morn, before the wedding, we can find out if your blade is as sharp as your wit."

"Madoc, join us," Gareth said without turning to his first in command. "I need no protection here."

Dante agreed while Madoc took his seat. "I'd venture you need no protection anywhere, Your Highness. Your skill was extraordinary today." He smiled when Gareth thanked him. "Did you learn to fight like that by battling Normans?"

"Nay." Gareth glanced up at the server setting a trencher down in front of him before moving on to Madoc. "By battling my brothers. I was four, the youngest of the brood when my father died and my mother sent us to live with my uncle in Deheubarth. We were immediately put to the training field, where my brothers repeatedly trounced me." His self-mocking grin worked well at disarming the two warriors facing him. "Taking pity on me, my uncle taught me how to avoid their fists by dancing."

"Dancing?" Brand asked.

Naked beneath the full moon, probably, Tanon thought, and then chased those images away with a drink of her cooled mead.

"Aye," Gareth explained. "Dancing helps you find your center of gravity. Balance," he added when both Brand and Dante cast him skeptical looks. "Balance and speed are integral to our training. I've since taught every person in my village."

"To fight or to dance?" Brand inquired, narrowing his eyes, curious to know more about his daughter's future husband.

"Both."

"I hate dancing." Oliver, Tanon's youngest brother, scowled and folded his arms over his chest.

"That's because your dances are solemn. We dance in celebration." Gareth winked at him, setting Tanon's nerves on fire.

"In celebration of what?" Brand asked him.

"Victories, a good harvest, the birth of a babe."

Tanon's other brother William snorted. "If we had to dance every time a babe was born, we'd be dancing all the time."

The warmth of Gareth's laughter caused even Brand to smile when Gareth looked around the table at his children, and then at him. "Six children is a good start, Lord Brand."

Tanon cut him a horrified look out of the corner of her eye. She hoped he was jesting. She'd watched her mother give birth to four of her six siblings, and she certainly didn't want to go through *that* more than a half dozen times.

"And we're expecting another," Brand replied proudly.

"My mother had twelve children," Gareth told him, finding it easier than he would have imagined a se'nnight ago to converse with a Norman warrior. Beside him, Tanon groaned. "My four sisters died at birth, and all of my brothers, save Cedric, were lost in battle over the years."

Tanon felt her heart lurch remembering the small army of boys when they'd visited Winchester. Almost all of them dead. She wondered if they had perished at the hands of Normans.

"All the more reason never to have children," she murmured.

"Nonsense," Rebecca scolded. "You shall have many little ones."

Tanon kicked her nurse beneath the table, but then she thought of a way to take Rebecca with her without Gareth's refusal. "If I'm to have so many children, I will need my most beloved nurse with me to help bring them into the world." She turned to Gareth. "Don't you agree?"

He took a bite of his heron and shook his head. "There are dozens of women in my village who know how to deliver babes."

Tanon's nostrils flared softly. Heavens, but he riled her. She was being denied her mother. She would not be denied her dearest friend as well. "If you insist that I conceive your babes, then Rebecca will have to be there to deliver them, else I will refuse to have them."

Gareth cut a side glance to Tanon's father and smiled. Warning the man's daughter that her refusal might make for a more interesting way of conceiving probably wasn't the best course to take.

He took a swig of ale instead. It wasn't like he didn't know Tanon possessed a fair amount of spiritedness. He welcomed it. Hell, she was going to need it in Wales. But the spark of stubbornness in her eyes when she defied him was another matter entirely. He wasn't used to being refused. His people obeyed him to stay alive, and so would she. There would be time to speak with her about it later. Now he would grant her request, hoping that having her nurse with her would help her adjust.

"Very well. Your nurse may come with us."

Sitting at Rebecca's right, Hereward closed his eyes and ground his teeth.

Gareth's voice settled over Tanon like a downy blanket, but his heavy lashes only half concealed the reluctance that cooled his eyes.

"Thank you," she whispered, knowing somehow that he just allowed her to win what could have become a heated battle. She smiled to show her appreciation, and his gaze softened. So close, she could almost read the thoughts he tried to hide behind his stoic expression. He liked her. But he didn't like being defied. According to her mother, no man did. And Gareth *was* a prince, after all, and arrogant to say the least. She would have to think about that later, though. Right now, she had a more pressing matter to worry about. Like how to keep from melting all over the table if he continued to look at her the way he did.

When she began to turn away, he covered her fingers with his.

"Tanon." He leaned in closer, addling her brains completely with his scent and the deep huskiness of his voice meant only for her ears. "I find I've missed the way you look when you smile. I would like you to do it more often."

He was arrogant, but her mouth went dry nonetheless, and her heart accelerated. She angled her head slightly to look at him and graced him with a smile that pulled a labored breath from his lungs.

How nice it was, Tanon decided while she returned her attention to her trencher, to have such an effect on a man.

Chapter Eight

~

TANON SAT BOLT UPRIGHT in her bed. Today she was
going to be bound to Gareth. Today he was going to take
her away from her family, away from Avarloch, to a land
as untamed as he was. She was going to be his wife, expected to share his bed.

But neither the unhappiness of leaving her family nor
the anxiety of being naked in a man's bed was the cause
of the panic rising in her chest now. It clutched at her
lungs until it erupted into a gasp.

She liked Gareth. She always had, and when he returned he brought with him something she had lost through
the years—her daydreams. Already she could feel the effects of other emotions stirring inside the place she kept
them. She had inherited a store of passions, and they were
being roused, evident in how quickly he could rile her
temper. The idea of living in Wales frightened her, but she
embraced her fear, absorbing its energy. It quickened her
heart and made her feel alive. She craved life with every
fiber of her being, but allowing herself to live it meant

exposing her heart to the misery of a loveless marriage—or worse, a one-sided one.

Non, *I will find a way to stop what he is doing to me.* She swung her legs over the side of the bed. The panic made her body tremble. She had to marry him. There was no stopping that. But if he didn't like her, if he stopped looking at her all the time and behaved a little more like Roger—well, then, she'd stop liking him and everything would return to normal.

A knock sounded at the door.

"Come," Tanon called, resolve squaring her shoulders and steadying her nerves. When she saw her aunt Gianelle and her two young cousins at their mother's skirt, she smiled and opened her arms to receive them.

Katherine and Cassandra leaped onto her bed and commenced chattering nonstop.

"Aunt Brynna is retching again," Katherine informed her with a sickly look of her own to emphasize.

"Are you going to be a princess?" the younger girl, six-year-old Casey, asked, crawling into her lap, her locks of honey gold spilling over her petite shoulders.

Katherine tugged on Tanon's shift. "Are you coming back?" Her large amber eyes solemnly awaited Tanon's answer.

Tanon couldn't bear giving it to her. It would be difficult to reenter England once she crossed into Wales. But not impossible, she thought, recalling Gareth's guarantee to William that he had crossed the marches without bloodshed. She simply had to find a way to convince Gareth to bring her back for a visit, at least once a year.

What was it her mother had told her when she was preparing to marry Cedric? A woman, if she was clever, should never try to rule her husband. But a soft touch and the feminine wiles God gave her worked well at bending a man to her will.

She smiled, kissed her cousin's head, and said, "Of course. I will visit you as soon as I am able. Now go below stairs with Casey. I wish to speak to your mother."

Gianelle watched her daughters leave the room. "Go find your papa, my darlings. Katherine, hold your sister's hand down the stairs," she called out after them, then turned back to Tanon. "Something troubles you?"

"*Oui*. I have a question to ask you about men and being married. It is of utmost importance."

Gianelle went to the bed and sat at the edge. She took Tanon's hand and gave it a firm pat. "I realize your betrothed looks a bit . . . primitive, but that is not necessarily a bad thing."

Tanon turned scarlet when her aunt blushed. "I was not talking about that! I just want to know what . . . Dear God, Aunt Gia, how can primitive not be a bad thing when your husband is tremendous and you are so delicate? *Non, non*, do not answer me. Just tell me, please, what are feminine wiles?"

Gianelle's huge topaz eyes narrowed on Tanon. "Wiles?" Her niece nodded. "Well, let me see now." She looked up, and then to the right, tapping her finger against her chin. "They are your brains."

Tanon giggled, knowing that couldn't be right. "But mother said *feminine* wiles. If they're brains, then men have them too, *oui?*"

Gianelle glanced at her and decided not to voice what she thought of *that* silly notion. "Well, of course, Dante has them. And your father is certainly intelligent, since he had the good sense to wed your mother." She stood up, reached for Tanon's brush, and began working the tangles out of her niece's long hair. "I suspect William has some brains beneath that gruff exterior."

Tanon closed her eyes to her aunt's ministrations and asked her how Dante had ever managed to win her heart. Gianelle certainly didn't think highly of men, save her husband. Then again, she had been a slave before she met Dante, suffering under the abuse of her masters.

Gianelle sighed, remembering the man who had given her freedom, and so much more. "Your uncle was kind and even-tempered, and so very patient."

"But I thought he was a womanizing snake?"

"Oh, he was." Gianelle snorted softly. "Before he met me, there was not a woman alive in England or Normandy who was safe from his bewitching charm and devilish dimple. The same dimple you have."

Tanon nodded and smiled, lost in the gentle tones of her aunt's voice.

"He made me laugh, and he gave me things I dreamed of all my life." Her voice grew softer, along with her brushstrokes. "How can you not fall in love with a man who gives you the sea?"

"You simply cannot," Tanon agreed with a wistful sigh, engrossed in her aunt's familiar tale of being rescued from the bonds of servitude by a dashing, loving man.

Eloise burst into the room, startling both women. "Forgive my tardiness, my lady," she begged with a curtsey, though the moment she straightened, her repentance ended. "Come, now, we've hours of preparation before the wedding, and less than that to see it all done." She nearly bolted across the room, heading straight for Tanon's emerald green wedding gown strewn across a high-backed chair.

"I still don't see what's the rush." Tanon watched her maid scurry by her, dress in hand, toward the door.

"'Tis wrinkled! I'll have to—" Eloise pulled the door open and staggered backward, then curtsied again at the man standing on the other side. "Your Majesty."

The years had been kind to William the Conqueror. Well past middle age, he still appeared handsome and commanding. Even more so this morn, garbed in full regalia for Tanon's wedding. He wore his shoulder-length hair, gone completely gray since the death of his wife, Matilda, a little over a year ago, in a neat queue tied with a black ribbon at the back of his head. A banded circlet of pure gold attested to his sovereignty, along with a breathtaking surcoat of scarlet with thick gold and silver thread stitched into the collar, cuffs, and hem. His deep gray gaze still possessed the power to thwart even the most resilient enemy. But when his eyes rested on Tanon, they were filled with regret.

"Leave us," he quietly commanded Eloise. He stepped inside and held up his palm to stop Gianelle when she moved to leave as well, his gaze never leaving Tanon's.

"How do you fare, *ma précieuse?*"

"I feel like everyone is eager to see me go. I know it's not so," she told him when he parted his lips to protest. "Everything has just happened rather quickly."

"*Oui,*" he agreed miserably. "Tomorrow you will leave us." Averting her gaze, he crossed the room and sat in the chair that had held Tanon's gown moments before. "Gareth must return to Wales with haste. His presence, as well as yours, is vital."

"If it wasn't, you wouldn't send me," Tanon told him, assuring him that she understood.

William's eyes met hers, and he couldn't help but smile. He had held her in his arms hours after her birth. He had loved her as his own from that moment on. It was her great importance to him that made her so valuable in Wales, and for that, he was truly sorry. He leaned forward in his chair and rested his elbows on his thighs.

"I know you've been taught about the land you were to share with Cedric, but I wish to give you a better understanding of where you're going. Wales is fraught with war. The natives fight us on the marches and each other in the wild lands." He gave her a look that said he would rather be telling her anything but this. "I don't mean to frighten you, Tanon. But you need be prepared."

"You are not frightening me," she promised him.

William regarded her with pride lighting his eyes, unsure if she reminded him more of her father or her mother.

"The country is not ruled by one king, but many, each governing regions in the north, south, east, and west," he continued. "The kings are enemies, but it is the princes who bring war against one another, vying to expand their territories. King Gruffydd's son, Dafydd of Gwynedd in the north, is the prince we thought had killed Gareth. You are a pledge of peace from a Norman king, not a Welsh one. Do you understand, *ma chère?* There will still be fighting in Wales, though you will not be in the middle of it. I have been assured that Gareth's region is peaceful."

Tanon nodded, thankful that Gareth was such a skilled warrior.

"I haven't had a chance to speak with you about all of

this." William looked away from her again. "I would have you know—"

"Non." Tanon sprang from her bed and knelt at his feet. "Whatever you wish to tell me, you already say with your eyes. I know how difficult some of your decisions have been. For I've seen you on your knees before God in the church. You are wise and merciful, forgiving even Hereward for his years of rebellion. You've been a friend to my parents and a loving guardian to me. I will not have you plead forgiveness again. There is no need." She took his large hand and brought it to her cheek. "All will be well with me," she promised, vowing to ease his concern.

William's battle-scarred fingers cupped her face, and when she looked up at him, he smiled so tenderly she nearly wept.

"I knew your mother would produce astonishing children. I was not wrong."

"You rarely are."

"Ask anything of me, Tanon Risande, and if it is in my power to grant it to you, I shall."

A mischievous grin spread over her face. "Tell me what feminine wiles are."

The king stared at her for a moment, wondering if he had heard her right. Then he blinked and shifted his gaze to Gianelle, hoping she would answer. When she didn't, he frowned and cleared his throat. "They are . . . they are . . ."

"Oui?"

He glanced down into Tanon's guileless expression and cleared his throat again. "They are the mystique of a woman. *Oui,* that is what they are."

"The mystique?" asked Gianelle, thoroughly confused. "Explain this, please."

William tucked his finger into his collar and gave it a yank. "A woman has many weapons to use on a man."

"Weapons?"

"*Oui,* Tanon. Weapons," the king said, looking toward the door, where he prayed Brynna would enter and take over this confounded conversation. "The sway of her . . . er . . . well, her hips, for one. She also possesses that 'come hither look.' 'Tis a certain thing she does with the lashes of her eyes."

"What certain thing?" Tanon pressed, eager now that she was getting to the bottom of it.

William looked directly at her and batted his lashes. Tanon burst into laughter.

"So feminine wiles are what a woman uses to soften a man." Gianelle wanted to smile for discovering what the king was trying to say. But she found the truth of it very unappealing.

"To bend him to her will." Tanon grinned when William nodded.

"It's trickery," Gianelle complained. "A husband deserves honest passion." She shook her head and gestured toward William with her chin. "You see now what I meant about his brains, *oui?*"

"What about my brains?" The king cast Gianelle a brooding look.

"Aunt Gia says you may have some under your gruff exterior," Tanon supplied.

"Don't be such a baby." Gianelle laughed at the king's wounded expression, then batted her eyelashes at him. "You know I adore you, *mon seigneur.*"

Tanon was married so quickly she didn't have time to worry about wiles, or passions, or anything at all. She guessed the priest might have rushed through the ceremony because of Roger mumbling angrily about his lost dowry. Or it could have been the way Madoc was glaring at the grumbling earl, daring him to continue. Of course, the speedy benediction could have been the result of the king's warning that he was about to trounce them both. Tanon's mother wept. One of Gareth's men hummed. And the tapping of her father's boot echoed through the church like a battle drum, giving fair warning to all that he was contemplating tearing his daughter from her groom's hands and killing anyone who tried to stop him.

Remarkably, Gareth remained unfazed throughout the ceremony. He even turned to Tanon once and winked at her. His calm reassurance soothed her nerves some, but the effect lasted only until the priest ended the benediction and the time came for Gareth to kiss her.

He smiled and, cupping his hand to her cheek, bent his head toward hers. His thumb caressed her lower lip while his warm breath washed over her. Tanon's body went stiff. But then, as his supple mouth molded to hers, teasing her, not with a long, possessive kiss, but with short, open-mouthed, excruciatingly tender kisses, her bones turned to tree sap. She clung to his shoulders for support and because she never wanted him to stop.

He withdrew slowly, only inches from the dreamy languor that glazed her eyes, and licked the taste of her from his lips.

"Thank the ancestors that's finally done." Alwyn's gravelly voice rang through the church. "Let's get to drinking!"

Still looking at Tanon, Gareth laughed and then held up her hand and turned toward the crowd. Some cheered, while others grumbled. Gareth's men all dropped to one knee to pay homage to their new princess.

Chapter Nine

THE GUESTS WERE LED to the great hall, where a grand feast awaited. There were minstrels and harpists, acrobats and jesters for entertainment. Barrels of William's finest wine, ale, and whiskey were cracked open for the celebration. Tables were lavishly decorated with fine linen and shiny silver and gold goblets. Cooked swan and pheasant, stuffed with various delicacies and refeathered, rested upon silver trays dusted with flower petals. The aroma of roasted lamb and shark sautéed in fresh mushrooms made mouths water and stomachs growl.

The king led the bride and groom, along with Tanon's parents, to a dais festooned with a lush array of colorful flowers.

Later, the hall grew quiet as Cian recited Welsh poetry. Tanon found it hard to believe when Gareth told her that the young poet was Madoc's brother. With a halo of shimmering bronze curls falling over huge eyes, he looked more like an angel than a warrior. Tanon listened to his tales of love and fidelity while she glanced at her husband beside her. She didn't hope for love, but would he take a mistress if she didn't please him? She didn't want him to. She didn't want him to kiss any other woman the way he had kissed her. Saints, but he was good at it. She wondered if other men kissed as wonderfully as he did. She doubted it. And he'd looked pleased with her afterward, though she'd done naught but stand there weak in his arms. She smiled at his profile before she realized she was doing it. He was well-mannered, too. Why, she—

"Hell," he growled, scowling at the crowd.

"Gareth," Tanon leaned in and whispered, "I do wish you would refrain from—"

"Damn fool is going to start another war." He rose from his chair and left her without another word.

Tanon watched him stride toward Alwyn, the brawniest of the four men who'd been following Gareth around for the last two days. At present, an even beefier Hereward the Wake was subduing the beefy Welshman.

"But that son of a whore called Cian a woman." Alwyn glared over Hereward's shoulder and yelled, "I'll break his skull with my fist and use it for a cup!"

"Alwyn." Gareth didn't shout, but his frosty tone silenced the growing murmurs of the guests. "Go outside and get some air."

Alwyn didn't protest. He yanked his arm free of Hereward's vise-like grip. Gareth plucked the goblet out of Alwyn's hand as he passed him. When the rowdy warrior was gone, Gareth looked to the Norman knight who had offended Cian and offered him a slanted grin, cooled with the promise of retribution should the offender open his mouth again. When Gareth turned back toward the dais, Roger stood in his path.

Tanon saw her father move to intervene, but William's hand on his shoulder stopped him. No one stopped Madoc, though, as he pushed his back off the wall a few feet away and narrowed his eyes on Roger.

"You're still an arrogant bastard," deCourtenay spat, then swayed on his feet. "You haven't changed."

Gareth glanced down at the empty flagon in Roger's hand and sighed impatiently. "You should mind how much you drink," he told him with the tiniest trace of menace lining his words. "It could be the death of you."

DeCourtenay was too drunk to heed the warning. "I should have killed you twelve years ago."

"That would have been impossible," Gareth assured him, and tried to step around him. Roger moved to block him again.

"You robbed her from me!" he suddenly roared, bringing Dante to his feet as well as Brand.

"Nay, in truth you robbed her from me," Gareth corrected him calmly. "But you had no way of knowing that, so I won't kill you."

Roger laughed, but an instant later his face contorted into a mask of fury. "Her dowry was to be mine. You made me look like a fool in the tourney. I will—"

"You *are* a fool, deCourtenay." Gareth's commanding voice overpowered his. "I knew that the moment I first laid eyes on you." He moved closer, his eyes sparking with challenge, his posture ready to end this altercation swiftly. "You lost to me because your skill is as poor as your taste in women. Will you tempt me now to wound more than your pride?" Though his words were meant as a warning, he sounded most eager to carry out the threat.

"Madoc." Gareth didn't take his eyes off Roger as his

first in command appeared beside him. "Move this drunk-ard out of my way. I don't want to soil my hands with his blood on my wedding night."

Tanon gasped from the dais when Madoc shoved the inebriated earl so hard he sailed into a nearby table.

Now that his path was clear, Gareth returned to the dais without so much as a glance to see where Roger landed.

"You handled that well," William commented before Gareth sat down. "DeCourtenay had that coming after his lewd behavior the other night."

"With all due respect, Your Majesty," Gareth said with a slight chuckle of disbelief. "Were you as drunk as deCourtenay when you promised Tanon to him? I told you how poorly he treated her that day with her pig, and yet you arranged for her to marry him?"

William regarded him for a moment with deadly still-ness, then leaned forward and smiled over Gareth's chest at Tanon. "*Ma chère,* go with your mother and speak to Dante and his lovely wife."

Tanon knew by William's tone of voice that he was angry with Gareth for what he'd just said. The king was sending her away so that he could throttle her husband. She was reluctant to go, because Gareth had spoken in such a manner in her defense. She cast her husband a nervous look and then excused herself.

"Gareth," William began in a low voice as soon as the women were gone. "If you ever speak to me like that again, I will cut off your head and hang it from the battle-ments. Clear?"

Gareth looked him dead in the eyes. "Aye." The chal-lenge in his cobalt stare surprised William and made him smile at the same time. He wouldn't have his Tanon marry a cowering dolt.

"I don't need to explain my decisions to you, but after seeing deCourtenay's actions myself, I find your question a valid one." William leaned back in his chair, bringing a flagon of wine with him. "DeCourtenay's father fought with me at Hastings. He was my friend, which is why I showed his son mercy after you confirmed his mistreatment of Tanon. It's true that Roger was a hellion as a child. I sent him to Normandy to channel that energy into something more constructive. When he returned, he seemed changed enough to be a suitable choice of husband for Tanon. He also inherited much land when his father died. Does that satisfy you?"

"Aye," Gareth said, relieved that he'd arrived at Winchester in time to save Tanon from Roger again. He scanned the hall for his wife.

"Good." William followed his gaze to Dante's table, where Tanon sat sipping a drink. "You may go to her."

When Gareth was gone, William turned to Brand. "I like him."

Brand laughed, caught his wife's eye, and beckoned her to come back to him. "Is that why you threatened to cut off his head?"

William nodded and swallowed a mouthful of wine. "I had to. He's a dangerous man, Brand. I have his respect. To lose it would be foolish and deadly indeed."

~

Tanon looked up from her cup and felt a smile creeping over her face when she saw Gareth moving toward her through the throng of guests. He had told William about

Roger and Petunia. He had not only rescued her from Roger that day, but for the next twelve years. Her smile softened. He was the reason Roger had been sent away. She hoped William wasn't too hard on him, but she was having difficulty remembering why William was angry. Her thoughts were all muddled. She was dizzy, too. Gareth and his strange effect on her were to blame. For the first time in years, she felt powerless over her emotions. Panic rose in her throat. She washed it down with another sip of her drink. She shivered as the warm liquid went down. He had rescued her from Roger, and this time her relief was even more intense than the first time.

She hoped Gareth kissed her again. She liked the way his callused fingers felt on her face, the way the hard angles of his body pressed so gently against her. Her gaze drifted over the length of him and settled on his hips, then on his thighs. She squeezed her eyes shut. Why did the sight of his legs make her spine feel like butter? She'd grown up around hundreds of men, and not a single one had ever tempted her thoughts to such wickedness. Now she was married, and she would be expected to perform her wifely duties with a clear head. Oh, God, how would she do it? She could barely remember her name, and he was fully dressed! And what would it be like with him later? Her nerve endings flamed. What if he was as feral in their marriage bed as he was on the field? Hadn't her aunt mentioned something about primitive men? She peeked up from her lashes and scanned the faces around her, praying that her flushed cheeks did not reveal her lewd thoughts.

Gareth was almost upon her. His steady gaze settled on her as palpable as a touch. His nostrils flared slightly, as if breathing in her scent. His mane of golden hair fanned outward while he walked, making him look like a lion stalking its mate.

Tanon finished off what was left of her drink and drew a curl around her finger when he reached the table. *Merde,* but he made her feel exhilarated. "I'm pleased that you still have your lips." She blinked again and went pale. "I mean your hips." Involuntarily, her gaze dipped to his thighs again. She shook her head to clear it, but it only made the hall spin in a sickening circle. "I'm pleased," she said, pronouncing each word with care, "that you have all your body parts. *Oui,* that's right."

"My body parts are fine," Gareth assured her with a rakish grin.

She laughed, but it sounded like a nervous chortle.

"Come." He held his hand out to her and lifted her to her feet. "I wish to be with you alone."

Her eyes grew wide. "But I don't know what to do!" she whispered as they left the table.

"About what?"

"About . . ." She leaned in close to him and stumbled into his chest. His arms came around her, holding her steady. She tilted her face up to meet his and whispered, ". . . later."

Gareth looked down into her eyes with an expression so soft, so heartwrenchingly tender that Tanon felt tempted to fling her arms around his neck and kiss him right there in the great hall.

"Don't worry over that." His voice was as warm as his breath falling against her lips.

"Oh, but I do!" She pushed herself off him. "I need to discuss this with my mother. She was ill this morn, and I did not wish to pester her with my concerns." Tanon spoke quickly, twisting a fistful of her gown in her hands. "She's with child, and I'm not even going to see the babe. Might we visit? My cousin asked me just this morn—"

"Nay."

"Nay?"

"It's too difficult to get across the marches, Tanon."

"We can have William send a missive." She blinked her eyes at him a few times, but the flashing torchlight of the great hall made her head spin again. Her wiles had failed her. Her shoulders slumped.

"Let's forget about coming back here and go . . ."

Tanon's lip trembled and tears spilled down her cheeks.

"Hell," she heard him swear. He raked his fingers through his hair. He looked so lost and helpless, Tanon would have laughed at this supremely skilled warrior's sudden discomposure if she weren't so sad.

"Stop it, Tanon," he demanded. "Whatever is causing this, we can discuss it in private."

"I miss my mother." She lowered her gaze, veiling her dewy green eyes beneath a spray of glistening black lashes.

"She's two bloody feet from you!"

"But after tomorrow . . ." She sniffed and heedlessly swiped at a fresh rush of tears.

"All right," Gareth conceded tersely, knowing he was going to regret this. "I will try. I'll find a way. Stop your weeping."

Tanon wiped her nose and stared up at him. "Do you mean it?"

He frowned at her. "I'm quite sure I just said it."

Her joy was instant. She leaped into his arms and clasped her arms around his neck. While a rush of happiness swept over her, she realized that she had just discovered the most powerful feminine wile of all. Tears.

"Are you ready for bed now?"

His voice against her ear was low, lulling. His body had gone tight. His arms slipped around her waist, drawing her into his coiled muscles. But Tanon only half noticed. Suddenly, she felt too exhausted to even return his smile.

She yawned. "*Oui,* I am very sleepy."

His smile faded. "Sleepy?" He leaned down and sniffed her breath. "Tanon, were you drinking whiskey?"

"Only a little." She rested her head on his chest and closed her eyes.

"How much?"

"Hmmm. Only one cup, I think. It tasted foul at first, but then it sweetened."

"You're drunk."

Her mouth opened. "I am not! Ladies do not get drunk!"

"Christ." He swooped down and lifted her in his arms when she leaned against him.

"You really must stop swearing, Gareth."

She held on to his neck while he strode toward the stairs. "Good night, Mother," she called out just before they left the great hall.

Chapter Ten

"YOU'RE VERY STRONG," Tanon purred against his chest on their way up the stairs.

Gareth tried to remain angry with her. But she looked so damned appealing nuzzled into him, wearing a smile of pure contentment, that he found his anger melting away.

"You're not heavy," he muttered, feeling weaker than he ever had in his life. The memory of the first time she had ever smiled at him with that adorable space where her tooth should have been came flooding back to him. Damn him, but she still possessed the power to render him helpless.

He carried her to his room and sat her on his bed. Her lids drifted open, revealing a flash of green. When she saw where she was, she tried to vault to her feet but swooned and grew pale.

"Sit." Gareth pushed her back down gently, then left her to retrieve a cloth from a small banqueting table that had been set up in the room for their wedding night. It was weighted with bowls of fruit, trenchers of bread and honeyed pastries, and two flagons of wine. He dipped the cloth into a small bowl of hand water and returned to the bed.

"This will help you feel better." He sat next to her and pressed the cloth to her forehead.

"But I—"

"Ssh," he quieted her. His touch was gentle, soothing, and soon Tanon closed her eyes and relaxed. A languorous sigh parted her lips.

Damned whiskey, Gareth thought miserably, gazing at her. He tugged at her wimple. Loathsome things they were, hiding the glory of a woman's hair beneath layers of veils. A curl fluttered over her cheek. He swept it away with his fingers. His gaze settled on the dainty curve of her jaw, then over her lips. He clenched his teeth at the throbbing beneath his navel. Hell, he had plans for those lips. He'd intended to kiss every inch of her, slowly, thoroughly, until she relaxed in his arms and ceased worrying about what to do in his bed.

"Tanon?"

Her lids fluttered open. She looked into his eyes and smiled. "Gareth," she whispered. "Do you remember the wonderful stories you used to tell me about Wales?"

"Aye," he murmured, sharing her enjoyment of their reunion.

"Were they true? I've heard so many terrible things."

She looked at him like she was ready to believe anything he told her. He told her the truth. "Aye, they were." He reached to pull the clips from her hair and watched, arrested, while her raven curls tumbled over her shoulders. This is how he remembered her.

"You're angry with me."

"Nay," he told her, sweeping his eyes over her bare face.

"But you're scowling." Her voice went a little soft as their gazes met again.

"That's because I've gone daft, and it worries me."

"It does?" she asked, acutely aware of his touch and the way the seductive lowness of his voice covered her.

"Aye." He nodded, giving her a smile so drenched in warmth she couldn't help but let it ignite her. "I find myself thinking about kissing you all the time."

The spark brought a memory with it of something important about not liking him, but all she could think of now was his mouth. "I admit," she told him with a flush of pink dusting her cheeks, "I've thought about kissing you as well."

He raised a surprised brow at her. "Have you?" When she nodded shyly, the slant of his sexy grin heated his eyes. He leaned forward, dropping the cloth from his fingers, and slipped his hand beneath her hair. "Come here," he whispered, using little of his strength to bring her mouth closer to his and the skill of an experienced lover to tilt her head to just the right angle to receive him fully.

His lips touched hers like a caress, stilling her breath. He did not ravish her with the hunger that tightened his loins, but with excruciating leisure and infinite control, he teased and tasted and nibbled her mouth. The tip of his tongue glided along the seam of her lips, dragging a languid sigh from the back of her throat.

The sound hardened Gareth's muscles. He shifted his body and engulfed her within the sleek steel of his embrace. With her mouth fully surrendered, he slid his tongue between the delicate barricade of her lips and entered her mouth with a rasping moan of his own.

Tanon went weak in his arms while his tongue flicked

over hers in a dance set to the rhythm of her heart, making her ache for something more. He flooded her senses with the wild scent of desire, the taste of danger and excitement. She felt his heart beating hard against her breast, his strong hands splaying over her back.

He tangled his hand in her curls, drawing her head back. Breaking their kiss, he grazed his lips over her chin and down the elegant column of her neck. When he pulled away, his breath came hard between his parted lips. His dusky gaze smoldered with dark intentions that made Tanon's pulse race.

"Don't fear me." His command was spoken with such alluring thickness, Tanon thought obeying it would be impossible.

He curled his finger around one of the laces tying the heavy bodice of her gown and gave it a gentle tug. Her gown loosened. He smoothed the shift underneath over her shoulders with his palms, exposing only her modest cleavage. His eyes soaked her in as if she stood naked before him. Tanon inhaled sharply, not from fear, but from the decadently wicked sensation of being desired. She felt stunned and shameful for delighting in such a depraved pleasure. But when she looked into his fevered gaze, discovering that his breath halted along with hers, she stopped thinking altogether. When he swept his fingertips over her flesh, tracing the milky soft mound of her breast, Tanon closed her eyes and arched her back.

Dipping his head, Gareth kissed her where his fingers had just been. He heard her husky moan before she fell back on the bed.

He lifted his head from her bosom. "Tanon?" When she didn't answer right away, he shook her softly. "Tanon.

Hell, wake up." She didn't move. His eyes flicked to the bowl of water across the room, and for an instant he considered pouring it over her head. "Christ!" He pushed off the bed and stared down at her unresponsive form. Now, this was something he wasn't accustomed to. No woman had ever fallen asleep on him before—and *while* he was kissing her!

He let his gaze drift over her body. Christ, what he wanted to do to her. But there was naught he could do now. He wasn't about to make love to an unconscious woman. Even if it was his wedding night. He didn't dare undress her, although her gown looked ridiculously cumbersome. Why did Normans feel the need to cover everything up with heavy fabrics as if it were the dead of winter?

Tearing himself away from the bed, he crossed the room and fell in a chair beside the hearth. He watched her. He had to have been daft to agree to take a wife. What he needed was peace in his life, not vexation. If he'd had an ounce of wits, he would have refused his exiled brother's promised bride and returned to Dafydd's fortress to finish what he should have done a year ago—cleave the bastard in half, then find out who among his men had betrayed him to the northern prince. He drew his hand through his hair, sweeping silky strands away from his face. Instead, here he sat, gaze fastened to his drunken wife. He thought about returning to the feast in the great hall, but Madoc and his men would never let him forget that he'd spent his wedding night with them rather than his beautiful bride.

Christ, she was breathtaking, he thought, tapping his fingers along the armrest of his chair. He found his heartbeat slowing when he recalled the guileless dip of her brow, the lush fan of her lashes against the cream of her skin when she told him that she didn't know what to do . . . later. That was most likely why she drank. She was probably scared to death of the marriage bed. But hell, she hadn't reacted to his touch with fear. He shifted in his seat as an uncomfortable thickness gripped his loins. The taste of her skin still lingered on his lips. His innocent had grown into a woman. Tonight she was open and honest, as if she knew no other way to be. He smiled. Tanon hadn't changed all that much.

"God help me," he mumbled and raked his hand over his jaw. "I'm going as soft on her as I was when I was ten!" With nothing but a smile, she had persuaded him to allow her nursemaid to come home with them. A few tears and he'd promised to find a way for her to visit her family. How in damnation was he going to accomplish that feat? Damn the *how*. *Why* would he want to return here? He'd come for what his people needed. He intended never to step foot in England again. He had more important matters to attend to, like visiting his uncle and seeing to his people after more than a year of his absence.

He kicked off his boots, stood up, and strode to the bed, tearing away at his clothes. He had planned this out carefully. He would strip her of her fear, her innocence . . . Nowhere in that plan did he intend to lose his heart to her again and turn into a pansy.

Peace: he reminded himself of his cause. He was doing this for peace. He climbed into bed and folded his hands beneath his head, staying clear of her. Tonight, he'd let her sleep. He didn't want to frighten her further by pawing at her. Tomorrow night, though, he'd have her, or he'd have Madoc thrash his good sense back into him.

Gareth opened his eyes the following morning and spat Tanon's hair out of his mouth. It took him a moment to realize the weight on his chest was his wife's. She was asleep, sprawled across him and snoring as if he were as soft as a pillow. He tried to move his arm, but it was numb. She must have been atop him all night. Christ, if that didn't stir him to a full state of wakefulness beneath his sheet. He flexed his fingers to circulate his blood, then wound his wrist a few times.

"Tanon." He tried to push her off, but she groaned, and his control nearly snapped. He moved his palm over her tempting rump and ground his teeth together. He'd been patient, but damn it, how could a man be expected to control himself engulfed in the warmth of his wife's body?

"Tanon, wake up."

She shifted, and he closed his eyes, fighting the urge to sweep her onto her back and take his pleasure.

"Oh," she moaned in agony and clutched her head. "It feels like a horse fell on my head."

Beneath her, Gareth cursed whiskey to Hades. "You deserve your discomfort for drinking whiskey." There, he wasn't as soft as her pillow, and now she knew it.

"Gareth, please lower your voice."

"Move away from me."

"I cannot."

"Tanon, I swear on the lives of my cattle that if you move like that again, I'm going to rip that gown off your body and do to you what I missed doing last eve."

Her eyes sprang open. She pushed herself off him,

ignoring the pounding in her head. Her hand touched his bare chest. She squeaked and pulled it away.

The instant he was free, Gareth lunged from the bed and strode across the room.

"Oh, dear God, you're naked!" The sight of his backside nearly made Tanon forget her throbbing head. Clothed in nothing but golden armbands and a torc, he was a sculpted masterpiece of honed muscle from his shoulders to his calves.

"I always sleep naked," he told her without turning. He headed for the small banquet table and picked up a bowl of plums and dates. He plucked a plum from its contents and turned to come back to bed.

Tanon's eyes opened wider, then squeezed shut.

"I'm your husband, Tanon. Open your eyes and eat something."

Oh, did he have to remind her? Did he have to sound so husky and warm doing it? And did he have to be so . . . large? She yanked the sheet from the bed and poked it at him, her eyes still tightly shut. A moment later, she felt the mattress sink a little. She peeked at him through a slit in her lids. Just as she feared, he was sitting beside her, but at least he'd wrapped his torso in the sheet. Tanon kept her gaze on his face, which was actually just as lethal as the rest of him.

Her head pounded. She had no memory of the previous night, and she preferred it that way. "I will leave so you can garb yourself." She moved to scramble out of bed. A wooden bowl in her face stopped her.

"Eat."

"Put your clothes on. I cannot—"

"Nay."

"My." Her eyes sparked at him. "You speak as primitively as you look."

"Not primitive enough to leave blood on these sheets." He fastened an icy blue glance on her. "But I can be pushed."

Looking down, Tanon brought her hand to the loosened laces of her gown, and then raised her accusing gaze at him.

His eyes dipped to her cleavage. He should have felt repentant that he'd tried to take her in her poor condition, but hell . . .

"You weren't unwilling."

She opened her mouth, but nothing came out.

He smiled and sank his teeth into a plum.

"Just what is that smirk supposed to mean?" she demanded, fisting her hand on his bent hips.

He looked her over with the kind of hungry appraisal she had seen on some of her father's knights when an interested wench sauntered by them.

"I'm a lady, in case you've forgotten." She fumbled with her laces, sensing his desire to remove her gown.

"You're a woman, and *you* haven't forgotten."

The blush of her cheeks against her wide emerald eyes was so appealing, Gareth thought he would be content to sit and look at her for the remainder of the day.

"What did I do?" she asked, lowering her voice and tightening her fingers on her laces.

"You drove me wild."

He didn't think her eyes could open any wider. He was wrong.

"I did?"

"Aye, and you're doing it again right now."

She liked the way he was looking at her mouth, the

same way she'd looked at his yesterday. He bent toward her, bringing his lips closer.

Non! She turned her face away from his. She didn't want him to like her, even if having him want her felt so exhilarating. She had to remind herself why a half dozen times before she felt strong enough to look at him again. Blast Roger for losing in the tourney. This would have been so much easier with him.

Someone rapped on the door. Tanon leaped from the bed, groping at her laces. Her head cleared instantly when she looked at the man still sitting on the bed, the sheet draped low on his hips, his flat, corded belly heaving above an enticing swath of golden curls. She met his gaze briefly, reading the frustration in his eyes.

"A moment, please!" she called out, frantically working the wrinkles out of her gown while Gareth casually rewrapped the sheet around his torso and propped his back against the pillows.

His eyes never left her as she raced for the door and pulled it open, allowing a trio of women to enter.

"Ah, good, you're up and about." Rebecca gave Tanon's hair an askew looking over, then licked her thumb and smoothed back a stray tendril. She turned to toss Gareth a polite smile, but then looked away, a bit flustered. Eloise and Lorette weren't handling the sight of him any better. Tanon glanced at him and tingled all the way to the soles of her feet. He lay there looking like a veritable god, all golden and relaxed, his honeyed mane dripping over molded bronze shoulders, taking each of them in with the brooding arrogance befitting his title.

"Well." Rebecca cleared her throat and clasped Tanon's wrist. "It's getting late, you know. We do have to get you dressed for your journey. Come, let's get you to your room and—"

"This is her room," Gareth corrected from the bed.

"Of course, my lord." Rebecca glanced in his direction but didn't look directly at him.

"And she can dress herself. Aye, Tanon?"

"Well." Tanon thought about it for a moment, then shook her head. "*Non.* My gowns are very intricate, and there is so much wear. It would take me hours."

Gareth sighed. "Very well, then." When he sat up, Lorette and Eloise turned swiftly toward the door. "You ladies leave while I dress, and then you can return to dress Tanon here."

He rose from the bed, clutching the sheet at his waist with one hand. Tanon's maids yanked open the door and hurried outside with Tanon close on their heels.

Gareth's voice stopped her. "You stay here."

Tanon pivoted around to face him. "But I . . ."

The raw command in his gaze stilled the rest of her words. She scowled at him and folded her hands in front of her.

"Shut the door," he called out to Rebecca, who was waiting in the hall.

"It's a sight you're going to have to get used to, wife," he said, letting go of the sheet and turning to reach for his clothes.

"Impossible," Tanon murmured, unable to look away from the tantalizing play of muscle that flexed in his thighs and shoulders while he dressed.

Gareth tossed her a grin over his shoulder and pulled his soft leather trousers over a thin breechcloth. He gave the laces low on his belly a firm tug before tying them.

"How's your head?" he asked, donning another sleeve-less tunic.

"Better," she had to admit, though her voice sounded faint in her ears. She pulled her gaze away from him and looked at everything else in the room. "But I don't care for you ordering me about. It is most impolite, and rather brutish."

He headed for the door but stopped when he reached her. Bending his mouth close to her ear, he felt her quiver close to him. "I'm pleased the sight of me had such a healing effect on you." The warmth of his teasing smile echoed in his voice. "And I will work on my manners," he promised before he opened the door again.

Tanon's nurse gave him a quick looking over when she returned and nodded her approval, though she still found his sleeveless tunic somewhat brash.

"We will bring her down to you shortly," the nurse advised him, sweeping past him with a rich burgundy gown draped over her arm. "There are steaming dumplings and warm mead awaiting you in the great hall, my lord."

"I'm not leaving." His grin flashed briefly when she turned to offer him an incredulous stare.

"Surely, you cannot mean to . . ." Her eyes widened as he strode toward a chair and sat down.

Tanon's mouth fell open. "You don't mean to watch."

"Why not? You're my wife." When she continued to gape at him, he gave her an impatient look. "Does your father leave the chamber when your mother is dressing?"

"Well . . . *non* . . . but . . ." Tanon's nostrils flared while he sat there waiting for her to continue. "I will not do it."

He stared at her, his gaze a direct challenge. He'd just finished promising her that he'd work on his manners.

And what the hell was wrong with his manners anyway? He sighed. He didn't want to go back on his word by demanding she do as he wished. He frowned, thinking of what a watered-down dolt he was swiftly becoming around her. If he didn't gain command over his marriage soon, he was going to turn into an indulgent, groveling peacock. He would have his way this morn, but he would need to think of a better way to achieve it.

"Do all Norman women refuse their husbands' every request?" he asked, knowing exactly how to get her to stop arguing. "Because I find it disturbing and very . . . discourteous."

Discourteous? Why, she had impeccable manners! She had never once brought shame to her family or her king.

For a tense moment, their gazes locked in a heated battle of wills. And then Tanon snatched the sheet up off the floor and handed it to Rebecca. "As you wish. But if you are disappointed, do keep it to yourself."

Gareth almost laughed, but Christ, she was serious. Could she truly not know what she was doing to him just standing there with her hair spilling in wild disarray around her shoulders? If they had been alone, he would have told her that it was taking every ounce of control he possessed not to get up and tear that gown off her himself. He would have said something if Lorette hadn't opened the sheet at that moment to conceal her while the other two began to undress her.

Chapter Eleven

⌒

Tanon thought undressing in front of her husband
would be mortifying. Instead, she found it to be one of the
most scintillating experiences of her life.

He watched in silence, comfortably sprawled in his
chair, elbows resting on his thighs. His smoky blue eyes
were fastened on the back of her shoulders as her gown
and shift fell to the floor. Tanon was grateful for the sheet
but still crossed her arms over her bare breasts when she
turned slightly to have another look at the man appraising
her. Like a sultan lounging on his throne, he took his
pleasure in her, seducing her without even a touch. His intense gaze soaked her in as if there were no barrier between them.

Her maids worked quickly, washing her with the same
cloth Gareth had used the night before. When Eloise fit a
fresh shift over her head, Gareth finally spoke.

"Turn around." His deep, lilting voice sizzled Tanon's
blood. He waved his finger at Rebecca, commanding her
without a word to discard the sheet. His eyes moved over

Tanon like a brushfire. Barely concealed beneath the thin creamy muslin fabric, her nipples were the first part of her to react. His gaze strayed to them briefly, then he raised his eyes to hers and winked, effortlessly dousing her fiery nerve endings with a more comforting kind of intimacy. He wanted her to feel at ease with him. It was a thoughtful gesture that earned him Tanon's most grateful smile.

Looking at him straight on now, Tanon could tell that she delighted him, excited him. That pang of desire she was beginning to grow accustomed to whenever he was near flooded through her. She didn't think herself homely. Her parents often called her beautiful. But she never credited it with much importance. Men looked at her, but never for too long. Even at home at Avarloch, her father's guards barely spoke to her. Most nobles' daughters her age were married with a child under each arm. But the only men who had sought Tanon's hand were old, withered, and half blind, save for Roger, who made it known to all the night before that he was more interested in her dowry than in her. But that was what she expected, what she told herself she wanted: no chance to lose her heart to a man who didn't love her.

But Gareth's eyes were always on her. On the crowded lawns, in the great hall, even on the competitors' field, his sultry gaze had found her. From the moment he'd stepped into Winchester's doors, he made her feel attractive. Her mother was right—he hadn't tried to kiss her in her room because her father would have taken the sword to him. He certainly looked like he wanted to kiss her now.

Gareth held her gaze while Lorette fit her into the soft woolen gown of rich burgundy with gold piping. The bodice fit snugly, accentuating her slim waist and softly rounded hips. When the handmaiden began to pin her hair up, Gareth stopped her.

"She prefers it loose."

Tanon arched a raven brow at him, then remembered complaining about all the pins in her hair the night Hubert led Gareth to her room. She was surprised he'd remembered and pleased that he didn't seem to mind if she didn't look her very best. "Just pin the sides, Lorette," she said softly. "To keep it out of my eyes."

Lorette ran her fingers through Tanon's curls and crowned her head with a gilt wimple and circlet.

Gareth felt his chest tighten looking at her. Before his eyes she had changed from a demure, sensual goddess to an equally breathtaking princess.

"Just her hose and we'll be done, my lord." Rebecca smiled, seeing the approval that lit his eyes.

"Nay. Leave now," he commanded without looking away from his wife.

"But . . . ," Rebecca began. He wasn't listening. He stood and went to Tanon as if lured by a siren song only he could hear. The nurse shooed Lorette and Eloise out of the chamber. They left, shutting the door softly.

"I will need my hose if it's cold where we're going," Tanon said, a bit unnerved by the staggering heat of his gaze.

"It's not. But if you wish to wear them, I will put them on you."

Tanon smiled nervously when she realized he was serious. "Don't be silly, Gareth."

He reached for the hose and ran their downy softness through his fingers. When he squatted before her, she glanced at the door. "This is mad. Husbands don't dress their wives."

He lifted the hem of her gown away from her leg, then handed it to her and cupped her ankle in his palm.

Tanon bit her lower lip as he rolled her hose over her pointed toes, then over her heel and up her calf. His deft fingers glided over her skin, whisper soft, bewitching her senses. "You will dress before me every day from now on." His fingers grazed across her sensitive inner thigh, and then, with even more provocative slowness, moved to the back of her knee. He secured the hose and then did the same with her other leg. When he finished, her breath came in heavy bursts. He straightened to his full height in front of her, and before she could calm the dizzying thud of her heart, he snaked one arm around her waist and dragged her into his arms. She sucked in a sharp breath, feeling his heavy arousal pressed against her.

"Never again think you disappoint me. You please me, Tanon. You always have." His gaze drifted over her features and then he lowered his mouth to hers. "Christ, you please me well."

~

Gareth clenched his teeth around a string of vile oaths when he stepped into the bailey and saw the four-horse carriage waiting there. The cumbersome coach would have been bad enough on its own, but piled high atop the roof were four wooden trunks of various sizes. Another was being hoisted up under the careful supervision of Lord Brand. A few feet away, Tanon exchanged farewells with the rest of her family amid a deluge of tears.

"What the hell is this?" Gareth stepped up to the car-

riage and tilted his head back to take in the complete horror of what he was seeing.

Appearing at his side, Madoc popped a sliver of hay into
his mouth and chewed. "Some of your wife's belongings."

"Some?" Gareth turned to him with disbelief widening
his eyes. "There's more?"

"Aye, but fortunately the rest is at Avarloch."

"With this beast slowing us up"—Alwyn stepped up
behind Gareth—"it'll take us an extra se'nnight to get
home."

Gareth set his glacial gaze on Tanon and then strode
toward her father. Just as he opened his mouth to question
Brand's sanity, the Earl of Avarloch turned and cast him a
look that asked the same question of Gareth.

"Last eve you filled my daughter's heart with the hope
of visiting her mother. This marriage was agreed to in the
hopes of putting an end to the fighting. It will not stop the
marcher lords from refusing to let you into England."

When Gareth tried to respond, Brand cut him off, causing his son-in-law's eyes to darken to midnight blue.

"As far as I know, you've made no arrangements with
King William to provide a safe return back to England, so
unless you plan on smuggling my daughter past armed
soldiers, which I would not recommend"—the lethal
warning in Brand's voice was unmistakable—"I ask you
if you think your promise was a wise one?"

"Nay, I don't." Gareth met Brand's level gaze head-on.
"In fact, I regretted my words the moment they left my
mouth. But your daughter was weeping all over me, and I
found it difficult to refuse her."

The harsh lines in Brand's expression faded. In fact,

his broad shoulders collapsed as relief settled over him. "I see. Well, I'm pleased that Tanon's feelings moved you."

"Her safety moves me even more." Gareth's voice was still clipped with anger. He glanced at the trunk being lifted to the carriage. "If you've traveled to the marches, then you know how dangerous it is. Even with the king's writ granting us safe passage into Wales, we will still need to move quickly through certain regions. How quickly do you think this carriage can move with all this weight?"

Brand narrowed his eyes on Gareth, then ground his jaw when the carriage creaked under the weight of the fifth trunk being set on it.

"Remove three of the trunks!" Brand ordered the hoisters in a loud voice.

When Tanon saw her boxes being removed from the coach, she hurried toward the men. "What are you doing?" she demanded, clutching her hands to her chest when another one of her trunks hit the floor.

"Lightening the load," Gareth replied succinctly. "It isn't safe to—"

"Lightening the load?" Tanon whirled around, her eyes wide with disbelief. "But those are my clothes! My lute, my parchments. How will I write to my mother?"

"Tanon, we cannot—"

"What about Rebecca's belongings?"

"Very well. One trunk for you. One for her. You'll both have until noontime to repack."

"But there are gifts from the people here in those trunks. How am I to stuff everything into one trunk? Please, allow me to at least bring—"

"Tanon," Gareth warned. "Noontime."

"Very well," she conceded through tight lips. She looked

like she wanted to say more, but she cut a quick glance to her father and smiled instead.

An hour later, the two trunks were lifted to the carriage while Gareth's men saddled their horses. After bidding her parents a final farewell, Tanon wiped her nose and ignored her husband when she passed him and Hereward on her way to the carriage.

"She's not usually so sour," Hereward pointed out, eyeing the stiff line of her back.

Gareth peered over Hereward's shoulder to watch her step up into the coach. "What is she usually? When you visited Cymru, you told me that her nose crinkles when she laughs. You didn't tell me that such an occurrence is rare."

The Saxon thought about his answer before he spoke. He'd known Tanon for many years. The Risandes spent much of their time with the king, and once Hereward made peace with William, he had come to know Brand and Dante, and their families. When he'd visited Wales several years past at the request of King William, he was surprised to find young Prince Gareth more curious about Brand's daughter than his older brother Cedric, who was not interested at all. "She's melancholy," he said, "but always kind."

"Melancholy," Gareth echoed, staring at her profile framed inside the window. A sudden pang of empathy tightened his chest. Why wouldn't she be? She'd been promised to his knave brother, who couldn't hide his hatred for the Normans even from an innocent little girl. Then to Roger deCourtenay, of all the detestable knaves, and now she was finally being carted off to the strange land she thought she'd escaped, with a man she had known for a few months when she was six. Gareth couldn't help but feel pity for her, and immense admiration. If he were a woman in her position, he'd probably be kicking and fighting to get out of the carriage. But there she sat, her expression stoic and resolved. It was difficult seeing her this way. He remembered a different Tanon. He was about to go to her when Brand joined them.

"You've but to send word to me and I will ride to the marches and escort you both back myself."

Gareth smiled at him, wanting to ease this notorious warrior's pain at losing his daughter. "I will consider it, my lord."

Brand looked at Hereward next, but the strapping Saxon's eyes were fastened on one of the two women approaching. Lady Brynna Risande curled her arm through her husband's when she reached him. Her longtime friend and children's nursemaid walked by Hereward without a glance in his direction and stopped before Brand.

"My lord." She offered him a slight bow before raising her eyes to his. "It has been an honor to serve you and your family these many years. Rest assured, I will continue to serve your daughter."

Brand pulled her into an embrace shared by his wife. "We will miss you, Rebecca."

"And I, you, my lord."

Hereward stepped away and proceeded toward his horse.

When they were finally ready to leave, the king handed his writ to Gareth, pounding him on the back with a warning to see to Tanon's protection. Then he flung open the carriage door and snatched Tanon up in an embrace that pressed the wind from her lungs.

"Please your king and find happiness with your husband, *ma belle*."

Tanon held on to him but didn't weep. She pledged to do her very best. She looked over his shoulder at her mother. She waved, wiped her eyes, and then put on the bravest face she could muster as her carriage rolled away from her family.

Chapter Twelve

~~~~~~

THEY RODE NORTH UNTIL nightfall and made camp in a hollowed clearing encompassed by dense forest.

Tanon had some difficulty adapting to her surroundings. Whenever she'd traveled with her family, they slept at an inn, in beds, with walls shielding them from the forest creatures. She knew she had nothing to fear. She wasn't alone, after all. Hereward was here with her. And Gareth stayed close when he went off to speak privately with Madoc. Still, sleeping in the woods was new to her. She doubted she would get an ounce of sleep tonight, what with her senses heightened by the echoing sounds of the wilderness surrounding her.

With Cian's help, she and Rebecca unpacked the food Brynna had prepared for the journey while Hereward built a small fire to keep them warm. Tomas and Alwyn scouted the surroundings, and the rest of the men spread out their pallets, claiming their places for the night.

"You're very thoughtful," Tanon acknowledged when Cian pulled a hidden dagger from his boot and began cutting the cheese into neat slices. She studied a soft curl dangling over his forehead, reflecting the light from Hereward's fire. "You certainly don't look like a warrior."

He chuckled and glanced up at her from his work. "I've killed over seventy Norm—" He stopped and grimaced, realizing too late what he'd just said. He went back to cutting without another word.

"None with that dagger, I hope," she said lightly, trying to disguise her horror.

"I didn't mean to offend you," he murmured quietly. "I fight only when there is no other choice." When he lifted his face to look at her fully, Tanon's expression couldn't help but soften at his boyish expression.

"How old are you, Cian?" she asked him.

"I'm ten and six." His posture straightened, and the glint of pride in his eyes revealed the warrior within.

For the first time, Tanon saw his resemblance to Madoc. She turned to where Cian's brother stood with Gareth closer to the darkness of the trees. She smiled when she caught Madoc's eye. His coal gaze lingered on her briefly, hard and detached, before he looked away. She didn't like him and decided to have a talk with Gareth about him later.

"I feel as if there are a hundred eyes watching me." Rebecca hugged herself and squeezed her eyes shut when an owl hooted somewhere above her.

"I'll be on watch tonight. You have naught to fear." From over the flames, Hereward's promise rolled off his tongue with such conviction, Rebecca opened her eyes to look at him.

"Who will be with you?"

"Who will be with me?" Hereward repeated with astonishment lifting his rusty brows. She knew him well enough to know he needed no help in defending those he chose to protect. "Woman, you sting my pride like a viper."

"Honorable men do not carry pride," Rebecca replied curtly.

"They do when they fight like me," he huffed with all the arrogance of a Celtic king. With his mane of deep vermilion and his cloak fashioned of wolf skin draping his broad shoulders, Hereward looked like one. "We're on the outside of the walls now, lady. Your comely blue eyes might begin to see things a bit differently."

Rebecca turned away from the meaning in his eyes and began pulling fruit, bread, and dried meat out of another sack.

"He's quite handsome, Rebecca," Tanon whispered while she laid the pretty butterfly-embroidered serviettes her mother had given her down on the grass.

"Hush. I've no interest in that Saxon."

"You're Saxon as well," Tanon reminded her while she arranged places in a large circle in the grass for each man to eat. "I daresay, he stares at you often." Tanon ignored Rebecca's mild oath and commissioned Cian to set each morsel of food atop each serviette. "If we are required to eat off the ground, it can at least look pleasing."

Kneeling beside her, Cian gazed down at her hair illuminated by the firelight. "Aye, 'tis pleasing, indeed." His voice sounder deeper, a bit rattled. It made Tanon look up at him. When she did, the firelight spread over her face. Her eyes sparkled like green stardust. Cian sighed and then went barreling to the left, thanks to a hefty shove from Gareth. Madoc chuckled as Gareth folded his legs and sat down beside his wife.

"That was a very thoughtless thing to do to poor Cian," Tanon admonished Gareth, then turned to Madoc while he took his place at the blanket. She offered the first in command a serene smile, even though she would have preferred to give him a good glare. If there was one thing she truly didn't like, it was laughter at someone else's expense. "That's the first time I've heard you laugh."

Madoc glanced at her, then looked down at his food. His bread and cheese were flanked neatly by two slices of dried meat. He looked at the other settings. They were all the same.

"I don't mean to sound presumptuous, since I don't know you, Madoc." She glowered at him when he picked up a piece of meat and shoved it into his mouth. "But do you think it was polite to laugh at your brother's humiliation?"

Madoc lifted his head slowly from his food and stared straight at her. Tanon wasn't sure which was blacker, his eyes or his expression. "I wasn't raised to be polite."

"Oh, please forgive me," she replied, sincerely regretful. "I shouldn't fault you, then, should I?"

He shook his head and looked at Gareth for some aid, but the prince was preoccupied with scowling at the butterflies on his serviette.

"Still," Tanon continued to scold him, gently, of course. She was a tad afraid of him, after all. "You might consider apologizing to Cian."

"Tanon," Gareth began just as she looked up and smiled at another man who hovered over her, looking for a place to sit.

"And what is your name, sir?" she inquired with a friendly smile that deepened her dimple. If she was going to be living among these men, she should get to know them.

"Bleddyn," he replied, darting a tentative glance toward Gareth.

"You may sit right there." She pointed to the space beside Madoc. "And please help yourself to another slice of meat. You are very handsome but terribly thin."

"Tanon!" Gareth's command startled her enough to make her leap almost into Madoc's lap.

"What?" She stared at him, her eyes large with surprise and anger.

"What the hell are you doing to my men?" He didn't shout but looked so incredulous, Tanon couldn't help but take offense.

"I'm being polite!" She righted herself and swept a mote of dust off her skirts. "Truly, Gareth, you would do well to follow my example. You frightened the wits out of me by bellowing so."

"I would do . . ." He was so incensed he couldn't finish speaking. A muscle flicked angrily in his jaw.

Tanon set her chin in a stubborn line.

"I will do as I see fit," he said through clenched teeth. "*You* will stop trying to turn my men into Norman peacocks with courtly manners. And never, *ever* tell any man again that he is handsome."

Why, she . . . He was . . . How dare he . . . Norman peacocks? Her mouth twisted into a wry smile, and even that took an enormous effort. She shouldn't argue with him in front of his men. But oh, when she found a moment alone with him, she was going to tell him just what a brute he was being. For now, she gave her full attention to her food, picking up a crumb from her bread and popping it into her mouth.

Satisfied that everything was back to the way it should be, Gareth began to eat.

"Had I known how incredibly rude you are," Tanon murmured under her breath, "I would have refused to marry you."

Rebecca cleared her throat. "This cheese is quite tasty," she said, trying to douse the flash of fire that had just gleamed in Gareth's eyes.

"And blemish your spotless reputation as a lady?" he asked in a deceptively cool voice. His mouth twisted into a smirk. "I think not."

Tanon continued to chew and looked up at the branches as if a bird had just chirped at her.

Gareth wanted to laugh—or wring her lovely neck—when she pretended to ignore him. He'd never suffered such belligerence before. He led men home alive from battle. No one ignored him. He guessed it was better than arguing with her at every turn. And he was rather enjoying watching the battle she fought with herself to maintain her mild-mannered temperament.

"Aye, silence suits you."

Tanon pivoted her head and stared at him. Anger flared to the surface as she rose to her feet. She tried to keep her temper in check by biting down on her tongue, but the task was becoming more difficult since he had strolled back into her life. She shouldn't care what he thought of her, but blast her, she did. His words stung, and she was good and tired of it.

"No wonder your poor men have no manners, what with an arrogant, mean-spirited . . ." The remainder of her insult disintegrated in her throat when Gareth stood up beside her. His cobalt eyes bore down into hers, daring her to continue.

Tanon's legs twitched, ready to run. She absolutely would not! She would never let a man bully her again, she reminded herself, girding herself to face his immobilizing gaze.

"Very well," she said more quietly, regaining her composure. "If it's silence you want . . ." Her dark brow tipped at him, then she turned and walked away without another word.

Without a moment's hesitation, Gareth took off after her.

"You will not run from me," he warned, snatching her wrist and turning her toward him.

She stared up at him, her chin impudent with challenge. "Let me go."

Christ, he wanted to kiss that mouth. "Nay, I'll not have my wife insult me in front of my men, Tanon," he said to keep his concentration where it belonged—on his anger.

"And I will not suffer the same from my husband," she flung back at him.

Gareth's jaw jumped. For a moment, he considered that his spirited woman might in fact be a little hellion. She looked very much like one right now with her springy curls peeping out from beneath her wimple and her green eyes shooting fire. She looked enticing. A pang of desire went straight to his groin, making him ache to find out if he was right.

"You will obey me, else I cannot—"

She feigned a yawn. "Are you going to go on much

longer? I'm very sleepy, and you're only adding to my drowsiness."

She listened to him growl something in Welsh. He turned away from her when Alwyn and Tomas burst through the trees.

"Gareth!" Alwyn vaulted from his saddle and ran to him. "There's a small band of men not two leagues from here. They're Cymry."

"Are you certain?" Gareth asked. "How did they get past the marches?"

Alwyn shook his head. "I don't know. Tomas and I were able to get close enough without being seen. They are planning an attack on Winchester."

"Non!" Tanon clutched his arm. "Gareth, you must do something!"

"Damn fools."

"Did you hear me?" She tugged on him again. "We have to warn the king. My family is there."

"Your family is in no danger," he assured her. "Those fools will be killed the instant they fire their first arrow on the castle." He turned to find Madoc across the fire. "Who the hell could have given them the order to attack when there are a thousand knights visiting for the tourney?"

"Gareth," Tomas said, returning his lord's attention to him, his dark eyes somber. "They carry your banner. They know they have no chance at victory. Their plan is to attack and make King William believe you are behind it."

Gareth's expression turned deadly in an instant. "How many are there?"

"At least fifty."

Hereward rose to his feet and went to stand beside

Gareth. "William knows you are not so foolish. He will never believe the order to attack came from you."

"He might," Gareth told him. "I don't intend to take that chance. Someone doesn't want peace with the Normans, and they want me to be William's first casualty." He flicked his gaze back to Madoc. "We take them out."

"Just before dawn," Madoc agreed and swung his gaze to Bleddyn.

Gareth nodded slightly and turned to Bleddyn next. "You will ride back to Winchester and inform the king that there is a plot to make us enemies. Tell him what we know and that we have put an end to it."

Gareth watched him mount his horse and ride away, disappearing into the trees.

"Who is behind this plot?" Hereward asked while Gareth returned to the fire. "We must find out and tell the king."

"I don't know. Prince Dafydd, any one of his brothers in the north . . . Prince Rhydderch of Powys, Cadwr of Glywysing . . . my brother." Gareth scanned his eyes across the shadows around them. "We will know soon enough."

~

Tanon couldn't sleep. She spent most of the night with Rebecca while Gareth sat with his men and Hereward, planning the attack on the Welshmen.

When Rebecca finally drifted off to sleep, Tanon returned to her pallet and watched her husband while he spoke. The wind stirred his hair around his shoulders. Firelight skittered across his face, tempting her to study the strength in his jaw, the firm set of his lips. He glanced at her, and she thought she saw his features soften.

She chewed her lower lip. In just a few hours he was going to fight against men who wanted him dead so badly they were willing to give their own lives to see it done. A quiver of dread coursed through her. She hugged her knees to her chest. What if they killed him tonight? She wasn't so angry with him that she wanted to see him dead. Just the thought of it tore at her chest. *Enfer,* she liked him, when he wasn't acting like an arrogant . . . prince. She almost pounded her fist on her thigh. She had tried not to, but he had a way of looking at her that felt so familiar, so safe. In fact, he was the only person who had protected her from Roger. Even William and her father hadn't done that.

She would be free to return home if Gareth was killed. *Non,* she admonished herself, that was a terrible thing to consider. Besides, God only knew whom she'd be forced to marry then. No one in her mind even came close to Gareth. Even if she had to live in Wales, he was her first choice for a husband. She pleased him, and heaven help her, he pleased her as well.

She didn't want him to fight, or get killed, but what could she do about it? Her mother always prayed for her father when he left for battle. Tanon thought about it. She was Gareth's wife. She should pray for him. Clasping her hands together, she lifted them to her mouth and closed her eyes.

"Dearest Father," she began out loud. "Please protect my husband from the wicked schemes and the merciless tip of his enemies' blades. I know I've already asked You tonight to punish him severely, but I've changed my mind. I don't want him to suffer in any way. Amen."

She opened her eyes and tilted her head up the length of Gareth's leather-clad legs. She hadn't heard his approach. He knelt in front of her, and she found herself staring into his eyes.

"Are you hungry?" he asked in a considerate tone.

She shook her head no and began to turn away from the warmth in his eyes. The last thing she needed to do was like him even more when he could be dead in the morning.

He touched his fingers to her cheek to draw her gaze back to his. "Don't worry over me, Tanon. I will return to you unscathed."

"My, but you're arrogant," she pointed out.

The corners of his mouth hooked into a smile that was so wondrously sweet, it tempted her to smile back.

"And quite brutish, too," she added. "You should know that I considered slapping you earlier. I've never slapped anyone before, and I would have had to have gone to penance for it." She narrowed her eyes on him. "You do have churches in Wales, *oui?*"

"Aye, but I would have deserved it, so there would be no penance due." His smile faded, and his expression grew serious again. "Tanon, I'm not accustomed to . . ."

What? He asked himself. Not accustomed to groveling? To worrying over the tender feelings of a woman? To feeling possessive, even jealous that she thought another man handsome? Christ, he was a prince, and the deadliest warrior in Cymru. He groveled to no one! Nay, not even when Dafydd had left him in the dungeons without food for over a se'nnight did he turn into such an abject pansy. He was commander of over four hundred men in Deheubarth, and not a single one had ever dared speak to him the way this woman had.

No one had ever prayed for him, either.

"Not accustomed to what?" she asked curiously.

He ran his hand over his jaw, looking at her. How was it possible that gazing into her eyes made him feel so powerless and weak? He had trouble breathing around her. Even when she questioned his every request, he ached to touch her.

"To apologizing."

"Oh." Her lips relaxed into a smile, and she gave his hand a reassuring pat. "I will help you get accustomed to that."

"I've no doubt you will," he said, his humor restored by her sweet innocence.

"Besides, you've much more pressing concerns to worry over tonight."

"Aye, I do." Like how to keep his mouth and his hands off her another second.

When he folded his knees and moved to sit behind her, she startled and almost moved away. He closed his arms loosely around her middle and stretched his legs out on either side of her. She didn't resist but let him mold her to his chest.

Gareth removed the wimple from her head and inhaled the hint of lavender that clung to her hair. He listened to the delicacy of her breathing, relished in the feel of protecting her. In a few hours his life would return to what he knew best. What he had trained his entire life to do. Fight. Kill. Win. Tomorrow he would know if one of his men had betrayed him yet again. But tonight he simply wanted to hold the woman he had married for peace. The woman who made him forget about war.

Chapter Thirteen

TANON'S EYES FLUTTERED open two hours later. The sky was still cloaked in darkness, but Gareth and all but one of his men were gone. She sat up, her heart racing wildly in her chest.

"Have they gone, then?"

Propped against a tree close to where she had slept, long legs stretched out before him, Cian nodded. "I'm to guard you and your nurse with my life."

Tanon looked around. Her voice had roused Rebecca from sleep, but beyond the soft amber hue of the fire, she could see nothing else.

"Fear not, lady," Cian reassured her when a small sound of panic parted her lips. "'Twas my brother, Madoc, who taught me to fight." He held up his palm to stop her when she stood up. "I must insist that you remain on your pallet."

"But it's so dark. How will they see?" She went to him, wringing her hands together until they ached. "They weren't supposed to leave until dawn." *Why didn't Gareth bid me farewell?* She closed her eyes and said another prayer that God would keep Gareth and his men safe.

"His suspicions against one of us have been raised," Cian explained quietly, his furrowed brow darkening his eyes when she began to pace in front of him. "If he is correct, then the traitor has not gone back to Winchester but has returned to warn his comrades about our attack."

"Bleddyn?" Tanon asked quietly.

Cian nodded. "Striking before our enemies expect it will give us a better chance at victory, since there are so many."

Rebecca came to stand beside Tanon. "But how does Prince Gareth know that Bleddyn has betrayed him and has not gone to the king as ordered?"

"He doesn't, yet. But someone has betrayed us," he told them quickly, "someone who betrayed Gareth before. These men know that Gareth has left Winchester. If they had attacked the castle while we were still in it, their scheme to involve the prince would have failed. Gareth would have killed them himself. Someone had to have informed them that we left."

Tanon drew in a nervous breath. "So, what do we do now?"

"We wait. Gareth and the others have already been gone over an hour. The sun will be up shortly. It shouldn't take too long. Why don't you and your nurse return to your pallets now."

Dear God, he was talking about killing fifty men as if it were nothing more than a slight inconvenience. She would never get used to their barbaric way of living.

Tanon took a step toward her pallet. A twig snapped. She looked down. Odd, the sound hadn't come from beneath her slipper. An instant later Cian was on his feet, grasping her arm.

"Get to your pallet, now!" He shook her when she didn't move quickly enough. Rebecca was already halfway there when Cian swept his long broadsword from its sheath.

Even before she reached her pallet, Tanon heard another man's voice behind her, chiding, tainted with arrogance.

"Cian, did Wyfyrn truly think my men and I would sit and wait for him to attack?"

Tanon spun around in time to see Bleddyn standing before Cian, a battle-ax dangling from his hand, a twisted smirk marring his features. That was all she saw before a huge hand covered her mouth and dragged her into the darkness of the trees. She bit down hard, and the man behind her growled out a sharp oath but held on. His other hand wrapped securely around Rebecca's mouth.

"Tanon, 'tis Hereward, blast you," the husky Saxon whispered against her ear. "Do not take a bite of me again."

Hereward? Her mind took a moment to comprehend that it was truly him. When it did, she became aware of more movements all around her. A flash of steel against a sliver of moonlight breaking through the canopy. A gurgling sound, and then a soft thump. Another swoosh of a blade and a muffled grunt. A bone cracking.

A battle was taking place in the darkness. And she was right in the center of it.

Eyes wide with terror, Tanon clutched Hereward's forearm.

"That clever bastard. Gareth is Wyfyrn," the Saxon whispered on a stunned growl. "And he was right, Bleddyn brought them to us." Tanon followed Hereward's gaze between the thick trunks into the illuminated camp.

Bleddyn stared into the trees, momentarily addled by the swift disappearance of the two women who were standing in the campsite seconds before. Tanon's expression matched his when she saw the figure creeping up behind him. He moved with absolute silence on the pads of his bare feet and stopped directly behind Bleddyn. The golden helm he wore molded to the angles of his face, ending just above the curl of his full upper lip. There was no visor but two intricately carved-out openings that revealed dark, deadly eyes. The metal was carved in the likeness of a dragon. Indeed, when he spoke, his voice consumed his victim in an unholy fire.

"Bleddyn, I knew precisely where you and your men would draw your last breaths."

Bleddyn paled and whirled around. He met the warrior's hard gaze as Wyfyrn swept his sword across his belly. Bleddyn sank to his knees and then fell forward at his feet. The notorious serpent dragon lifted his eyes to the spot where Tanon stood frozen, watching him.

The clearing came alive with shouts and men from both sides swinging their weapons. Wyfyrn leaped to his right, easily eluding a slice at his head. Madoc dropped from the branch of a tree to Tanon's right and landed on his haunches. For a moment he fought from that position, jabbing his blade into the back of the man who had swung at Wyfyrn.

Terrified, Tanon turned into Hereward's big body and squeezed her eyes shut. But he was already pulling away from her.

"You are safe here." When Hereward released

Rebecca, Tanon clung to his arm. "They need me." He gestured toward the fighting. "Stay here," Hereward warned her. "Do not move from this spot, Tanon. Wait for him." She shook her head, but he stepped past her and into the clearing. He looked around, his red hair spilling down between his shoulder blades like blood.

"Ah, 'tis a good night for fighting." He drew in a deep, hearty breath before a man came at him from his right. The mighty Saxon swung his fist. Bones crunched and blood splattered, and then Hereward raised his sword high over his head to finish his victim.

Tanon wanted to run, but she was too afraid to move. She felt Rebecca tug on her skirts.

"Get down lest they see you!" Her nurse tugged her harder.

Numbly, Tanon fell to her knees. She'd been raised around warriors, watched her father's men honing their battle skills in the lists of Avarloch for years. Some had even bled from the ferocity of their practice. She had seen melees at William's tourneys where dozens of men fought in a writhing mass of wooden swords and swinging fists. But this was real. This was gruesome. Her nostrils tingled with the acrid scent of blood; her stomach twisted at the sight of dead bodies not twelve feet from her. She wanted to go home.

She caught a movement out of the corner of her eye. Someone in the trees on the other side of the camp was scurrying toward the battle. He moved again, closer to the edge of the trees. Tanon's wide gaze cut to Cian's halo of burnished curls. The young warrior fought with his back to the forest, unaware that his life was in peril.

Tanon's eyes darted to Gareth fighting two men too far

from Cian to offer him assistance. Madoc was the closest, but there was no time for her to run around the perimeter of trees and warn him before Cian was struck down. Her throat convulsed. Panic engulfed her. Before she had time to consider what she was about to do, she sprang to her feet and lunged forward into the clearing.

"Cian! Behind you!" she screamed. He turned and stabbed at the man about to bring his sword down on his head.

Tanon didn't have time to breathe a sigh of relief before another man knocked her to the ground. She tried to scream, but strong fingers clamped down hard on her throat, cutting off her air. His other hand lifted over his head, a dagger clutched within his fingers. Another blood-stained hand appeared over her, lifting the man off her.

Madoc stood over her attacker. His eyes were no longer cold but black with a tempest fury that promised no mercy. He pulled a second sword from its sheath and crisscrossed both of his blades against the man's throat.

As the sheer horror of what he was about to do settled over her, Tanon bolted upright and skirted backward on her rump. She turned her face away just in time. She didn't waste another moment to look back but scrambled on her hands and knees into the cover of the trees.

With the sides more evenly balanced—after the killing of half the ruffians while they hid in the darkness, waiting to attack—the battle ended as the sun spread its soft golden hues over the forest.

From her place crouching behind a thick oak, Tanon watched Wyfyrn tear off his dragon helm and head directly for her. A swath of dark crimson stained his shirt, but to Tanon's great relief, it was not his blood. The rest of his men bore the same battle marks, with blood smeared across their arms, chests, and faces.

Her husband broke through the trees and hauled her to her feet. "Are you injured?" He ran his hands over her face. He looked so pained, Tanon thought her first assessment of him was wrong and he had been wounded.

"I'm not hurt," she assured him, though she trembled. She lifted her hand cautiously to the bloodstain on his chest. "Are you?"

He clasped her fingers before she touched him and brought them to his lips. "Nay."

As Tanon watched Gareth kiss her knuckles, Hereward crashed through the web of trees, releasing a deep sigh of relief when he saw her unharmed. He turned next to Rebecca and reached out to swipe away a tear running down her cheek.

"Hereward," Gareth said, glancing at the bodies scattering the clearing. "Take Rebecca with you to get cleaned up while the men clear the campsite." He left Tanon for a moment to call to Madoc. "Bring the fallen into the woods, then have the men get some sleep before we leave. Cian, toss me a fresh tunic from my pack."

Cian ran to his task. After handing over Gareth's tunic, the youngest of Gareth's warriors stopped before Tanon and offered her a heartwrenching grin. "Thank you," he said softly, then returned to the campsite.

Tanon could feel Gareth's eyes on her, but she didn't look at him lest he see the raw emotions in her eyes. Fear from standing in the center of a battle still made her legs weak. Relief that Gareth and Cian weren't killed made her feel light-headed. She clung to the one thing that prevented her from throwing herself into his arms. Her husband was Wyfyrn.

~

Tanon let Gareth lead her deeper into the labyrinth of trees, away from the bodies of the men they had ambushed. Sunshine spilled through the canopy, creating columns of hazy amber light.

Gareth stopped and pulled his bloodied shirt away. "It was a brave thing you did for Cian," he said. "But you scared the hell out of me."

She watched the way the light fell over his hair, his sleek muscles. "I did not feel brave at the time," she admitted. She didn't feel brave now, either, alone with him. But looking at him was better than dwelling on the massacre she'd just witnessed.

He smiled. "Without fear, courage doesn't exist."

Her raven brow enthralled him when it wrinkled above her eyes. "How did you know they would come to our campsite?"

"I realized that if Bleddyn told them I was coming, they wouldn't sit around waiting. He would lead them to us, thinking to catch us unaware before we left. Ambushing them in the woods gave us a better chance at victory. You and your nurse were supposed to be asleep on your pallets. Hereward's task was to bring the both of you to safety."

Tanon nodded, losing herself in the husky velvet of his voice, in the staggering depths of his eyes. A chill snaked up her spine. The ruffians would have killed her, and Rebecca, and Cian had Gareth not been so clever. But Wyfyrn was rumored to be a crafty warrior.

"You are the sworn enemy of my people."

He broke their gaze to sit on the dewy grass, moving like liquid returning to liquid, stealthy and sinuous. "Enemy only to those who would try to bring harm to what I love."

Tanon stared down at him. "You lied to William and to my father."

Dear God, what would William do if he ever discovered that he'd wed her to Wyfyrn? She joined Gareth on the grass, lured by a desire to be near him.

"I had to," he told her quietly. "My death will not bring an end to the warring between our people, Tanon."

Tanon wound her finger around one of the curls that had escaped her clips. She'd spent too many hours already pondering his death. She didn't want to think about the vibrancy in his eyes fading as his spirit left him.

"You love your people well," she said, feeling a hook of envy piercing deep. "You would do anything for them."

He swept his gaze over the forest in front of him and nodded. "Aye, I would."

"Even wed a Norman."

His eyes slid to her first before he angled his head and gave her a humorous look. Was that the reason she kept her laughter from him? She thought he wasn't pleased about marrying her? Hell, he had never told her any different.

"I was reluctant to wed you at first, but . . ."

She offered him a cool smile and turned away, giving her attention to a rock.

"Even though you constantly try my good nature, I—"

"*I* try *your* good nature?" She snapped back around. "I don't even have to try not to like you. You make it—"

He covered her mouth with his, curling his fingers around her nape to hold her captive. He didn't have to. Tanon went soft against him. When he pushed her back, she fell into the grass, accepting him into her arms. His mouth devoured her, feeding on her breath, her last shred of will. When he withdrew, it was only to seal her fate with a tender smile. For she surrendered her hopes of making him dislike her, and with it, the comfortable, dispassionate life she'd prepared herself for. There was no more use in denying it. She liked Gareth very much, and she wanted him to like her, too.

He shifted his hard body. His eyes grew hot with dark desire as he settled his hips over hers. "You make it hard to be gentle." His mouth dipped to her throat. She closed her eyes and lifted her hands to his lower back, instinctively pressing herself to the thickness between his legs.

She heard a sound to her left, like footsteps or . . . flapping. A shrill scream pierced the morning, followed by an equally chilling screech from Tanon.

Gareth rolled off her, tearing two daggers from his belt while vaulting to his feet. He looked down at the raven cocking its head at him.

Tanon sat up. Her smile deepened into a giggle at the sight of him standing ready to defend her life against a bird. "My champion."

Gareth tucked his blades back into his belt and cut her a wry look. "You're quite mouthy for a lady."

"You're quite slow for a warrior," she tossed back at him, up for the playful challenge that ignited his eyes with blue fire. *Enfer,* there was naught courtly about him. She was glad. "That raven could have plucked out ten strands of your hair before you took notice."

He shrugged and crooked his mouth into a smile that kindled her blood. "My thoughts were occupied with what part of you I wanted to taste next."

Tanon's nipples tightened instantly. Instead of blushing, she felt her lips curl into a curious smile. She'd grown up a lady, but he made her feel like a woman.

Gareth's eyes raked over her, settling on the firm tips of her breasts pushing against her gown. He felt himself go hard again. He watched her gaze dip there, surprise spreading across her features at the sight of his powerful arousal.

He glanced down at himself, and then back at her. "Aye, I'd say you needed protection from what I wanted to do to you."

The notion of him doing anything to her with . . . *that* made her so nervous, she giggled into her hand.

"You're laughing?" He sounded so astonished and insulted it made her laugh even harder.

"Christ, I'm doomed," he murmured, but then he smiled. Her gown was dirty, and there were leaves in her hair. She looked more beautiful to him than the day before or the day before that. The winsome sound of her mirth filled his soul, pulling him back to a time when he'd been innocent, too. Before he became prince and before he took up arms against his enemies in a struggle to regain what his people needed to survive. What his soul had ached for since he was a boy. Peace.

Chapter Fourteen

"I WANT MY WAR." Cedric, son of King Rhys's brother, Owain, stared out over the timber palisade encompassing one of the twin towers of Prince Dafydd ap Gruffydd's fortress. His dark gaze spread over the steep mountain slopes and wooded hillsides in the distance. Gwynedd. He enjoyed a deep inhalation of cool, pine-scented air. So much of the north was still unsullied by Norman invasion. The land here was as wild and as brutal as his dreams. His jaw, lightly dusted with chestnut stubble, tightened. This was where he would make his home after the war. Indeed, he decided he would live in this very fortress once its current owner was removed.

"Rhydderch of Powys and that dolt Prince Amren of Gwent do naught while the Normans slowly advance deeper into Cymru. I understand some of Lord Benevere's men on the central marches have taken Cymry wives. Our enemy is seeping into our lives and our land like a disease."

Standing beside him, Prince Dafydd nodded. "Your brother follows their example by marrying a Norman."

"Aye, and after all the Normans have done." Cedric returned his cool gaze to the landscape. "They attacked Ystrad Towi and left Llandovery in ruins before my uncle handed it all over to Gareth. They killed many, and my brother repays them by taking one as a wife."

"Have you forgotten what your man Bleddyn told us?" Dafydd asked him. "Gareth is Wyfyrn. If he spoke the truth, then your brother has killed many Normans."

Cedric's mouth twisted into a smirk. "Wyfyrn, the people's hero who hides behind a helm." He laughed, but the sound was void of any mirth. "He is afraid of the Normans. From the day we first met the king, my brother has preached peace. King William frightened him with his vast armies. That is why Wyfyrn hides. He killed a few Normans because they raped a peasant or burned a few huts down. He does not possess the passion for war, the pride of the Cymry."

Beneath his bushy brown beard, Dafydd's jaw twitched and his lips tightened. "Afraid or not, he snatches life from his victims like a wraith. Are we wise to underestimate a man who held Lord Hamilton of Chepstow captive on his own land, in his own castle, after he decimated the warlord's garrison?"

"Of course not, Dafydd," Cedric assured him, softening his voice. "That is why we have not attacked Gareth's village outright but have meticulously planned his death, along with my uncle's. That is, unless King William kills Gareth before we do."

"Do you think the Norman king will believe the attack on Winchester was ordered by Gareth?"

"Aye. My men carry Gareth's banner. But then, I don't really care whose order he thinks it was. One way or another, I will force the Normans onto the battlefield, where I will rid Cymru of them for good."

"Can Bleddyn be trusted?"

"He's been in my service for three years."

"And the other?"

Cedric's lips curled into a grisly smile. "He wants Gareth dead as badly as we do. He will lead Gareth straight to us. My brother has betrayed his people by marrying a Norman. It is a sin not so easily forgiven. Not even by his closest friends."

Gareth and his group made camp on the outskirts of Herefordshire two days later. Tanon sat with Rebecca while they ate with the rest of the men around a small campfire. She listened quietly while Hereward finally confronted Gareth about his true identity.

"The Cymry cannot help but rebel against invasion." Gareth spoke calmly, but his eyes, over the glowing embers, shone with unshakable conviction. "When the Normans try to raid the land I rule, I hold them back with the sword and with my army. But the people who live along the marches have no defense. They are mostly peasants who have been abandoned by their princes. Some marcher lords treat them kindly. Some do not. I cannot sit by and do nothing while children are taken as serfs and women and old men are beaten or killed because they refuse to swear fealty to their overlords."

Tanon's gaze drifted over her husband while he spoke. Though his words were chilling to her ears, they settled warmly over her heart. Her childhood hero had become a champion to his people.

"Why do you fight them as Wyfyrn?" Hereward asked.

"If the Normans knew who I was, my villagers would suffer the consequences."

"But if you fought them openly, as a prince . . ."

Madoc tossed his uneaten bread into the fire and turned his dark eyes on Hereward. "You were once a rebel against the same men who took your land. You did not fight openly but eluded them for years. Why do you judge Gareth for doing the same thing?"

"I don't," Hereward tossed back at him. "I understand his cause. But if he fought as a prince, making his reasons known, other princes might stand with him."

"My reasons are known to them who die by my hand," Gareth replied in a thoroughly controlled voice. "And tell me, Hereward, when I fought against Lord Fitzgerald while he tried to advance into Ystrad Towi, what princes drew swords by my side?" Gareth didn't wait for an answer. They all knew what it was. "If we are not united, how can we stand against an army that stretches as far as Normandy? I don't want to plunge Cymru into a war we cannot win."

"Yet you kill Norman noblemen in their *beds,*" Hereward argued.

"I exact justice to those who deserve it."

"There have only been . . ." Cian closed his eyes and moved his lips, counting out how many. "Three, nay, four marcher lords we've killed, aye, Gareth?"

"And their entire garrisons, lest you've forgotten," Hereward reminded them succinctly.

Tomas nodded and spat a twig from his mouth. "Aye, and the circumstances of their deaths have instilled fear in the rest, making further bloodshed unnecessary."

"And if your identity is discovered?" Hereward asked Gareth, the concern in his voice conveying his fondness for the Welsh prince. He'd spent a full year with him in Wales and had come to think highly of King Rhys's youngest nephew.

Alwyn guzzled the last of his ale, then swiped his knuckles across his mouth and raised his gaze to Tanon. "The Normans will not find out who Wyfyrn is unless someone tells their king."

Tanon regarded the hefty warrior, who clearly didn't like her. She understood now why he didn't. But not all Normans were cruel lords. Her father and her uncle, and even William, treated their vassals kindly. "I am loyal to my king, Alwyn," she told him. "But I would not betray my husband."

"King William has left the laws of Wales to the Welsh and to the Normans who govern them." Hereward grazed his eyes over Alwyn and then settled them on Gareth. "Else he would have already sent troops to hunt down and capture Wyfyrn. He is not the merciless tyrant you imagine. He pardoned me, and I've killed even more Normans than you."

Tanon hugged herself and shivered. She'd heard enough about killing Normans. She didn't want to think about death and war and deceit. She looked around the twilit glade, praying that no men were hiding in the shadows. She met Gareth's gaze across the fire, and he winked at her. Mayhap it was his confidence, or the tenderness in his eyes, but he soothed her. She offered him a grateful smile in return.

Rising to his feet, Gareth stepped around Alwyn's hulking form to reach her. "Come." He held out his hand

and she took it, letting him lead her to her pallet. When he lay beside her, she didn't protest.

Spooning her against his body, he closed his arms around her. "You've nothing to fear," he whispered when he felt her trembling.

Tanon wanted to tell him that she wasn't afraid, but it would have been a lie. Her defenses crumbled every time he looked at her, touched her, smiled at her, and she had no idea what to do without them.

~

Someone watched them from across the campsite. Over the flickering flames, his eyes reflected the stark darkness of the night.

Alwyn sat beside him and followed his gaze before Madoc blinked it away.

"He's falling for her," Alwyn grumbled and slipped a sliver of apple into his mouth. "He assured us he wouldn't. What does he have in common with a Norman?"

"Shut up," Madoc growled at him.

"She's comely, aye. But there are dozens of comely women in Llandovery. He assured us all, even the villagers, that this marriage was for peace only."

"And it is. Now shut up, damn you," Madoc warned him again.

"But look at her all tangled up in his arms. She's got him—"

Madoc's elbow smashed into Alwyn's nose with a resounding crack that made even Hereward cringe.

"Don't speak of her as if she were the same shit you take to your bed, Alwyn. I warn you for the last time."

Holding his nose that had already been broken so many

times it refused to bleed now, Alwyn cast Madoc a look of pure astonishment.

"Don't speak the treason of what you're thinking, either." Madoc's voice was low, deadly. "She is *his* wife. She put her life at risk for my brother, and for that, I owe her mine."

He stood up and called to Cian. When his brother reached him, Madoc swung his arm around his neck and walked him to his pallet.

Tanon was the first to awaken the next morning. She began to move away from Gareth, taking care not to wake him. But the sight of his sleeping face made her heart grow still. Saints, but he was handsome. The longer she looked at him, the more she wanted him to wake up. She wanted to see those incredible blue eyes looking back at her, so strong, so reassuring. She sighed. Fighting his effect on her was futile and tiresome. She would simply have to keep herself from expecting anything more from him. She nodded to herself and stood up. She must remember that he had returned for peace. Not for her. She was fortunate that they liked each other, but she would not let herself hope for more than that. She would not end up like Rebecca.

Smoothing the wrinkles from her gown, she looked around the camp. Rebecca was still asleep, curled up on her pallet. Tanon quirked her brow, certain that Hereward hadn't placed his sleeping bed so close to Rebecca's the night before. She shrugged her shoulders and stepped over Tomas's sleeping body, then made her way to the dying campfire. She picked up a stick and poked it into the embers, sending them into the air.

"Needs more leaves."

Madoc's voice above her sent her sprawling to the right. Without looking at her, he squatted and dumped a handful of dried leaves and twigs into the fire.

"You frightened me." She righted herself and glanced at him out of the corner of her eye.

"You should be used to that by now."

"What do you mean?"

"You avoid my gaze since the night of the attack." He turned to look directly at her, testing his theory.

Tanon blinked but fought the urge to look away from the depthless charcoal of his gaze. He had such a hard face, like that of a warlord detached from the blood that drenched his sword. She tried to forget the merciless rage in his eyes just before he sliced the head from the man who had tried to kill her, but every time she looked at him she saw the face of a cold, unyielding warrior.

"You have my allegiance for what you did for Cian."

She nodded but said nothing and finally lowered her gaze.

"You're afraid of me."

She laughed softly, pride forcing her to look at him again. "*Non,* I am not."

"Aye, you are. But you don't let your fear stop you from doing what's needed. Even as a babe you faced down a tyrant."

"Pardon?"

"Roger deCourtenay and your pig, Lily," he explained.

"Petunia," Tanon corrected him with curiosity knitting her brow.

"Aye, Petunia," he agreed with a smile etching his mouth. "Gareth and I were friends when he first traveled to Winchester. When he returned he told me about the day he met you."

"That wasn't the first day," she said faintly. There was something terribly heartwarming about Gareth telling his best friend about her twelve years ago.

Madoc shrugged his shoulders and returned his gaze to the flames. "It was for him."

It was the first day of their friendship, Tanon recalled. It was the day she finally told the truth about how she lost her tooth. It had felt so good to do so. Even though they'd had some trouble communicating, it hadn't stopped them from filling their days with laughter. Tanon didn't realize how much she missed those days, until now.

"I used to wish he was my brother." She laughed at herself. "My own were too young to play with. I wished that he lived with . . ." Realizing what she was saying, she glanced at Madoc and blushed.

"Working your magic on my woman?" Gareth came up behind her so quietly, she didn't notice him until he squatted beside her. He smiled at her when she looked at him, scattering the thousands of butterflies already fluttering in her belly. His very presence next to her shattered her nerves. She was beginning to love the way he always smiled at her. Goodness, but she must look hideous with her hair so untidy and her gown wrinkled from sleeping in it night after night. Still, he looked at her as if she had just stepped out of her room after hours of preparation. Something clutched at her heart, making her want what she thought she would never have.

Tomas joined them, scratching his dark, shadowed jaw as he sat. He offered Madoc a distasteful grimace across the fire. "Madoc couldn't work magic on a wrinkled old hag who was blind and hadn't had herself a man in a score of years."

Gareth laughed, and Tanon poked him in the ribs. "I think Madoc can be quite nice when he isn't—"

"Slicing someone's head off their shoulders," Alwyn offered over his shoulder on his way to the carriage for something to drink.

"I'd prefer to forget that, if you please, Alwyn," Tanon called back. Then, putting it out of her mind completely, she turned to offer Madoc her kindest smile. "I would even chance to say, he's quite thoughtful."

"I wouldn't chance saying that, were I you." Tomas snorted and caught the skin of water Alwyn tossed him.

"Nonsense," Tanon huffed at him.

"Lady," Madoc said, back to brooding, "he's right. Never call me such a detestable thing again."

Tanon stared at him and then turned to Gareth when he began to laugh again. Tomas joined him, as did Alwyn when he sat down.

She shook her head at the lot of them and realized just how much she was going to have to get used to living among such a motley bunch of Welshmen.

After everyone rose from their pallets and ate, Rebecca brushed the tangles out of Tanon's hair while the men cleared the campsite. Tanon watched her husband as he folded their pallet and took it to his horse. He flicked back his hair, but it fell like beaten gold around his face, making him look sensuous and wild.

Something moved in the line of her vision. She looked up and smiled at Hereward.

His verdant gaze shifted to Rebecca. "I'm driving the carriage today and thought you might like to sit with me."

"Of course I wouldn't." Rebecca nearly scoffed right in his face. "I could fall and break my leg. Have you gone daft?"

Hereward's lips twitched beneath his closely cropped beard, but he laughed softly. "Aye. I think I have."

When he walked away without another word, Tanon sighed and shook her head. "Must you be so cruel to him? He has always been kind to you, but you continue to rebuke him."

"I don't wish to discuss him," Rebecca said tersely and continued weaving Tanon's hair into a long plait down her back.

"Why do you dislike him so?" Tanon scowled when her nurse yanked on a stubborn curl.

"Who says I don't like him? I simply have no interest in him."

"Because of my father."

The moment the words left her mouth, Tanon regretted them. But, dear God, how could the woman continue to love a man who would never love her back?

"I have no idea what you mean," Rebecca snapped, releasing Tanon's braid before it was completed.

She could deny it until she lay dying in her bed alone, but Tanon had grown up watching Rebecca's lingering gazes on her father, the smiles that slowly faded over the years and finally barely existed at all. How did she do it? How had she remained with them for so long, giving up her happiness for naught? "Rebecca, if there's nothing stopping you, then just sit with him. Honestly, what could it hurt?"

Her nurse sighed, glanced at Hereward climbing to the

bench, then gained her feet. "I don't see any purpose to this," she mumbled, trudging toward the carriage.

Tanon watched Rebecca go with a trace of a smile lifting her mouth. Her gaze returned to Gareth. Her eyes drank in the sight of him. Even his hands pulling at the straps of his saddle invited unbidden thoughts of him ripping off her gown.

She could never stand loving him if he didn't love her in return. But mayhap he would come to love her in time. He was nothing like Roger. She had known that from the moment Gareth first looked at her the night he stepped into Winchester Castle. He wasn't deeply in love with someone else. Perhaps she could win his heart. She doubted they would ever have what her parents had, but . . .

He turned, as if sensing her eyes on him. Their gazes met; his was warm and wonderfully inviting. Suddenly conscious of her appearance, she swept her curls away from her face. His eyes followed, grazing over her unkempt tresses. He crooked his finger at her. She took a step to go to him and tripped.

She didn't fall flat on her face, but she did go sprawling a few steps. She heard his rich laughter before she lifted her head and narrowed her eyes on him.

"Christ, we have to do something about that." He let his laughter fade to a smile as he reached her and took her arm.

Tanon yanked it away.

"You're not hurt, are you?"

"Not at all." She bit off each word with equal venom, then gave her hair a prim pat.

"Good, because I want you to ride with me today."

"I'd rather you strap me to the wheel of the carriage," she murmured.

He had the audacity to chuckle! She was torn between gaping at him and giving him the glare he deserved. "My goodness, but you have to be the rudest man in all of Wales."

"Cymru," he corrected, grinning at her loss of composure. "After I teach you how to walk without falling, I'll teach you more Cymraeg."

Her mouth dropped open and then snapped shut again before she stormed away from him. She made it to the carriage at the same time Gareth reached his horse. He leaped into the saddle and whirled the steed around in her direction.

Tanon yanked on the door, her eyes opening wider as he cantered closer. Without slowing his horse's pace, he reached down and gathered her under his arm, lifting her feet off the carriage step. She landed hard enough on his lap to make her teeth knock together.

Snapping her head around, she fastened her scalding gaze on him. "That was quite an impressive feat. What might you do next, strip naked and kill a wild boar with your bare hands?"

Gareth stared at her, his honeyed brow rising with surprise. "Christ, you have a mouth like a she-devil. I thought you were a lady, Tanon."

"Did you have an actual thought?" she shot back before she could stop herself. "Or were there just grunting sounds inside your empty head?"

He still wore that infuriating smile, but his eyes flashed at her with warning.

"Woman, you try my patience."

"And you try mine!" She turned to face the road and swatted a curl away from her face.

"Don't raise your voice to me again."

"Don't raise yours to me," she countered. She felt his entire body go stiff behind her. She waited for him to say something else. When he didn't, she peeked over her shoulder. "Well?"

"Well what?"

"Aren't you going to order me to apologize to you now?"

"Nay, I'm considering that the best way to avoid tossing you off my horse is to avoid speaking to you at all."

She spun around to face him, her green eyes blazing with insult. "There will be no need for threats. I will do my best never to speak to you again!"

He grinned. "You would do that for me?"

Tanon bristled in his lap. "I would if you promised to learn how to behave like a civilized man," she retorted and pulled away from him. He hauled her back. She tried to ignore him and the way his large hand covered most of her belly. The contact was hot, needful, suddenly possessive.

"You won't make a peacock out of me, Tanon." A broad sweep of his thumb just below her breasts made her quiver against him.

"And what is so terrible about peacocks?" she challenged him. "They diligently preen themselves to woo a female, proudly displaying their magnificent feathers for all to see."

He nuzzled through the abundance of her hair until he found her ear. "Would you like me to display my feathers, then?" His husky, melodious offer sent a heated fissure to her groin.

She fought her reaction to his touch, but it was no use. His hard body behind her felt even harder, even tighter. Being with him every day, looking at him, sleeping with him, was slowly driving her mad. At first, she had thought him a savage, but he hadn't tried to force himself on her. He hadn't even kissed her again since the morning after the attack. He simply tortured her beyond mercy by giving her all his attention and by being a complete gentleman— when he wasn't tossing her onto his horse.

She opened her mouth but found that her retort had gone sour. For some horrible reason, she suddenly envisioned him naked with a dozen eager women all around him. Women who knew exactly what to do with all that man. The thought of it made her grind her teeth and curl her hands into fists.

"These women that you've been with, did you care for any of them?" She swore to herself that she would ignore him for the rest of the day, no matter how much she would rather be kissing him, if he said that he had.

"What women?"

She rolled her eyes and sighed exhaustively in front of him. "All the women who fawn over you."

"I wasn't aware of any fawning."

"Oh, please, Gareth," she said, turning to give him a skeptical smirk. "You are an extremely virile man. My goodness, you walk like you've just laid claim to a sultan's entire harem. Why, Eleanor Fitzdrummond offered herself to you one day after she met you!"

"Tanon." His eyes softened on her. The warmth in their

heavily fringed depths made her scalp tingle. "If I didn't know any better, I would think you are falling for a savage."

"Don't be ridiculous." Her gaze strayed to his lips, and she licked her own, trying to remember to breathe. "You've proven you're no savage."

"Have I?" he drawled. "Then you're no longer afraid to make love to me?"

"I wasn't afraid of you. I was unsure of what . . ."

Shifting slightly, he fit her rump neatly between his thighs.

Tanon's eyes grew wide at how hard he suddenly felt there.

"You were saying?"

"I was saying . . . I think . . ." She swallowed. That was the problem. She hadn't thought at all. He ignited fires in her and then left her burning. He seduced and intoxicated her. He made her ache to do things she knew naught about, but she didn't think about *how* she would accomplish them. Good God, the man was enormous! "Will it hurt much?" she asked, too curious now to care what he thought of her query.

"Not if it's done right." His sensual grin convinced her that not only did he know how to do it right, but he did it marvelously well.

"Will you kiss me while you do it?" she asked him breathily, eager for his mouth only a scant few inches from hers.

"Aye. I'll kiss you before, during, and after, and in places you never dreamed of being kissed."

He lowered his head and brushed his mouth over hers, giving her a teasing taste of the tender prince he could be.

He withdrew slowly and lingered only a breath away so that she could see the hunger that gleamed in his eyes.

Tanon's breath quavered, and a delicious tightness spasmed between her legs. She was wrong. The savage was here, only controlled. His passion had been carefully harnessed while he watched her being undressed, when he fit her hose over her legs, and every night while he held her until she slept.

"Is it only fighting that sets free the beast?"

The raw, sexual heat in his gaze impaled her; his rough, ragged voice weakened her against him. "Be wary of what you ask for, lady, else I might show you."

"Aw, Christ!" Alwyn trotted up to them to have a word with Gareth. He blanched in his saddle when he saw his lord about to kiss his wife. He turned to the others behind him. "He's going to kiss her! What did I tell you bastards? Soon there will be a brood of little Cymry–Norman brats all over Wales!"

Tanon melted all over again when her husband tossed his head back and laughed.

Chapter Fifteen

THEY REACHED THE WELSH marches two days later. Tanon clutched the window frame of her coach when they passed dozens of small villages, the inhabitants watching her troupe with frightened, suspicious eyes. She saw a grand castle in the distance, built high above a carved-out niche of hundreds of cottages. They crossed Offa's Dyke and continued on unhindered for another two leagues before they were stopped by a group of mounted Norman knights bearing an unfamiliar standard of a hawk with four outspread wings.

When the carriage rolled to a halt, Tanon stuck her head out the window. A guardhouse made of stone and timber, with more armed knights patrolling the low battlements, loomed before her.

"Quelles sont vos affaires au Pays de Galles?" one guard with flaxen hair peeking from beneath his helm called out. Twelve other guards flanked Gareth and his men on every side. The one who had spoken rode toward Gareth with one hand on the hilt at his side.

"Speak the language of the Angles and the Saxons as your king has ordered," Hereward called out from atop the carriage.

The flaxen-haired knight turned to him. "Who addresses me?"

"Hereward the Wake, friend of King William, who himself speaks in the tongue of those he has conquered."

A flurry of whispers rose up from the knights as Hereward announced his name. Many of them still harbored ill will toward the Saxon rebel for his years spent fighting against their king, but none considered laying a finger on him. Not only was it known throughout the land that King William had pardoned him, but none of them wanted to fight with six feet four inches of pure brawn.

"Very well. I am Sir Philip Bonvalet, commander of Lord Richard D'Avre's first regiment. Now, I ask you again in your own tongue, what business have you in Wales?"

"My chickens need tending to," Gareth called out, offering Sir Bonvalet a pleasant smile when the knight snapped his attention back to him. "They haven't eaten in a fortnight, and I'm overcome with worry."

"Welshmen!" Bonvalet reared back on his horse and drew his sword. His action was echoed by the other twelve surrounding Gareth's group.

"Ease yourselves, men." Gareth held up the king's missive. "Being saddled all day in piss-soaked breeches will make you disagreeable. You have naught to fear from me."

"How did you gain entry into England?" Bonvalet demanded.

Gareth shrugged. "The same way a group of fifty other Welshmen did. You soldiers are grossly lax in your duty."

Beside him, Madoc chuckled. Bonvalet glowered at him from under his helm. "You find that humorous, knave?"

"Aye." Madoc's posture on his horse remained relaxed, but his eyes bore into Bonvalet. "But I was also thinking about how quickly I could kick your arse back to Normandy."

For a moment, Bonvalet simply stared at Madoc's audacity, doubting his ears. Then his lip curled into a challenging snarl, and he urged Madoc forward with a wave of his gloved hand.

"Norman." The force in Gareth's voice made every head turn to him. "Read the missive before I let him do it."

"I've no interest in missives," the knight sneered, then pointed to the carriage. "But she might be able to persuade me to let you live, if she begs hard enough."

The malevolent curl of Gareth's lips sparked an equally deadly glint in his eyes. "If you make it to the carriage door alive, you are welcome to her."

Inside the carriage, Tanon took hold of Rebecca's hand and squeezed. She wasn't worried about being given to the Norman knight. Her husband was a confident warrior who knew he could fight this entire regiment and win, else he would never had made the challenge. But she didn't want to see any more men killed before her eyes.

The carriage bounced slightly as Hereward leaped from the upper bench and landed on his feet. Without pause, he strode directly to the Norman soldier. He reached up, gripped the knight by the back of the neck, and pulled him off his horse.

"The lady is Lord Brand Risande's daughter." He gave the man a teeth-throttling shake and then set his burning green eyes on the rest of the knaves. "That's the Earl of

Avarloch I refer to, if any of you bastards don't know. I warn you now, if any one of you even looks at her again, I will personally skin you alive."

Within the coach, Rebecca arched her neck to have a better look at the brutish Saxon.

Hereward swiped the rolled missive from Gareth's hand and shoved it in Bonvalet's face. "If you can read, you had better begin now." While the knight tore open the missive with shaky fingers, Hereward released him and grumbled under his breath about foolish whelps, lightning-quick serpents, and crazed earls.

While they waited for Bonvalet to read King William's missive, Gareth sighed impatiently. If he didn't get Tanon home where he could make love to her in private soon, he was going to start removing some heads.

The guard finally looked up. "The Earl of Avarloch gives his daughter to a Welshman in marriage?"

"To His Highness, Prince Gareth of Ystrad Towi," Cian called out with a measure of pride straining his voice that made Tanon smile hearing him. "Nephew to King Rhys of Deheubarth."

"Your king desires peace," Hereward announced to the guardsmen, raking his gaze over each. "Which one of you will defy him?" When no one answered, he gave Bonvalet a hard shove. "Do we pass, or do you wish to send for your priest to pray over your bodies?"

Bonvalet vaulted to his horse and called out to his men. "Let them go by order of King William." The knights parted, creating a wide path for Gareth's men and the carriage. As Gareth passed Bonvalet, the Norman eyed him warily.

"I shall remember your face, Welshman."

Gareth nodded, his confident smirk belying the icy contempt that made his eyes frost like blue glaciers. "And I shall remember that you wanted to make my wife beg."

As Tanon's coach tottered by him, Gareth's eyes found hers. Then he flicked his reins and entered Cymru behind her.

～

The land of the savages looked nothing like Tanon had expected. In fact, she was certain she'd never seen any land more beautiful. Oh, Gareth's stories had been true. White wooly sheep scampered across lush green rolling hills as serene as a summer loch. Windswept moorlands festooned with blossoms bursting with color filled her vision and tickled her nose with sweet perfume. Riverbanks and woodland met along the winding Wye River. As they rode onward, the landscape grew wilder, even more glorious with low, grassy mountains and razor-sharp ridges. In the distance, farmsteads speckled sprawling vales, where more sheep and cattle grazed.

They reached Gareth's home two days later. His village, which was actually larger than some towns Tanon had seen in England, was sheltered in a valley of wild rolling hills and glistening rivers, set against the magnificent mountain ranges in the east.

A defensive earth bank and ditch were built around the village. The ditch was topped with a timber palisade wall of carefully arranged oak planks. Inside the palisade was a footbridge where dozens of men paced, looking out over the populace. There was no castle jutting toward the vast swath of powdery blue sky, but dozens of large, well-kept cottages nestled close together. Some structures were not cottages at all, but craftmen's shops. Blacksmiths, leather-workers, weavers, and potters all busy with the day's tasks stopped and followed Gareth's men to the front of a large tavern in the center of the village. Children dressed in linen smocks ran alongside the carriage, calling out greetings of *Bore da!* and *Croeso!* Dogs and even squeal-ing pigs ran at the children's sides. The sounds of harps and stringed lyre, pipes and drums, permeated the fragrant air with lively music.

Tanon marveled, gazing out her window. Everywhere she looked, women, dressed in gowns of patterned linen, some with colorful overskirts and aprons stained with the food they'd been preparing, stopped to have a look at her. Some carried large baskets piled with laundry under their arms, and others wielded wooden paddles Tanon hoped were used to beat the dust out of bedding, rather than chil-dren's hides. None offered her a smile or a scowl. The men were a different tale altogether. They wore shirts of dyed hide over loose hose or dusty kidskin breeches. They raked their gazes over her quite brazenly when she stepped out of the carriage. Some smiled, looking a bit like wolves that had just spotted an unguarded sheep ripe for the devouring. A few of the men narrowed their gazes on her moments before coming to some conclusion that made them spit and look away.

Tanon looked around. Gareth was talking to an older man, far enough away to make calling him difficult, nev-ermind mortifying. Hereward began the task of untying the trunks. He must not have been doing it to Rebecca's liking, because she hurried to him, abandoning Tanon altogether.

"Are you coming?"

Tanon looked up and thought she would never feel so relieved to see Madoc standing beside her. She nodded. "Thank you."

"*Diolch*," he corrected her woodenly and walked away. When she didn't follow him directly, he turned and flicked his wrist at her. When they reached Gareth's side, Madoc left her and continued on his way toward the tavern.

Tanon took a step after him, not sure where she was supposed to go or what she was supposed to do. Gareth caught her wrist and riled her when he cast her a cool look.

"What? You left me alone in the carriage!" she charged, mindless of the utter silence that had descended on the growing crowd facing her. "How was I to . . ." Her words faded as she looked around and found dozens of faces staring back at her. She took a step closer to Gareth.

"She's wrinkly!" a child called out, and another giggled, only to be silenced by a swift slap to his shoulder.

Tanon's face grew flush. She lifted her fingers to her cheek. "Wrinkly? Why, I am only ten and eight." Her eyes found a young woman in the crowd. She had minky braids and huge dark eyes, and a belly as huge and as round as Tanon's mother's had been when she'd carried Anne and Ellie. The woman giggled and pointed to Tanon's gown. The fabric was a maze of wrinkles from hem to waist. Tanon lowered her hand, aching to smooth the fabric, but then realized the effort would be fruitless. It would take her a se'nnight to get all the creases out.

"This is Lady Tanon." Gareth's voice boomed so loudly in her ear, she nearly toppled over. "As you all know, she's a Norman—"

"Norman and Saxon," Tanon called out, correcting him

with a smile. When no one smiled back, she cleared her throat and moved farther behind her husband. He turned and gave her an exhausted sigh.

"You will not interrupt me again, aye?"

She nodded, and he returned his attention to the crowd.

"Since you all—"

"It was very rude, forgive me."

Gareth closed his eyes and waited a moment. When she remained quiet, he opened his eyes and continued. "Since you all speak the language of the Saxons, you will use those words when addressing my wife until she learns Cymraeg. You will show her kindness and respect, and offer her aid should she request it." He reached behind him and took her hand. "I care for her, and it would please me if my people do as well."

Tanon gazed up at his profile and felt her knees buckle at his declaration. He cared for her? What did that mean, exactly? Her head reeled. She hadn't expected to hear such words come from him, but she couldn't deny how pleasing they were.

The women in the crowd whispered among themselves. The wolves suddenly fidgeted nervously and smiled at her more politely. Hereward and Cian, and Tomas, who stood now with his arm tossed around the pretty pregnant woman, smiled at her.

"Did you have to take her by force?" someone called out.

"Aye, did you fight any Normans, lord?" called another man from the crowd.

Gareth nodded and offered his people what they wanted, a victorious smile. "Aye. I fought her betrothed at the king's tourney, and won."

"Her betrothed," Cian added with a shout, "and eight of his men."

After a chorus of cheers, the crowd dispersed. Gareth shackled his fingers around her wrist and gave her a slight tug. "Come, let's go home." He paused when she called to Rebecca to join them. He thought about telling her that her nurse would not be living with them but decided to wait a little while longer. Let her first recover from seeing her new home. Turning to look over his shoulder, Gareth motioned to Hereward and two other men to follow with the women's trunks. Rebecca eyed the Saxon while he lifted the largest trunk to his shoulder. The other two men shared the weight of one trunk between them.

"Where's your castle?" Tanon asked a few minutes later when her legs began to ache from trying to keep up with Gareth's long strides. They had left the main village and were crossing a wide, open glen dotted with more cottages and a rich harvest of barley, wheat, and various vegetables. To her right, a small group of villagers, both men and women, returned to a grassy field. They picked up wooden lances that had been discarded upon Gareth's return and waited while minstrels began plucking their instruments once again.

Gareth pointed to a cottage, slightly bigger than the ones his people occupied. It was ringed on two sides by a low stone wall that separated it from the harvest. The walls of the cottage were washed white beneath a thick thatched roof and stone chimney. There were windows along the wall facing east, and in the center, a small wooden door with a bronze handle. Tall columns of trees swept upward behind the cottage, their rustling crowns adding more music to the air.

"You live there?" Tanon didn't realize she had stopped walking until she noticed that Gareth had stopped as well. He was staring at her with a slight scowl marring his golden brow.

"I know it's not what you're used to, but it will have to suit you."

"It's . . ." God's breath, it was small. There wasn't even a second landing! She swallowed and tried to smile. She didn't want to hurt his feelings. ". . . cozy." She blinked at Rebecca. "Isn't it, Rebecca?"

"Aye," the nurse sighed solemnly. "Cozy."

Gareth studied his home, tilting his head to look at it from a different angle.

"It needs a few things, that is all," Tanon pressed on. "I simply expected something a bit larger. You are a prince, after all."

"A fortress separates you from your people. I prefer to live as they do." He sounded somewhat apologetic before he picked up his steps again.

To live as they do. Tanon chewed her lip. That had to mean no vassals, no handmaidens, no cooks. "That's very noble of you," she told him, hurrying to catch up, and aware of his sudden brooding mood. If she'd married Roger, she would be the lady of a fine castle, complete with every comfort . . . and so miserable she would probably have tossed herself off the highest battlements by now. She sighed silently. Gareth's home wasn't a mighty stronghold, but it was where he ate, slept, and returned after battling his enemies. She envisioned him walking about inside, sitting in a comfortable chair by the hearth, chopping wood for his fire. A sense of warmth settled over her. With some colorful drapes and pretty flowers planted around the outside wall, his cottage would be pleasant, indeed.

"I like it," she said, this time with a convincing enough smile to make Gareth stare at her.

He wondered if she had banged her head inside the carriage. She was used to finery. Her chambers at Avarloch were larger than his entire house. His scowl faded. It was thoughtful of her to pretend fondness for his home. She was, above all else, polite.

When they reached the cottage, he gave the door a slight shove, then stepped inside, followed by Hereward and the two men hefting the other trunk.

Tanon and Rebecca stood in the doorway, peering into the darkness. Something smelled foul. Tanon wrinkled her nose while Gareth dismissed his men and lit a few candles. When the interior illuminated in the soft amber glow, Tanon wanted to race to the flames and blow them out again.

"I'm afraid it has suffered neglect in my long absence," Gareth said as Tanon braved the task of entering. "But once it's cleaned, it won't be so bad."

Tanon's nose itched from the musty rushes on the floor. The windows didn't need drapes, after all. They were already covered with fur, which accounted for the darkness. A small bed with moldy straw poking out of tears in the mattress was pushed up against a corner wall. Against the opposite wall, a hand-carved, heavy oak wardrobe reached halfway up to the ceiling. Beside it, various-sized daggers, swords, and axes hung from a wooden shelf. A trivet for cooking blocked her path to the hearth, where Gareth was now squatting and peering up into the chimney chute.

Other than a table and a single chair, there was nothing else in the house.

Tanon bit her lower lip. This was going to take a much firmer resolve than she believed she possessed.

"Is there a garderobe?" she asked her husband.

"Through there." He pointed to a door at the far end of the cottage. Tanon went to it, opened it, and then returned, pale.

"It's a stream."

Hereward suppressed a smile. He felt sorry for the girl. This place was as different from Avarloch as he was from . . . Brand Risande. His gaze slid to Rebecca, who looked away from him when their eyes met, and his smile faded.

"There's only one bed." Rebecca stalled, still huddled in the doorway. "And no walls to separate our sleeping chambers."

Gareth swore an oath under his breath at the chute, then straightened and walked toward the nurse. "You won't be staying here. I'll go and find a place for you." He gave her a reassuring nod when she looked about to protest. "Not too far from your lady, I know."

He passed Hereward on his way out. "You coming?"

The hulking Saxon shook his head. "Nay, I'll wait here for your return. I promised your wife's father I'd keep my eye on her."

Gareth cut a knowing glance toward Rebecca, then left the cottage.

"Gareth." Tanon followed him outside. "I need Rebecca here to . . ."

He stopped and turned to face her, and suddenly Tanon couldn't think straight. Streaks of golden light spilled around him, glinting off his golden armbands and torc, making him look like some invincible god of legend. Beneath the thick sweep of his lashes, his eyes probed hers, waiting for her to go on.

"Um . . . to help me dress."

An intimate smile teased his lips, coaxing memories of how his fingers felt on her legs when he helped her into her hose. She drew in a shuddering breath and forbade herself to step closer to him.

"I need her to tie up my hair in the mornings."

His gaze swept over the long, wild curls draping her shoulders. "Your hair is perfect the way it is."

She brought her fingers to it and smiled. "But it is unkempt. I look—"

"Ravishing."

Tanon sighed, thoroughly enchanted. Did he truly think her ravishing without even a single hour of work?

"Tanon." He closed the distance between them by slipping his finger beneath the neckline of her gown and pulling her to him. "I have done everything in my power to stop myself from ripping off this blasted gown and spreading you beneath me. But if I don't have you alone very soon, I'm afraid I'm going to become the savage you fear."

He made every part of her tighten and burn. Madly, she almost held him there longer to find out if he spoke the truth. "Go," she said on a ragged breath.

⌒

Gareth returned quickly and escorted Rebecca, with Hereward in tow, carrying the nurse's trunk, to the home of Tomas and his wife, Adara, whom Tanon found out was the comely pregnant woman from the village.

Left alone in the cottage, Tanon eyed her dusty, moldy surroundings. She sank to the bed, cringing when the mattress crunched beneath her. Dear God, but she had to relieve herself, and after having to do the like behind the trees for the last se'nnight, she had so hoped for a proper garderobe. She looked at the front door, willing Gareth to open it, bringing something beautiful into this gloomy place. How was she ever going to survive here? She could throw herself at his mercy and cry until he took her home—tears had, after all, worked for her once. She worried her lip, thinking of writing to her parents and begging them to come get her. She slammed her palm down on the mattress. Heavens, but she was made of better stuff than this, wasn't she? Besides, she didn't want to go home. *That* notion came with a serious jolt, almost as shocking as the revelation that she didn't want to leave Gareth. Besides, she had promised William she would try to find happiness here. "I will not fall to pieces." She eyed the broom propped against the wall and gritted her teeth. If she was going to learn how to be a wife, it was best to begin now. She stood and reached for the broom when the door opened. Cian stepped inside, followed by Alwyn.

"Well, what do you think of Cymru so far?" Cian grinned at her.

Tanon smiled and gazed across the dirty floor. "It's lovely," she answered, not having the heart to say anything less.

Alwyn did nothing to mask his amusement as he looked around the cottage and then at her. "Do you know how to use that?" He gestured to the broom in her hands and chuckled, making it quite clear that he doubted she did.

"Of course I do," Tanon retorted, not liking his mocking tone one bit.

"I'd be happy to help you clean up the place," Cian offered gallantly.

She softened her gaze on him. "*Non,* I can manage perfectly, thank you." She swiped the broom across the floor to prove it and sent a cloud of crumbling rushes flying in Alwyn's direction.

"Oh, dear!" She covered her mouth with her hand as he began to cough and wave his hands in front of his face.

Cian turned away and smiled as the grumbling giant left the cottage. "You're certain you need no aid?" the young poet asked again when they were alone. Tanon shook her head no, leaving Cian to stare at her for a moment before he left the cottage.

Tanon smiled at the door and then pushed the broom across the rushes again, gently this time, and with familiar ease. Foolish Alwyn to assume she'd never swept before. She stopped and looked around the cottage. Then again, she'd never cleaned as much as this place would require. Gareth was untidy as well as arrogant. Why, then, couldn't she stop smiling?

Chapter Sixteen

GARETH LEFT IOAN'S COTTAGE and walked home as night
settled over the glen. He set his eyes on his cottage and
frowned. Hell, he hadn't planned on leaving Tanon alone
all day, but he should have realized his people had much
to tell him. He'd been away from them far too long. He'd
returned to Llandovery after his imprisonment in Dafydd's
dungeon, only to leave again soon after to claim his Norman bride.

He told them about Bleddyn's death and the plot to
turn King William against him. A plot birthed by his own
countrymen. He had secured peace with the Normans, but
the northern princes were a different matter entirely. Peace
in that quarter of the land could be found, it seemed, only
through battle. The sooner he met with his uncle, the
sooner the fighting would end.

Tonight, though, his people didn't want to think of wars.
They wanted to celebrate his return. He had almost denied
their request, wanting to spend the night alone with Tanon.

But he could not refuse them. They needed a reprieve from their daily lives. They needed celebration.

He smiled and waved at the group of women carrying blankets and satchels of food toward the glen, and pushed open his front door.

Gareth had always known he'd been born to a warrior's life. His wife would be expected to live that life with him. He'd never thought anymore about it. But when he stepped into his cottage and saw the scrubbed floor, he felt a measure of pride that nearly brought him to his knees.

He walked quietly to the bed. Crouching at the edge, he simply gazed at his sleeping wife. Here she was, a seemingly delicate lady with the fortitude of a warrior. Her clips had long since fallen from her hair. Coal black curls hung limply over the delicate contour of her jaw. He smoothed them away, familiar with the heavy tightness in his chest that came whenever he looked at her. She'd endured sleeping on a thin pallet on the forest floor for over a se'nnight without so much as a sigh. She'd been attacked and watched men die not a foot away from her, and she hadn't begged him to return her to the safe arms of her father. He dumped her in a filthy house, and she cleaned it. A smudge of dirt shadowed her chin. He wiped his thumb over it. He looked at her hands, swollen and red from scrubbing. Bringing them to his lips, he kissed each finger. She should be sitting on a throne, enchanting hapless men with her dimpled smiles. Selfish or no, he didn't care. He wanted her here with him. Every time she smiled at him, she swept his heart away to a time before he'd come to understand the hardship of war. He wanted to protect her, make her laugh, make love to her.

Her eyelids fluttered open slightly.

Gareth traced the perfect line of her brow with his finger.

She gave him a sleepy smile that would have doubled him over if he wasn't already hanging over her. "I've missed you." She stretched and then grimaced in pain. Reaching behind her, she pulled a stiff sliver of straw out of her back.

"I've missed you, too." He leaned down and kissed her eyelids.

"You have?"

"Aye," he whispered close to her lips. He climbed onto the bed, above her, splaying his palms on either side of her head. "I fear I think of you too often." He kissed her smile and then her chin, grazing his teeth down her throat. "Forgive me for leaving you all day. Everyone needed me . . ."

Tanon tunneled her fingers through his hair and pulled his face back up to hers to meet his gaze. "I understand the need for you, husband." And she did. His smoldering smiles had excited her from the first night in the great hall. His kisses and his gentle, teasing touches made her desire him in the most basely primitive ways. Ways she was not even sure she understood but wanted to explore. Every nerve ending seared for him, every muscle clenched at his nearness.

She had been wary at first of his feral appearance, anxious about his touch, certain that he would ravish her as soon as their vows were spoken. In the forest, she was sure the savage would finally show himself and tear away her virtue with careless disregard. But Gareth's kisses left her wanting more of him. His control made her even more curious to discover what he might do when that control snapped. She didn't want to wait any longer.

She closed her teeth around his lower lip and sucked softly, tasting him. Her hands reveled in the awesome strength of his banded arms. When he lowered his weight on top of her, a tremor quaked her to her soul. He captured her mouth, sweeping his tongue over hers like a scalding flame. As his passion grew more urgent, Tanon tested her boldness by stroking her finger along the broad curves of his shoulders, his back, and then his hips. He pressed into her, grinding an erection as hard as forged steel against her warm, wet niche.

"Wait." She pushed her palms against him.

He groaned and lifted his head from his thorough assault on her neck, his eyes lit with desire, his mouth ready to brand her flesh again. The sight of him so eager for her nearly made her body spasm. She bit down, trying to calm herself.

"I should have a bath first," she breathed.

His slow, sexy grin seduced every one of her senses while he shook his head. "A waste of time. We're going to get very dirty."

The sensual dip in his voice made her nipples throb beneath her gown. She wanted to tear it off and offer herself up to him in any way he wanted her.

The door burst open, and Cian and Tomas plunged into the cottage, looked around, then slowly, and in unison, turned their heads toward the bed.

Tanon pushed her husband off her with surprising strength and sat up. Her flushed cheeks went pale, then flushed again before she lowered her head to escape their knowing looks. A single black curl slipped over her forehead.

In contrast to Tanon's mortification, Gareth sat up slowly. His jaw clenched, and his glare made Cian and Tomas back up. "You will never enter this house again without knocking first." He didn't shout. The warning in his steady voice was daunting enough.

"Apologies, Gareth," Tomas murmured, keeping his eyes averted from Gareth's wife.

Cian, on the other hand, couldn't take his eyes off her. Her beauty entranced him, gave birth to sonnets capable of causing great men to fall in love with her without ever seeing her. Cian's gaze angled to Gareth. Great men like him. He cleared his throat.

"The people await their lord who has brought them peace. Though without any discourtesy meant to you, Gareth, the sacrifice made is not a great one."

Tomas gave his younger brother a shove between the shoulders. Gareth's hand on Cian's chest stopped him from falling into Tanon's lap.

"Adara wanted you to have this." Tomas held out a folded swath of cloth and handed it to Tanon. "It's a gown, I think. She says the lord's wife shouldn't be dressed in wrinkles. And your nurse, Rebecca, is doing well."

Tanon accepted the offering with a grateful smile that made Cian stifle a sigh.

"All right, off with you both now." Gareth pushed them toward the door. "We'll be out shortly."

When the men were gone, Tanon unfolded the bundle and left the bed. "Oh, Gareth," she whispered, revealing a gown of feathery soft yellow wool. She held it up to her body. The cut was simple with a low-scooped neckline and short puffed sleeves. The fabric gathered at her waist, falling in thick flowing folds to her ankles. A beautiful red shawl accompanied the gown, along with a wide waistband of red leather, beaten to buttery softness.

Gareth stared at her, arrested by the look of wonder on her face, and then gathered her into his arms. "You tempt me beyond reason, but my people await us outside."

She looked up into his dusky gaze. "They await us for what?"

"Celebration. It's a custom. Come, they've prepared the food and the music. We have only to enjoy the night. Our time together will come soon enough."

Not too much longer, she hoped, but didn't speak her wanton thoughts. She could scarcely believe what a trollop she'd become for him. Why, if Cian and Tomas hadn't arrived when they did, she was certain she would have torn Gareth's tunic off and sunk her teeth into his body.

She patted her flushed cheek and stepped away from him. "I will wear Adara's gift."

"I'd better wait outside, then, while you dress," Gareth said, knowing if he stayed while she stripped, they would never make it to Celebration. He went to the front door but stopped and turned to give her a look that darkened his eyes with desire. "You asked about my control. This is the last shred of it." He closed the door behind him.

Heavens, but he certainly knew how to ignite her blood. When she had first seen him, she wondered how untamed he truly was. She was sure tonight she would find out. She hurried into her new gown, wondering how on earth she could have tried to dislike him. She couldn't wait to be in his arms again.

The gown fit loosely, and Tanon was a bit horrified

when she realized there was no shift to wear underneath. She thought about wearing her own, but it was too soiled, and none of her other gowns were unpacked yet. *Non,* this would have to do. Besides, the wool was thick enough to conceal her properly, though her nipples, still erect from Gareth's touch, pushed up against the fabric. She tied the wide belt to her slender waist, tossed her shawl over her shoulders, and freed her curls from beneath.

She was ready, and how utterly delightful it was not to have three maids pulling and tugging at her for over an hour to make her presentable. Oh, *this* she could get used to.

Smiling, she pulled on the door and stepped outside and into a twinkling paradise. Hundreds of torches lit the darkening glen like stars sprinkled across velvet. Music filled the cool night air. The mouthwatering aromas of roasting rabbit and freshly baked bread invaded her senses and made her stomach rumble. She slipped past Gareth waiting beside the door, her vision taking in the view of people gathered around dozens of small bonfires, laughing, drinking, and slowly turning to look at her.

His people weren't the only ones staring at her. Gareth couldn't take his eyes off her. His heartbeat accelerated, pounding hard in his chest. When she turned to him, her eyes wide with surprise, her lips parted on a stunned breath, he could barely form a smile, so enthralled was he just looking at her. She might have been raised a stately noble lady, but tonight she looked like she belonged here in Cymru with its wild landscapes and fiery sunsets.

"Do you know how completely breathtaking you are, Tanon?"

Her smile washed over him, making his jaw tighten. "I do as of late, husband."

He pushed himself off the wall and wove his fingers through hers. He swept his mouth over hers, tantalizing her with the brevity of his kiss. "Come, my people await you." He walked her through the glen, stopping at different groups of people for more personal introductions.

She met Cadwyn, a cheery, rotund woman who offered her a skein of indigo muslin. Llwyd, Cadwyn's husband and master blacksmith, greeted Tanon next, presenting her with a deadly-looking dagger and a softly spoken prayer that she would never have to use it. Ioan and his wife, Dierdre, gave Tanon three freshly killed rabbits along with a promise to teach her how to cook *Caws Pobi,* a traditional dish prepared with rabbit, toast, and melted cheese.

More gifts were given as Tanon and Gareth made their way around the large glen. They received food, linens dyed in various colors, beads, and cooking ware. Tanon accepted each offering with sincere gratitude and even embraced some of the women, causing their polite smiles to widen into friendlier ones as Gareth led her away. Cian was happy to keep two steps behind them, gathering what gifts he could carry in his arms. Alwyn and Hereward took those that he couldn't carry directly to Gareth's cottage.

"You win the hearts of my people with natural ease," Gareth, leaning down, whispered in Tanon's ear. He was pleased, but not surprised. She'd won the affection of his men easily enough, as was evident when they finally reached his blanket. Every trencher was decorated with a sprig of heather.

Tanon sat down, embraced Rebecca as if she hadn't seen her nurse in a pair of years, and then thanked Adara for her gown with a kiss to the cheek.

"Oh, Cian," she cooed over the youngest member of

Gareth's *Teulu* when she noticed the carefully arranged trenchers. "You are going to make a very fortunate lady quite happy someday."

Gareth shook his head at the poor condition of such a fearless warrior when Cian sighed like a love-struck squire.

"Madoc helped me gather the heather before you joined us tonight," Cian advised her.

Lifting a curious brow, Gareth looked across the glen at his best friend, astonished at what he'd just heard.

"Well, *his* wife will need a bit more resolve than yours." Tanon pulled her slippers off when she noticed that no one was wearing any footwear. "But I told you all that Madoc was sweet."

"As sweet as sour goat's milk," Tomas interjected while he poured Tanon a drink of blended ale, honey, and spices.

"It's called *Bragawd*," Gareth told her, sitting beside her. He laughed softly when she tried to repeat the word. "Don't drink too much," he added with a lecherous wink that reminded her why she shouldn't.

"Tell me"—Tanon lifted the cup to her mouth, tasted the drink, and sighed at its heavenly flavor—"is it a Welsh custom to go barefoot?"

"Most of my people could not afford leather for many years," Gareth explained. "They went barefoot because they had to. Now we choose to forgo our footwear for a better grip on the ground. Bare feet provide better balance."

Tanon propped her elbows on her bent knees while she listened to him. She loved his voice, his deep, lyrical accent.

"You are one of us now," he continued, giving her a

meaningful smile. "We do not call ourselves Welsh. We are Cymry."

"Cymry," she echoed and crinkled her nose at him when he nodded. "Teach me more of your words."

He looked up as Madoc approached. "*Noswaith dda,* Madoc."

"*Noswaith dda.*" His first in command nodded at him, then bent his head to Tanon next. "My lady."

"They bid each other good evening," Cian told her, leaning in close. "I could teach you to speak Cymraeg while Gareth visits the king."

Tanon turned to her husband and tugged on his tunic while he spoke to Madoc. "You're going away?"

"Aye, I must meet with my uncle in Llandeilo."

"When?"

"In a few days." He dipped his head to hers. "You will be well cared for while I'm gone," he promised quietly. "Ioan will watch over you, as will Hereward. You will be safe."

"I know." She looked away when understanding settled over his features.

He leaned closer, dragging his lips across her temple while he spoke. "Will you miss me, then?"

"*Oui,*" she relinquished.

Christ, he loved how she spoke that powerful word so delicately.

He withdrew to look into her eyes. "I will make haste with my uncle."

She smiled, feeling a cascade of warmth flow through her.

"Allow me a toast," Madoc requested, pulling their attention to him. He held his cup aloft when Gareth nodded.

"Hear me!" Madoc's strong voice carried over the gathering, and soon everyone turned to listen. "Tonight we give thanks for many things. Our prince has returned to us!" A round of cheers arose, but Madoc held up his palm after a moment to quiet them. "With him comes the promise of the Norman king. Her name is peace . . . beauty, bravery." His eyes fell on Tanon briefly before he raised his gaze back to the crowd. "May peace find her way among us and be cherished by us all. For Cymru!"

"For Cymru!" the people cheered.

"That was beautiful." Alwyn sniffed and wiped an imaginary tear from his eye.

Madoc's smile was every bit as menacing as the glint in his eye when he turned his cup upside down, pouring the remainder of his drink on Alwyn's head. He ignored the flurry of blasphemies spilling from Alwyn's lips while he sat down beside Gareth. "Sincerest apologies for getting you wet."

"Aye, now there's something no woman has ever heard you say, eh, you bastard?" Alwyn retorted, wiping his hand down his face.

"You speak true," Madoc told him with a trace of humor lifting the corners of his mouth. "I didn't apologize to your sister."

The string of threats Alwyn shot at him next were thankfully drowned out by the glorious sound of harp, lute, and tabor drums.

Everyone ate together, filling their bellies with bowls of steaming *Cawl* and savory lamb pie. Alwyn's mood lightened considerably after three helpings. When a small group of the villagers began to dance in the center of the glen, he joined them.

Adara eyed Hereward from across the fire while he chewed his supper. "Is it true that you're a Saxon warrior?" she asked him when his gaze met hers.

He nodded and went back to his food.

"My father once knew a man who claimed to have seen Saxons," Adara continued. "This man told us that they danced almost as well as the Cymry."

Beside her, Tomas snorted.

Hereward cut him a warning glance. "What's so humorous about that?"

"Naught, save that the Saxons are too dull witted to . . ." Tomas's voice faded when Hereward scowled at him. "No offense intended," he amended nervously.

"Offense taken," Hereward replied and laid his trencher down in front of him.

"Our people are as old as yours," Rebecca offered gently. "And dancing is as ancient as time."

Ringed within the glimmering vermeil of his mustache and beard, Hereward's mouth curled into a grin at the pride for her heritage lacing her voice.

"I didn't know you, too, were Saxon." Adara clutched Rebecca's hand. "Do show us how you dance. I've never seen any other movements but our own."

"Oh, I couldn't." Rebecca blushed and shook her head. "I haven't danced in over a score of years."

"Hereward looks that rusty," Madoc threw at the Saxon, a mischievous gleam flitting across his dark eyes. "Dancing with him will be easy for you, Rebecca."

The nurse glanced at Hereward. Their eyes met briefly before he looked away, expecting her refusal.

Hereward the Wake was a frightening man, with a reputation as gruesome as King William's, but he'd always been kind to her. He wasn't talkative, saying barely a handful of words to her when she rode with him on the carriage. She hadn't minded, though. She had no idea what to talk to him about, anyway. Lately, though, she found herself noticing the strong angles of his brawny physique, the way the sunlight set his hair ablaze with streaks of cinnamon, scarlet, gold, and bronze. His features were hard and forbidding, nothing at all like Brand's beguiling beauty. But Hereward possessed an intense male magnetism that grew more captivating each time she looked at him.

She had been nothing short of rude to him over the years when the Risandes visited the king. How could she have possibly shown him any interest when her heart ached for another?

"Very well," she said, watching the firelight play over his arching brow. She came to her feet and dusted off her skirts. "Hereward?" She motioned for him to follow her when he looked up, astounded by her invitation.

"Go on, Hereward. Dance with her," Gareth urged with a wink.

"All right, then." The burly warrior stood up, offered Rebecca a handsome smile, and then walked her toward the center of the glen.

Tanon saw her first dancing circle that night. It was one of twelve scattered over the enormous glen. Ringed by torches jammed into the earth, the inner perimeter was illuminated beneath the vast heavens. The music didn't stop as Hereward and Rebecca stepped forward to join the other dancers.

Hereward looked as regal as any king, his spine arrow straight, one arm folded neatly behind his back while the other extended to clasp Rebecca by the hand. Compared to the movements of the others around them, the Saxons' dance was slow, but no less enchanting. Tanon watched them with a happy heart, for Rebecca's smile was more profound than any she had ever offered to Brand Risande.

"No dancing tonight, my lord?"

Tanon turned to the woman hovering beside Gareth. She remembered meeting her earlier. Her name was Isolde, daughter of Padrig the carpenter. Her russet braid dangled to her buttocks, and her eyes deepened to a darker shade of blue when she smiled at Gareth.

"Mayhap later, Isolde."

"But it's Celebration," Isolde insisted with a pout that lasted only for an instant. "And I've been practicing. I'm sure I could best you," she challenged. "I bested Ioan."

Cian snorted a laugh. "Ioan isn't Gareth."

"Mayhap," Isolde countered with a pitying sigh, "Prince Gareth left Wyfyrn in Dafydd's dungeon."

Her eyes flashed with victory when Gareth swept his arm in front of him. "After you."

"Prince Gareth dances!" Cian shouted, clearing a path for Gareth to take. Around her, Tanon heard some of the men offering sheep and geese to anyone willing to bet against the stealth of Wyfyrn, and win.

The air was charged with excitement as Gareth and Isolde approached the other dancers with Cian racing on ahead, crying for all to make way.

"You're scowling," Madoc pointed out to Tanon, whose eyes were fastened on Isolde.

"She's very beautiful." Tanon drew her lower lip between her teeth, creasing the dimple in her cheek.

"So?" Madoc asked, bringing the cup he carried with him to his lips.

"So?" She turned a quelling look on the baleful warrior. "So, my husband is about to dance with her. I've heard many tales of how your people dance, Madoc."

His gaze on her softened at the worrisome frown marring her lovely features. "Your husband is going to dance, but not with her. For that, she must best him. And trust me, my lovely princess, that is quite impossible."

Tanon offered him a befuddled look, but instead of giving an explanation, he moved closer to the gathering crowd, turned, and crooked his fingers at her.

The dancers, including Hereward and Rebecca, made room when Gareth and Isolde entered the ring. The night grew silent as musicians paused, awaiting Gareth's order.

Facing Isolde, Gareth tossed his head back, clearing his golden hair away from his face. "Something spirited," he commanded the players. Isolde nodded and folded her hands behind her back.

Drums pounded and boomed in Tanon's ears as fiercely as her heart. Lute and viol picked up the tempo, and Isolde kicked up her feet.

"She thinks she can touch him with her feet alone," someone shouted directly behind Tanon. Others around her laughed. Madoc leaned closer to her so that she could hear him over the music.

"Isolde's feet are quick, and she is well balanced. She *has* been practicing." When Tanon glared at him, he laughed softly. "No one is as fast as he. But if she comes so close to striking Wyfyrn, imagine what damage she could inflict against a slower man who intends her harm. Watch, lady," he whispered. "Imagine a spear or ax in her hands. She would have killed, or at least wounded, her attacker by now. Everyone here has been taught to defend themselves through dancing, ensuring that this village will never fall to any enemy again."

Understanding a little better now but still not liking it one bit, Tanon looked on, twirling a stray curl around her finger.

Isolde advanced on him, her feet keeping perfect rhythm with the music as she kicked and spun, then kicked up her skirts again. The two appeared to be engaged in a feigned battle. The sinuous elegance of their dance blended perfectly with their complex maneuvers of striking and skirting. Gareth's movements were purely defensive, avoiding Isolde's touch with amazing ease. He coaxed her to kick faster, higher. He stretched his carved arms outward, daring her to make contact, his feet so light and quick that Tanon blinked to make certain he was touching the grass. Isolde clutched fistfuls of her skirts and lifted the hem to her knees. Gareth laughed and shook his head at her when her steps grew more complex, one leg crossing over the other in a blur that would surely have landed Tanon flat on her face.

Gareth arched his back with nimble grace when Isolde's hand shot out before him, bending his legs to avoid a swipe to his head.

Mesmerized by their movements, Tanon began to recognize each fluid motion as the same Gareth had used at the tourney when he'd beaten eight of Roger's men without losing one point. As swift as a fox, he eluded every blow, all the while moving to the lively pitch of the music. Entranced, Tanon smiled when he sprang backward, escaping a kick to his groin. He cast Isolde a teasing glare and then swept past her before her offending foot touched the ground. Like molten gold, his hair shuddered across his shoulders, falling around his face, full and wild, while his feet traipsed the verdant carpet beneath him.

"Her defeat comes swiftly," Tomas called out, and the crowd shouted with agreement.

"Let his wife have a go!"

Tanon paled and turned to see who had shouted *that* ridiculous suggestion. Someone else cheered, and then the entire village joined in. Tanon shook her head and backed into Madoc's side.

"I cannot dance like that." She looked sick to her stomach.

"You won't be dancing unless you touch him," Madoc reminded her, and gave her a gentle shove forward.

Tanon stood at the edge of the circle and watched the sinfully seductive man who turned her insides to mud. Gareth's breath came in short bursts, his hair tousled and his smile challenging. He came toward her, pulsing with unleashed energy and a blazing fire from his eyes that made her insides tingle. She stood on a battlefield with the warrior who had first awakened her, close enough to touch his heaving chest, to smell his feral scent. She swallowed, thinking she could not bear being this close to him when he looked so untamed, so dangerously exciting.

He held his hand out to her, but when she reached for it, he snapped it back and flashed her a mischievous grin. Her feet felt rooted to the ground. Then he began to move, and the stars came undone. At first, Tanon could do nothing more than stare breathlessly at him before he danced behind her and bent to her ear.

"One touch and I am yours."

She quivered as his hot breath parted her curls and fell against her nape. He appeared in front of her again, so close she could feel the alluring heat of his body. But she didn't try to touch him. His smile widened into a sensual grin, his gaze seething with fierce emotion.

Tanon remembered that Gareth fought defensively. He was impossible to strike, and trying to do so was his opponents' error. She had to make him come to her. She knew how to win, but she dreaded doing it. Still, she was not about to chase him around a circle or stand here as still as a tree and have his people laugh at her anyway.

She backed away from him and carefully shielded her satisfaction when he moved forward with her. Now, how difficult could it be to spin on one's heel? Tanon twirled, albeit not nearly as fast as Isolde's practiced spins, and smiled at her victory. He was close, advancing cautiously now, his eyes sharp on her limbs, her eyes.

Taking more steps backward, Tanon laughed, goading him to follow. Suddenly her left foot crossed over her right and she fell backward on her rump. Gareth rushed to her, trying to keep his grin from spreading over his face as he reached for her. No one laughed outright, and Tanon was grateful for that while she closed her arms around his neck and flashed her dimple at him. "I win."

Leaning over her, Gareth lifted his brows and then laughed. "What a devious woman I married." He swept her to her feet, his laughter fading into a smile so heated, Tanon almost kissed him right there in front of his villagers.

"Wyfyrn has been slain," someone called out. When Tanon turned toward the crowd, Madoc lifted his cup to Gareth first, and then to her. She smiled at him, and he smiled back, not looking anywhere near as dangerous as he had a se'nnight ago.

"Dance with her now," Adara called out.

"Non." Tanon tilted her face to Gareth's. "Take me home."

Gareth almost lifted her in his arms to get her to his cottage faster, but he knew her courtly manners would lead her to protest. So he curled his fingers around hers and pulled her toward the crowd, shoving Alwyn out of his path.

The moment they were away from the villagers, Gareth hauled her into his arms, lifting her off her feet.

"My, but you're eager." She giggled nervously.

"Hell, you've no idea."

He reached the door and pushed it open with his foot, then slammed it shut the same way. He began to kiss her even before he set her feet on the floor. She clung to him, her heart battering against her chest with excitement and a spark of fear. Her nerve endings sizzled. She felt alive and on fire. The urgency in his kiss, and in his hands as they worked to untie the thick belt at her waist, seized the breath from her lungs. His tongue plunged deep, laving her mouth with long, masterful strokes. Her belt dropped to her feet. His broad hands splayed across her waist and then quickened her breath as they cupped and caressed her breasts. Her nipples grew hard under his hot palms. He squeezed them gently between his thumb and index fingers. Grasping her bottom lip between his teeth, he surged the full length of his stiff erection against her.

The size of him sent a spasm to Tanon's core. Needing satisfaction only her instincts understood, her legs opened wider. Shamelessly, she rubbed her hips against his and scored her fingers through his hair. She had wanted to touch him this way since the day she watched him fight at the tourney. She had ached to feel his strong heartbeat beneath his bare skin. Needing to run her fingers over his lean muscles, she cast the last shred of propriety she possessed to the wind and tugged at the leather laces of his shirt. She tore his shirt away, groaning inside his mouth. She didn't realize he'd lifted her skirts until she felt his rough hands on her skin caressing her buttocks and gliding her up and down against him.

Wanting to look at her while he stripped her, Gareth broke their fevered kiss and pulled her gown over her head.

She stood before him naked, cloaked only by her hair.

The raw, torrid need in his eyes was so arousing when he raked his gaze over her body, her nipples hardened instantly.

His lips parted seconds before they sank to take her nipple into his mouth. He swirled his tongue over the sensitive bud and then sucked deeper. Tanon rolled her head back, burrowing her fingers through his hair, dragging him closer.

She felt bold. Feverish. Each salacious stroke of his tongue threatened to ignite her into flames. With an instinct born of primal desire, she slipped her hand between their bodies and traced her fingers over his arousal, sensually caressed in leather.

Gareth's control finally shattered. Grasping her hands, he shoved her back against the wall. His eyes impaled her. Something wicked flared within their indigo depths. "If it's gentle you really want, Tanon"—he breathed against her face—"I'll treat you like a sprig of heather."

"*Non,*" she panted, aroused beyond endurance.

His slow, lusty smile convinced her that she had made the right choice.

He wanted to take her untried body slowly. But her wanton kisses shredded his control until nothing remained.

He bent his mouth to her throat and spread his tongue over her pulse, whetting his appetite with a taste that fevered his blood.

Tanon groaned beneath his ravenous mouth, but his assault continued as he moved down her body. He flicked his tongue over the peak of her coral nipple, making her body quake in his arms, then bent his knees before her and kissed her soft belly. The rough stubble of his jaw pricked her flesh. His hot breath set fire to it.

He spread her legs with a scandalous lick that made Tanon gasp and her muscles jolt. She tried to pull away, but his broad hands splayed across her thighs, holding her immobile while he tasted her in the most intimate way. He paused to suckle the bud at her tender crest. The masterful savagery of his mouth, his teeth, his tongue, drove her pelvis upward, offering herself to him more fully. When she lifted her foot to his shoulder, he rose up, curling his fingers under her thigh. He used his other hand to free himself of his trousers.

"This is going to hurt . . . a little." A titillating smile caressed his lips. He brought his index and middle finger to his mouth and moistened them with a tantalizing brush of his tongue.

Dipping his hand between their bodies, he caressed her engorged apex, stroking and petting her until she began to shudder in his hand. He covered her mouth with his, kissing her harsh gasps from her lips as he thrust into her, tearing away the last remaining barrier of her innocence.

"*Non!*" Tanon cried out as her pleasure ebbed and a bolt of white-hot pain shot through her.

"Aye." His voice was a guttural tangle of desire and ecstasy. "I'm taking you. Feel it."

So close to the zenith of her release, it took only a few more tender strokes of his fingers to make her climax. A shuddering spasm closed her muscles tighter around his rigid flesh. She cried out, and with one last powerful surge that lifted her feet off the floor, they found their release together.

Spent, Gareth pulled Tanon into his arms and carried her to the stream. He washed the evidence of her lost virginity away with tender fingers, kissing her face while he promised he would not take her again this night.

"You are a brutal beast." She snuggled against his chest as he carried her back inside.

"And you are a wanton wench," he told her.

Tanon could hear the playful smile in his words. "I am, aren't I?" She felt drunk with wine, heady with happiness as he laid her in his bed and climbed in beside her, collapsing with a lusty sigh.

When Tanon rested her head beneath the crook of his shoulder, his arm came around her and pulled her closer.

"Gareth?"

"Aye?"

"I'm happy we married." She closed her eyes, waiting for his reply, hoping, praying that he would give her one.

"So am I, Tanon."

A radiant grin spread over her face, and she snuggled deeper against him, finally ready to relinquish her heart to a man who would cherish it. Her champion.

Chapter Seventeen

CEDRIC WATCHED THE CELEBRATION from a densely wooded hilltop, alone and obscured from the view of the guards keeping watch from the tall footbridge. His eyes drifted back to the cottage barely illuminated by the bonfires, his thoughts preoccupied with the woman who'd disappeared inside with his brother. The Norman. The girl who was to be his. The peace he had rejected.

He decided, while he had watched her earlier, her long raven ringlets swinging carelessly about her face, that he would not take her life right away. Nay, though she was his sworn enemy, she was far too lovely for him to deny himself the pleasures of her body first. He would take his time with her, avenging the blood of his people with her flesh. But not too much time. He wanted his war. Taking over Deheubarth and withdrawing the peace treaty would bring the Normans to Cymru, but killing her would bring them here faster.

Someone moved along the line of trees to his right.

Cedric gazed toward the sound. "I had no idea my brother's wife was so lovely."

The figure stepped beside him and followed his gaze when it returned to the villagers. "She is a Norman bitch, nothing more."

Cedric aimed his chilling smile on his clandestine companion. "You are not tempted by such beauty, then, Madoc?"

"Every man is tempted by beauty, Cedric. Not all succumb to it," Madoc replied tightly and swung his gaze to the rogue prince. "Why didn't you tell me that Bleddyn was one of us?"

"Because I needed someone to make certain you weren't betraying me."

Bleddyn had been watching him. Madoc's mouth hooked into a grim smile as another truth became evident. "It was Bleddyn who betrayed Gareth to Dafydd."

"Aye," Cedric boasted. "He is a most loyal vassal."

"Was," Madoc corrected him succinctly.

"Ah." Cedric extracted a heavy sigh. "I assumed he didn't make it to Winchester when I saw Gareth still alive."

Madoc shook his head. "Not even close."

"Pity. I'd hoped to turn the Norman king against my brother. But it will not matter in the end." His gaze hardened on Gareth's cottage. "He weds our enemy and takes her to his bed, betraying our people and their families. He does not care how many Cymry have died at the hands of the Normans. He is a traitor to our land, as my uncle is. I'm going to rid Cymru of them, and then of the Normans, beginning with her."

Madoc's unblinking eyes fixed on the people below.

The flickering flames of the glen reflected in his cool sable eyes, hinting at the anger burning beneath.

"Where is Prince Dafydd?" he asked benignly.

"He is close." Cedric returned his attention to the Celebration.

"He'd best not deceive us, Cedric," Madoc warned.

"Dafydd is as eager to war with the Normans as I am," Cedric reassured him. "The northern princes are no longer our enemy. Not until I am king of Cymru, at least." He gave Madoc a wink that looked much like Gareth's. "His army will be waiting for us outside my uncle's fortress in Llandeilo. They will be ready if we need them."

"Are you certain that Dafydd and his men are well armed?" Madoc asked. "King Rhys has an army of over five hundred men in his garrison. Remember, we cannot use arrows or the people will suspect foul play. You must have the favor of the people in order to—"

"Dafydd's men are fine warriors," Cedric cut him off, glancing at him. "But it will not come to fighting. There will be no war in Llandeilo if what you told me is correct."

"It is," Madoc vowed. "You know your uncle's affinity for music. Gareth shares that fondness. As long as you and your men are well disguised as troubadours, you will be granted a private audience."

"We must time it right," Cedric added. "I want Gareth with the king when we meet. We will strike swiftly, killing them both, and then we will kill Rhys's young bratlings. No one knows that I have returned. You are certain Gareth doesn't suspect you?"

Madoc's only reply was a thin smile.

"You will bear witness that Gareth murdered his uncle and his nephew and niece." Cedric repeated their plan with chilling satisfaction. "I will return from exile to take my place as the only surviving heir to the throne. Once I am king, all peace agreements with England will be canceled, and when the Normans hear that I have taken Risande's daughter it will seal their rage and they will declare war. With Prince Dafydd at my side, the north and the south will unite. We will defeat the conqueror's men and kill every marcher lord from here to Chester."

Madoc nodded but said nothing.

"Tell me," Cedric asked, eyeing the crowd again. "What is Hereward the Wake doing here?"

"We were not told, though my belief is that he was asked by the Norman king to keep watch over Risande's daughter."

"I see." Cedric watched the hefty red-haired warrior leaning into a woman with pale yellow tresses. "Another traitor to his people."

"I must go. I will be missed," Madoc said evenly, taking a step away toward the glen.

"Wait." Cedric stopped him with a hand to his shoulder, though he knew Madoc didn't like to be touched. "Swear to me now that you will never betray me as you betray him."

Madoc moved away from Cedric's fingers. "If you kill him, I will swear fealty to you at the throne of Llandeilo."

Cedric smiled in the darkness. "I'll be in contact with you before we leave for Llandeilo."

~

Gareth drifted somewhere between the realms of sleep and wakefulness. He heard Tanon's voice in his thoughts and began to stir.

"Really, William. I've made such a mess of everything. When you think about it, though, it is all Gareth's fault."

He was dreaming. Why else would she be speaking to the Norman king? Surely he would have been informed if King William had arrived in Cymru.

"I don't know what to do." Her soft voice was so riddled with anxiety, it yanked Gareth awake with the need to go to her.

"I fear Gareth is going to kill me for this."

Kill her? Christ, how could she think so poorly of him? He sat up and waited a moment to let the murky effects of sleep wear off completely before he left his bed. If King William was here, he wanted to be fully awake. But first, his wife needed to know that he would never harm her.

"Tanon, whatever you've done, I . . ."

Dressed in the gown Tomas's wife had given her, at least Gareth assumed it was the same gown, Tanon sat in his lone chair with—he blinked, feeling like he'd been transported back in time—a little black pig in her lap. Thick soot covered every inch of them both. A thin layer blanketed the walls of the cottage as well.

"What the hell happened in here? And who the devil are you talking to?"

At the sound of his voice, Tanon cringed and turned to face him, her eyes wide with apprehension. The sight of them, vividly green against her soot-covered face, was so comical, Gareth had to bite down on his tongue to keep himself from smiling.

"I was just trying to clean the hearth. How was I to know you haven't swept the chimney since you built it?"

Gareth looked around the cottage. They were alone.

His eyes settled on the pig. "Where the hell did that come from?"

"I found him in the glen this morn. He followed me back here."

Gareth aimed his incredulous stare at her. "And you named him William?"

"*Oui.*" She coughed. "I almost choked to death on all the soot!" She sniffed and then flung her head back and sneezed, losing the pig from her arms. The hog scrambled toward Gareth and plopped itself at his feet.

"I wanted you to be able to light the hearth fire. It would have been cozy, and now everything is a mess." A single tear slid down her blackened cheek, creating a pink path to her jaw. "I was so afraid to wake you. I knew you would be angry."

"Aye, mayhap even kill you."

"*Oui.*" She nodded, and more tears striped her face. Gareth knew she was about to erupt. He wanted to tell her that there was no reason to weep. He didn't care about the mess. But hell, did she still think he was such a monster that he'd put his hands to her over it?

"Come." He went to her and lifted her in his arms. "Let's get you some fresh air before you pass out."

Tanon was so relieved that he didn't hate her for destroying his home, she buried her face in his neck and kissed him there, leaving a sooty print.

"Thank you for not bellowing," she murmured while he opened the back door and carried her outside. "You know, when you put your mind to it, you can be such a tender, kind spirited—"

He let her go.

Tanon's arms flailed wildly for one dreadful moment

before she hit the cool water. She sank, and Gareth was tempted to jump in after her. He turned around instead and strode back into the house.

"How could you, Gareth?" He heard her shouting furiously while he searched for a clean drying cloth.

"Gareth!" she screeched, sounding like the pig squealing at his heels.

He returned to her with the cloth in one hand and the soap in the other. "Quit your bellowing, woman." He tossed her the soap. "You're fortunate I didn't hang you by your feet from the rafters. It's a slow death we savages enjoy inflicting on others now and then."

She glared up at him, long black strands of dripping hair falling over her eyes. "I could have drowned, you uncaring lout."

He stood there in the grass, six feet of naked male insolence, and grinned at her. "It's two feet deep where you're standing. But you're making me rethink the rafter option."

Tanon opened her mouth into a wide O and swept both hands across the surface of the water. She managed to soak Gareth quite well on her first attempt.

He gaped at her, sincerely stunned that she had the audacity to douse him. She did it again. He didn't even shiver at the icy water, but he glared at her impish smile.

"I'm warning you, Tanon. Don't do that—"

She did it a third time, giggled, and then spun around to swim away when he took off after her. She should have known her husband would be as quick in the water as he was out of it. When she felt his hands span her waist, she squealed with laughter.

Pulling her against him, he gazed into her eyes and felt his heart melt all over his ribs. Her eyes glimmered with happiness that seeped into his bones like sweet summer sunshine. Her wet hair clung to her face, and he smoothed it away, inhaling a shuddering breath when she closed her eyes at his touch. He'd kissed other women, but each time he kissed Tanon, hell, every time he looked at her, she claimed more of his heart.

He cleaned her as thoroughly as he kissed her, plucking the soap from the water and gently scrubbing her cheeks and forehead with his soapy fingers. His lips sent molten fissures down her spine when he kissed each of her fingers, after cleaning them as well. When he slipped her gown over her head and rubbed his rough, sudsy palms over her breasts, her belly, Tanon sucked in a gasp of the torrid air that enveloped them. His hand slipped around her back to caress her buttocks. With little strength, he held her firmly against his hard, hot passion. He bent his lips to hers, but instead of kissing her, he grazed his mouth over her chin, the alluring softness of her jaw, telling her what he wanted to do to her.

"In the water?" Tanon whispered, surprise and excitement lighting her languid gaze.

He answered her with an erotic slant of his mouth and a seductive grunt that lifted her onto him. He moved slowly, knowing she was sore.

Tanon gripped his shoulders and rested her forehead against his as pain ebbed and she became weightless in his arms. She coiled her legs loosely around his waist, and his smile nearly took her to the edge of reason. He angled his hips lazily, taking pleasure and giving it with long, unhurried thrusts. His body was warm, his muscles sleek with water. He clenched a fistful of her hair and tipped her head back until her lips were but a breath from his.

"You're perfect," he whispered before he molded his mouth to hers in a kiss that was as languorously sensual as his undulating hips. But soon his long, deep plunges quickened. His kiss became more demanding, until he pulled her head back and grazed his mouth, his teeth, over her throat. Clamping his hand to her hips, he pushed her body upward, then drove her back down his full swollen length. He straightened when she cried out, his gaze on her laden with emotion while they found their release.

Later, Gareth found a thin shift for her to wear, while he donned a fresh pair of dark kidskin pants. They returned to the edge of the stream and lay facing each other beneath the shade of an old oak.

"When I was little, I dreamed about you returning."

Gareth pulled her closer into his arms and kissed her forehead. "I thought my life had taken a different path from yours."

She looked deep into his eyes, wanting to know him again. "What has your path been like?"

"Same as yours, dutiful."

Tanon thought about it, moving from his embrace to stare up at the clouds. Leaning up on his elbow, Gareth traced the quirk of her brow. "What are you thinking about?" he asked her.

"My parents." It wasn't really a lie. She did miss them terribly, but she was thinking of their happiness. She wanted her marriage to Gareth to work. How was it possible that he had shed her of her defenses so easily? She knew how. He made her feel alive again. Even when he angered her, it felt exhilarating not having to hide behind a forced smile. He excited her. He made her laugh. God's blood, she had forgotten who she was, and he helped her remember. Once, long ago, she wasn't afraid to love him. She realized, looking into his gaze, that she wasn't afraid anymore. He made her feel safe. He always had.

Neither of them heard Madoc's approach until his voice broke the comforting silence. "What the hell happened to the cottage?" he asked, carefully averting his eyes from the sweet contours of Tanon's form.

Gareth turned toward his friend and sat up. "Tanon was cleaning."

Tanon would have defended herself, but she was too busy scrambling for the drying cloth to cover herself. She sat up and tossed her husband a scathing look.

"I knocked." Madoc averted his gaze from Tanon's calf when the covering she pulled over her lap dragged her shift up. "It's getting late in the day, and you said you wanted to work in the fields today."

"Aye." Gareth nodded. "I'll be out shortly. Have Cadwyn and Dierdre come by to help clean the cottage, and then—"

"But I made the mess, Gareth," Tanon reminded him. "I will clean it." She offered Madoc a polite smile. "Disregard what Gareth said. I will do it myself."

"Disregard what Gareth said?" Gareth repeated, raising an incredulous eyebrow at her. "Did I just hear you right?"

"Oui," she said pointedly.

His jaw flexed. "Everyone here—"

"I won't have these women thinking that I refuse to lift a finger—"

"Tanon, stop talking."

Her green eyes flared with indignation. "I most certainly will not stop talking."

Gareth's eyes glinted dangerously at her. "Madoc, you may go," he commanded without taking his eyes off his wife.

"Madoc, *do not* bring Cadwyn and Dierdre to this cottage," Tanon warned him through clenched teeth. Oh, she had had enough of Gareth's arrogance. Who did he think he was, telling her to stop talking? How could she have even considered caring for him? Why, he was looking at her like he wanted to throttle her senseless.

"Madoc," Gareth growled.

"I'm going." His first in command slipped back into the house without another word.

When they were alone, Gareth leaped to his feet and stared down at his wife as if he'd never met her before.

The hellion had been set free.

"Does your father allow you to argue with him this way?"

"Of course not," she replied curtly. "But then, he is not a brute."

Gareth glanced at the tree behind her and thought about smashing his head against it. It would be more satisfying than trying to reason with such a stubborn little . . .

"Tanon, hear me. You will not argue so openly with me."

"I wasn't arguing with you. I was merely telling you . . ." She frowned at him when he closed his eyes and raked both hands through his damp hair.

"You're arguing with me right now," he insisted in a deceptively calm voice.

"I certainly am not." She pounded her fist on the ground and then scooted away from him when he bent over her. "Mayhap, if you weren't so prone to telling me what to do. I would—"

"Silence!" he roared, then ground his teeth, trying to control his temper. "You will be silent while I speak."

She opened her mouth, but Gareth's icy gaze made her think twice about saying anything. Her lips grew tight instead.

"I'm lord here. My people . . . my men accept what I tell them. And so will you."

Her nostrils flared, and she stared at him in mute fury while she rose to her feet.

"I am not one of your men."

"Nay," he agreed. "If you were, you'd be in the circle with me right now getting your arse whipped."

Tanon's fingers curled into her palms. "Oh! You crass, uncaring son of a—"

"Tanon!" His eyes widened with stark disbelief, but when he spoke her name his voice dripped with warning that she should stop now before she regretted it.

That fired up her nerve endings.

"Can William swim?" she demanded.

Gareth's face contorted into a scowl of pure confusion. "What?"

"Can that pig swim, Your Royal Pompousness?" She shot out her arm and pointed to the sooty swine watching them from the door.

"How the hell should I know?"

"You should discover if he can," she shouted at him. "Because when I see him swimming the length of this stream, *I will obey you!*"

She whirled on her heel and stomped away toward the cottage. Gareth thought about going after her but then decided he was daft for even considering it. He stormed away toward the front of the house instead, glaring at the pig as he went.

Chapter Eighteen

GARETH SWIPED HIS FOREARM across his sweaty brow and lifted his face to the afternoon sun. He'd been working his field for the past two hours, plowing and sowing grain and various seed. Cian, Alwyn, Madoc, and Hereward planted vegetables with hoe and spade. He barely saw his wife at all in that time, save for when she opened the door to greet Cadwyn and Dierdre, and then sent them away.

Brooding, Gareth pushed his body against the plow and continued working. He glanced at the cottage from time to time, hating that Tanon was inside cleaning again. At least Rebecca was with her. Still, he didn't understand why his wife refused help from his people. Everyone here worked together. Tanon would be expected to help the other women with a task should they ask her. Their unity made them an invincible army—not of brute strength or military force, but of courage. His people worked hard together and trained even harder. Every accomplishment they achieved rewarded them with greater strength of will, a tenacious sense of pride, and a firm resolve to protect not only themselves, but their neighbors as well. And it was Gareth who taught them. He led them. He'd gained their respect by fighting for them and always returning when the battle was over. They trusted him to see to their needs, to treat them fairly, and to teach them how to survive with or without him. Tanon hadn't given him a chance to explain any of this to her. She had angered him. Hell, she riled him more than any other living being. She needed to learn to trust him. If their village was ever attacked again, she would have to obey him in order to stay alive.

The thought of losing her terrified him. God's blood, he would annihilate the entire north region if harm came to her.

Pushing those thoughts from his mind, he sent Cian to the cottage to find some food that wasn't spoiled by chimney soot. A short while later, Tanon returned carrying two trenchers. The gushing, golden-haired dolt at her side balanced another three trenchers in his arms.

"Your fair wife was gracious enough to prepare us a fine meal," Cian announced while Madoc, Hereward, and Alwyn accepted their trenchers from him.

"The bread was wrapped, and the fruit was easy enough to clean and slice," Tanon said stiffly. She handed Gareth his trencher without a word and then passed the last to Cian with a warm smile before returning to the cottage.

Gareth watched her with a mixture of stubborn pride tightening his jaw and powerful feeling softening his gaze.

Hereward elbowed Madoc to have a look at his lord.

"They quarreled," Madoc explained and began eating.

"Ah, that explains why the mighty Wyfyrn looks about to drop to his knees," Hereward chuckled. "Felled by the anger of a woman." He shook his head. "Bloody shame."

Gareth slid his gaze to Hereward, a wry smile creeping over his lips. "Look behind you, Saxon. Your own defeat quickly approaches."

Hereward looked over his shoulder at the glorious flaxen-haired Rebecca leaving the cottage and making her way toward them. His ruddy cheeks burned to match his hair. He straightened his shoulders and turned away from her when he heard Madoc and Cian snicker.

"Remember"—Alwyn shoved a slice of pear into his mouth and nodded toward Gareth—"your wife's a Norman. You haven't forgotten, have you?"

"She's Cymry now," Gareth corrected him flatly.

"She's always been Cymry," Hereward pointed out to them all. "The Celts were driven out of Briton by the Saxons. Most of them migrated here, to Wales. Tanon's grandmother was a Celt, from what I understand. The blood of your people flows in Tanon's veins, along with Norman and Saxon."

"Whatever she is"—Madoc looked up at Hereward from his trencher—"she's fearless beneath her delicacy."

"Aye," the Saxon agreed, along with Tomas and Cian. "A good combination, that. I remember a day when she was yet a child. I had traveled with the king to Avarloch to visit the Risandes after the birth of their son Oliver. Dante Risande and his wife were there as well. Tanon wanted to ride her uncle's mare. A magnificent white Arabian beast as untamed as the sea. Her father wouldn't permit it. It was the only time she had ever disobeyed him. She stole into the stable and mounted the horse. Of course, she was thrown. For no one, I am told, was able to ride that horse but the Earl of Graycliff. Tanon suffered a broken arm and vowed to her father that she would never go near the mare again. She kept her word, and it was difficult, believe me. For every time she laid eyes on that glorious beast, those wide green eyes of hers lit up brighter than the sun." Hereward looked at Gareth. A faint, knowing smile curled his lips as Gareth fastened his eyes on the cottage. "She's not as fragile as you think, Gareth. She just hasn't had a chance to prove it yet."

"Hereward the Wake." Rebecca's voice pricked his ears. He pivoted slowly and was surprised to find her gaze as soft as if she were looking at another man with aqua-colored eyes. "That was a very thoughtful thing to say about Tanon. You surprise me."

His gaze swept over her face, potent and intent, and for a moment, Rebecca imagined how fearsome he must have appeared to his Norman enemies when he fought them.

"Allow me, lady, and I promise I will astonish you."

She raised a curious brow at him. A faint blush stole across her cheeks, making her appear younger as years of stern resignation and loneliness slipped from her face. "Very well. I will allow it."

Hereward slammed his trencher into Alwyn's chest and crooked his arm at the beautiful maiden before him. When she slipped her hand inside, a warm grin spread across his handsome features before he led her away.

"Oh, I almost forgot," Rebecca said, turning back to Gareth. "Tanon asks that Cian bring her three sacks of feathers."

"Feathers?" Gareth stopped Cian from rushing off to do Tanon's bidding. "What does she need feathers for?"

Rebecca smiled secretively, then turned away. "She asked me not to say."

"Another one lost to a Norman," Alwyn muttered, watching Hereward and Rebecca leave.

"She's a Saxon, like him," Madoc drawled and cast Gareth a look that said Alwyn had to be the dullest dimwit in Cymru.

Gareth barely acknowledged him. Hereward was wrong about one thing. Tanon had proven her courage over and over again. First by facing a life with Roger deCourtenay, and then with him. Gareth knew what his wife had endured over the last few weeks. He had known how difficult all this would be for her since before they left Winchester. But she didn't falter. She didn't fall apart and weep. She was trying to adapt.

"Hell, I'll see you bastards later." He threw down his trencher and headed home.

~

Tanon smiled watching Hereward and Rebecca leave the field together. She prayed the powerful Saxon could persuade her nurse to forget her father and give herself a chance at finding real love.

Tanon cut her gaze to Gareth. She was still angry with him, but that didn't stop her from sighing like one under a spell. She'd been enchanted by a handsome prince. There was nothing she could do about it. *Enfer,* nothing she wanted to do about it, save listen to his endless apologies. She'd been tempted to speak to him when she'd taken him his food. Either that, or hit him over the head with the trencher, which she came quite close to doing when he didn't say a word to her. How could he ignore her all day? She was angry with herself for peeking out the window every time she passed it. He certainly wasn't pining over her. She doubted she'd even crossed his mind while he plowed and smiled with his friends. She sighed. Why did he have to look so marvelously fit and healthy out there under the sun? He . . . He was coming!

She spun around and looked for something to make her look busy. She had already emptied her trunk and made room in his wardrobe for her gowns. The cottage was spotless. Not a smudge of soot remained, even on the walls. Her eyes dropped to three of the carefully tied sacks the villagers had given her the night before, piled in one corner.

The front door swung open and sunlight spilled into the cottage, falling on Tanon, squatting beside a large bag, her fingers working diligently to untie the knotted twine.

"Oh, it's you," she said vaguely, glancing up.

Gareth stood in the doorway, his body outlined by light and shadows. He stepped inside and smiled at the two butterfly serviettes spread out on the table.

"I need to build another chair," he said, his gaze returning to her.

"*Oui,* and more shelves." She tugged on the twine and swore under her breath. "And mayhap a cushioned settee to place before the fire, once we get one started."

"Whatever you want," he vowed on a ragged whisper as he moved toward her.

"I want"—she straightened and crossed the room to the bed where she left the dagger Llwyd had given her—"to get this sack open." She stomped back to the bag and knelt before it again.

"Tanon, forgive me for being a—" Gareth's gaze settled on the bed. The mattress was empty. A poor hollowed-out shell, stripped of its insides. For one maddening instant, he felt so much in common with that mattress he groaned out loud.

"What did you do to the bed?"

Tanon's nostrils widened. "The straw was old and prickly." She waited for him to begin bellowing. "I intend to fill it with feathers." She swiped the sharp blade across the twine. The tip of the dagger punctured the bag, and a cloud of flour erupted upward. She pointed the dagger at him while she wiggled her nose. "And I'll have you know that I'm good and tired of your unfeeling nature, Gareth."

He watched the blade waving in her hand when she cleared the flour away from her face. When she wiped her hand across her nose, almost slicing her throat, Gareth moved in a blur of speed.

Snatching her wrist with one hand, he carefully removed the blade from her fingers with the other. He exhaled so powerfully his breath fanned a stray lock of her hair off her cheek. "God's teeth, woman." He kissed her knuckles. "You scared the hell out of me."

She cast him a narrowed look. "Gareth, I had no intentions of attacking you. I may have lost my temper, but I would never—"

He laughed softly and then hauled her into his arms, snatching her words right out of her with his mouth. He withdrew slightly to stare into her eyes and smooth her curls away from her face with his palms. "I missed you today. Christ, I've missed you for twelve years."

Tanon blinked into his gaze and smiled at him. He had not only stirred her childhood fantasies of love, he made her desire it again. Who cared if he did a little bellowing every now and then if his apologies were going to be like this? So, he was a bit arrogant. The man could kiss better than . . . Well, she had nothing to compare it to, but she was sure no other man's kisses could have ever tasted so sweet on her lips. His touch made her feel reckless, willing to chance loving him, whatever might come. She surrendered to the fire he had ignited in her and delighted in the thrill of discovering how to unleash the savage he tried to control, until he left her panting and completely spent, sprawled on her belly across his table. Which is exactly what he did.

Chapter Nineteen

THE NEXT TWO DAYS were the happiest in Tanon's life so far. She worked alongside Deirdre and Isolde, clawing at soil that often found its way to her face. While they planted leeks and other vegetables beneath the comforting warmth of the sun, Tanon learned that the Norman invaders had once burned this village to the ground. With nothing left but charred timber and ashes, the villagers had grown ill and lost a number of children to starvation. At the time, Ystrad Towi belonged to Prince Cedric, but he had abandoned the people to their own defenses and diseases. After his exile, the village became part of Prince Gareth's inheritance from the king. From the day he arrived, he took his place among them and helped them rebuild what they'd lost, even better than before. He suffered their hardships with them and basked in the rewards of their labor. He went to battle for them, and for the Cymry who lived along the marches, exacting justice as Wyfyrn to the cruel Norman overlords who thought to rule them.

Hearing of her husband's gallant deeds compelled

Tanon's gaze to find him where he stood across the glen watching Cian and Llwyd's son, Gruffyn, practice with their swords. The music of tabor drums and lute orchestrated their pace. The young warriors looked to be of the same age, but they were not evenly matched. Though Gruffyn was indeed quick on his feet, Cian had almost perfected the art of speed and balance.

Gareth's eyes followed their every move, every parry and jab. Watching him, Tanon wondered how the weight of keeping this village alive and thriving didn't crush his shoulders. *Non*, his responsibility was what drove him. She prayed that William never discovered the truth of who he was. Gareth's people needed him. Wales needed him, and so did she.

Goodness, but he had to hate the Normans for the land they had taken from his countrymen, the suffering they caused. But he had put that hatred aside and married one of them. Tanon suddenly understood what kind of sacrifice Gareth had made by taking her as his wife. She admired him for his dedication, but she worried over it as well. Could he ever grow to love her, or did he make her so happy simply to keep the peace between their people? When he turned, as if sensing her eyes on him, he flashed her an intimate grin that convinced her she had come to mean more to him than a vow of peace.

The need to be near him summoned her to her feet just as Cian feigned a jab and struck Gruffyn in the face with his other fist. Gareth stepped forward into the circle while Cian helped his fallen opponent to his feet. Patting Gruffyn on the back, Gareth sent him back to Madoc and the others watching from the perimeter. He faced Cian unarmed and folded his arms neatly behind his back.

Beginning a slow, watchful pace, Madoc called out over the vivacious music to his youngest brother.

"Cian, watch your sword, and stay focused!"

"Aye," Tomas shouted after him. "Don't let him get too close."

Tanon stopped when she reached the men, taking a place beside Madoc. She looked to Cian in time to see his angelic features harden with stern determination as he prepared to practice with Gareth.

Gareth smiled at him, a challenge answered by Cian's tightened jaw. Gareth's feet thumped the ground, instantly picking up the rhythm pulsing around them. His legs carried him left two steps, and then back one. Cian matched his movements, advancing on him, yet keeping a careful few feet away. He arched his sword upward, feinting a crushing blow to Gareth's head, but at the last instant he changed direction and stabbed from the right instead.

Gareth pivoted on the pads of his sure feet, crouched low, and came back up almost behind Cian. With a snatch of his hand, he reached over the younger warrior's shoulder and wrested Cian's sword from his hand.

Alwyn's rowdy laughter earned him a shove from Tomas. Madoc only shook his head at his brother's swift defeat.

There was no shame in Cian's expression when Gareth faced him again and handed him back his sword. They repeated their previous movements four more times, until Cian learned exactly where Gareth would appear behind him and how he had arrived there.

When Cian left the circle, Gareth's gaze found Tanon. His eyes gleamed with the residue of battle practice. He beckoned her forward with a wave of his hand and a slight curling of his lips. She laughed, about to refuse his tempting invitation, when the playful goading of his men urged her on. She entered the circle even while her logic told her she could never learn such complex maneuvers as his other pupils. She expected him to spring away from her when she lifted her hand to his jaw, but he wove his fingers through hers and pulled her closer.

"We'll start slow," he promised in a low, lilting voice. "Watch my feet."

She looked down and tried to pull away. "I'll step on your toes! Let me remove my—"

The instant Gareth moved her, she knew his toes were not in jeopardy. He moved with weightless delicacy, though there was nothing elegant about him. His virility permeated the air like musk, heightening her awareness of the breadth of his shoulders, his heated exhalation of breath hovering above her lips.

He brought her hand to his chest and spread her fingers over his strong heartbeat, melding with the beat of the tabors. She let his body guide her as she danced with him around the ring. He swept her up as the tempo increased and pointed out what steps he took when he hooked his foot between hers and she fell backward into his waiting arms. The pleasure of dancing with Gareth was intense, and Tanon understood why any woman in this village would want to best him at a challenge.

Tanon wasn't certain how she managed it, but she didn't fall. She wasn't truly sure if her feet touched the ground at all.

He taught her the first basic lessxon in balance that day and the day after that. At night, he took her with a need far more primitive.

Chapter Twenty

ADARA GRIPPED HER BEDSHEETS late the following afternoon and wailed for all she was worth as her fifth hour of labor came upon her. Hovering beside her, Tanon wiped Adara's forehead with a damp cloth, reassuring her that all was well. Soon her babe would arrive.

"Aye, 'tis stubborn." Rebecca stood on the other side of Adara's bed and rubbed ointment on her belly, her voice as soothing as her fingers. "The first ones usually are." She grinned at Tanon and then called out to Cadwyn. "Fifteen."

Adara squeezed her eyes shut, gritted her teeth, and then spewed a flurry of Welsh words that made Cadwyn and Isolde blush.

"There, now," Tanon soothed in a gentle whisper, gripping Adara's hand. "It will not be much longer. You are already at fifteen pangs. Take courage. The pain is normal."

"It cannot be!" Adara screeched. "Something is wrong."

"*Non.*" Tanon stroked her cheeks with the backs of her fingers. "Adara, look at me. My mother did this seven times and will do so again in a few short months."

"And each time it pained her," Rebecca added, moving away to fetch another folded bedsheet.

"I will slice Tomas's throat if he thinks I will do this seven more times." Adara bore down, squeezing Tanon's hand until it went numb.

"Aye, she's ready," Rebecca said calmly, glancing between Adara's legs.

Tanon shut her eyes. She hated this part even more than the pangs of labor. A woman had to be strong of body, mind, and spirit to push a babe out of her. Her mother possessed such great strength, and still she had cried out in pain when the twins were born.

"Cadwyn." Rebecca's tone snapped with control. "Warm the swaddling cloth by the hearth. Isolde, the bath is ready?"

"Aye, everything is prepared." Isolde looked as resolute as Rebecca. Tanon straightened her shoulders and patted Adara's shoulder.

"Tanon, take her hands now," Rebecca commanded. "Pull her up."

"But she should be lying still." Cadwyn rushed forward, concern twisting her chubby features.

"Nay, she shouldn't." Rebecca positioned herself between Adara's thighs and pressed her palms on either side of Adara's belly. "Lady Brynna delivered her children sitting up. Some Turkish women, I am told, deliver squatting. It's more natural."

Cadwyn gasped, bringing the swaddling cloth to her chest. Isolde rushed to stand behind Adara, helping her to bear down, while Tanon pulled her forward, urging her to push on Rebecca's command.

Ten minutes later, Adara's son was born, gray, greasy,

and howling. Rebecca cut the birthing cord, and Tanon cleaned the babe's mouth and nose. She wrapped him in warm linens and handed him over to his mother. Cadwyn wept while Isolde prepared mother and babe for their bath.

"That wasn't so terrible." Rebecca cut a glance to Tanon while she changed the bedsheets.

Tanon scoffed at her. "It was horrendous. As it always is." She cleaned her hands and stepped toward the door. "I'll fetch Tomas."

Adara barely lifted her teary, joyful face from her infant.

Stepping outside, Tanon had an instant to inhale a breath of cool, fresh air before Tomas was upon her.

"Well?" He looked about to pass out at her feet.

Tanon smiled and reached out for his hand. "You have a son."

"And Adara?"

"Is alive and well."

Tomas clutched her shoulders and hauled her close for a kiss to her cheek, then dashed into the cottage.

Looking up, Tanon's heart fluttered at the sight of her husband pushing off the wall he'd been leaning against. He walked toward her, framed against the afterglow of a smoldering sunset. He wore a close-fitting olive green tunic oddly fashioned with tiny silver clasps securing the fabric from the front of his neck to his lean hips. Braided stitching of the same color outlined the elegant cut. Long sleeves stretched over his smooth, sleek muscles and tapered at the cuffs, where more clasps were sewn up to his elbows. His legs, which, as always, caused Tanon to skip a breath, were encased in thin kidskin breeches of light tan. Flat boots, also made of kidskin, laced up his strong calves.

When he reached her, he didn't speak but slipped one arm around her shoulder and drew her in close.

"How do you fare?" he asked softly.

"I am well." She inhaled his musky scent and closed her arms around his waist. "I've done this more than once."

He moved away just enough to look at her. "Aye." His smile was tender; his long, honey-streaked hair snapped around his shoulders at the breeze that cooled the air. "I've a feeling you won't even cry out when our babe is born."

Tanon wanted to tell him that she never wanted to suffer as Adara had today, but the words sounded cowardly as they formed in her head. The feel of his strong, sure embrace, the potent emotion in his gaze stopped her as well. The idea of bearing his child suddenly filled her heart with longing.

Tomas's return only fueled her mad desire. With his son swathed in warm linen and clutched to his chest, he approached them.

"Gareth, my son, Deiniol."

Tanon watched Gareth take the infant in his arms. With one finger, he carefully moved the swaddling cloth to reveal the babe's face. And then he melted.

"A son," he murmured on a deep, meaningful breath, his smile so wonderfully warm that Tanon's head felt light just looking at him. "You are richly blessed this night, Tomas."

He would love their babe. She knew it by the warmth lighting his lapis eyes. Dear God, she wanted him to love her that much.

Cian and Madoc called out as they approached from the center of the glen, where another great celebration was already taking place to honor the arrival of Tomas and Adara's babe. Gareth turned toward them, facing Tanon fully. For one shockingly blissful instant, Tanon imagined that the child he held so tenderly was theirs. He looked more irresistible than ever before.

Cian wiped his misty eyes, and Madoc smacked him on the back of the head. But then the usually stoic warrior graced his new nephew with a touching grin and promised to teach him how to fight.

"You will announce him to the others, Gareth?" Tomas asked, taking Deiniol back into his arms. "I may attend Celebration later, but now I want to remain with Adara."

Promising that he would, Gareth curled his fingers around Tanon's and nodded when Cian and Madoc told him they would join him later as well. When the three brothers entered the cottage, Tanon leaned her head on her husband's shoulder.

"Would a daughter be as much of a blessing?"

"Aye." He turned her in his arms to look deep into her eyes. "Especially if she is anything like her mother."

He made her feel fevered . . . and cherished. "Mayhap, then"—she tilted her head to whisper close to his mouth—"I shall give you one of each."

His eyes glinted beneath golden brows, and his mouth curved into that sensual half-grin that turned her kneecaps to honey. "Then let's get to it."

They didn't make it to the cottage until early the next morn. When Gareth stopped the music to announce the birth of

Deiniol, his people were eager to hear more about the newest arrival to their large family, as well as the details of the birth, which Tanon simplified by saying, "It went well," and "Adara was quite wonderful." This, of course, earned a round of cheers from the people. They sat and ate steaming bowls of lamb stew and washed it down with heavy tankards of freshly brewed *Bragawd*. The mood was joyful and the music merry. Tanon found herself laughing with Hereward, and even Alwyn shared a few gracious smiles with her. When Rebecca finally joined them, Tanon was pleased to lose Hereward to her. The two laughed and shared a trencher of fruit and sweet cheese. Tanon was certain her nurse had never looked happier.

When Ioan asked her to dance with him, Tanon declined at first, but after two more tankards of *Bragawd*, she flung away her courtly manners to show him what she had learned so far with Gareth.

She felt her husband watching her in the bronze glow of torchlight. She could hear his laughter mixing with her own. When he finally met her in the center of the circle writhing with dancers, he took her in his arms and swept her off her feet.

～

Madoc stepped out of Tomas's cottage with Cian and made his way across the glen toward the Celebration. He stopped when he glanced at his cottage, down the hill. Normally, the sight of his door hanging slightly ajar would not have alerted him to anything out of the ordinary. Cian ofttimes forgot to close it behind him. But a shadow crossed the firelight inside, and since he shared his home with Cian, and his brother was standing right beside him, there should not have been anyone inside.

"Cian." He laid his hand on his brother's back. "Go on ahead. I will join you shortly." When Cian turned to offer him a questioning look, Madoc pushed him along. "Go now, brother. I won't be but a few breaths."

The moment Cian walked away, Madoc dashed toward his dwelling. When he reached the threshold, he paused and slowed his breath before stepping inside.

"What the hell are you doing in here?"

Cedric looked up from a small chair set before the hearth and smiled. "There is a matter we must discuss."

"It could not wait?" Madoc demanded, entering and closing the door behind him. "You could have been seen. My brother could have come here instead of me."

Cedric rolled his eyes heavenward. "I wasn't seen. Think you Gareth is the only one who learned from my uncle to be crafty? Besides"—he shrugged—"everyone is in the glen. I found it quite easy to enter the village. As for Cian, I would have slipped through the back door had he wandered here. Really, Madoc, you insult me."

"One err, Cedric." Madoc closed the distance between them in two strides. "One err and everything would have been over. Now tell me what is so urgent that you risked all to come here to tell me?"

"Very well." Cedric gave him a long-suffering sigh. "You must kill the Saxon."

Madoc simply stared at him. "What?"

"The Saxon. Hereward the Wake. Do it immediately after Gareth leaves for Llandeilo."

"Cedric." Madoc set his hard eyes on Gareth's brother. "I will be with Gareth when he leaves."

"Nay, there has been a slight change in our plans. You will not travel with Gareth, but with me. And you will bring with you my brother's Norman wife."

"Nay," Madoc whispered through tightly clenched teeth. "There can be no change. She is to remain here. We agreed that you would return for her after you are king."

Cedric was already shaking his head, not listening to Madoc's reasoning. "I want her brought to me after Gareth leaves. She will come with us to Llandeilo."

"Why? For what purpose?" Madoc pressed almost urgently.

"He cares for her." Cedric left his chair and began a measured pace before Madoc. "I have been watching him. His eyes follow her. His laughter can be heard on the wind." He stopped and gazed into the small hearth fire. "My uncle preferred Gareth's ways of thinking. Fool. Gareth took everything that was mine." His voice was even and quiet with the promise of retribution. "I want him to know clearly that I will reclaim it all. When he sees his wife in my arms, he will know."

Madoc glanced at the door and then rushed at Cedric. "Think, man! Your brother is no fool. He will suspect something is amiss if I do not go with him. We must not alter the course. We will be crushed under his feet if he is prepared for us. I will travel with Gareth and meet with you in Llandeilo. We will return for the girl later, as planned."

"Nay," Cedric repeated, the warning edge in his voice cautioning Madoc not to argue with him further. "Convince Gareth that you are too ill to travel. Injure yourself with your sword, do whatever you like. But convince him that you cannot go. He may not protest overmuch, since you will promise to join with Hereward in keeping his wife safe during his absence." When Madoc remained silent, Cedric cocked a curious brow at him. "She means naught to you, aye?"

"I told you, she's a Norman."

"Good, then I shall see you both in three days."

Madoc finally conceded with a slight, stiff nod, then turned to leave the cottage. "You know your way out."

~

Before he entered the glen, Madoc stopped just beyond the perimeter of warm firelight. It was easy to find Gareth and Tanon amid the crowd, for something between them drew others closer. They shared smiles charged with profound emotion, laughter that rang out with more joy than the laughter of those around them. They touched, and one could feel the shuddering effects of their attraction toward each other. Cedric was correct—Gareth cared for her. Madoc saw it plainly in the way Gareth's eyes pored over her as if drenching his soul with her captivating visage. Tanon's affection was no less evident. For no matter whom she spoke to, her gaze drifted back to her husband, her expression a mixture of subtle surprise, relief, and contentment. As if the happiness she felt was unexpected.

With a determined set of his jaw, Madoc stepped into the glen and made his way toward them.

"We missed you, brother." Gareth turned from his conversation with Hereward when Madoc reached him. "All is well?"

"Aye." Madoc met his gaze directly and then looked around the glen. "Where is Cian?"

"I sent him on an errand."

Madoc snatched a cup from a passing server and downed its contents. He swiped the back of his hand across his lips and glanced at Tanon.

"Mind if I dance with your wife?"

"Not at all." Gareth accepted the empty cup Madoc handed him and winked at Tanon when she followed Madoc to the center of the glen.

"I was not aware that you danced, Madoc," Tanon teased with a merry lilt to her voice when they stood facing each other a few moments later.

Madoc's gaze brushed hers briefly before he fit her hands into his. "King Rhys made us learn the art of movement to melody. Gareth and I learned together as boys. Swerve and strike. Defense first"—he spun to her left, and then to her right so quickly she giggled—"and then offense." He swept his boot beneath hers and caught her in the crook of his arm when she stumbled backward. "Remember this, Tanon." He leaned over her, his piercing dark eyes holding her still. "No one is as deadly as your husband, save me. I will let nothing and no one destroy what I value."

Tanon searched his shadowed gaze. His words sounded like a warning. There was more he wanted to say, something he was keeping from her. She pushed her palms against his chest to break away from his grasp. "What is it? Why are you telling me this?"

He straightened, letting her go. "Just . . . remember."

She didn't understand, nor did she like the way his mood changed. He looked like the dangerous man she'd seen in Winchester before she knew him. Taking a step away, Tanon bumped into something immovable. She turned and blinked up into Gareth's eyes.

He looked over her head at Madoc. "Tanon, find Rebecca and Hereward and stay with them while I have a word with my friend."

She went without quarrel, much to Gareth's amazement. Beneath his thick lashes, a glint of firelight sparked his eyes when he returned them to Madoc. "Come, let's talk."

Chapter Twenty-One

GARETH HADN'T SMILED in two days. Tanon noted that his mood had gone sour since he spoke with Madoc at the Celebration. When she questioned him, he insisted that all was well. But he shouted at Alwyn and Tomas when they brought him the wrong-sized wood for the new chairs he was building. He barely noticed the lovely amber window coverings she'd hung or the matching tablecloth she had sewn. He called William a filthy pig—the hog, not the king, but it offended Tanon just the same. He hammered and brooded and bellowed from dawn to dusk. And when night fell on the glen, he made rough, passionate love to Tanon on their new feather-stuffed mattress, and then held her until the morning.

On the morn of the third day, she woke to an empty bed. The sound of wood being chopped outside drew her to the front door. She tossed her nightdress over her head and stepped outside.

The air was cool with the coming of autumn, but her husband's bare chest glistened with sweat as he brought down his ax on a vertical slab of wood, cleaving it in half. He didn't look up at first, and Tanon let her hungry gaze revel in his flat belly and the long, lithe muscles that pulsed in his arms as he lifted another piece of wood to the chopping block. His long, sun-burnished mane rippled as he brought his ax down once again.

When had she begun to love him so fiercely? Dear God, it frightened her. She hadn't wanted to come to Wales, but now she didn't know what she would do without him. Something was terribly wrong. She could feel it in the marrow of her bones. Where was Cian? He had not yet returned from his errand. What had happened between Gareth and Madoc to cause her husband to behave so unbearably these last few days? Did it have something to do with her? The Normans? Tanon knew William would never go back on his word and bring battle to Wales.

"Gareth?"

He brought down his ax, hard, splintering the wood. He glanced up at her. His rugged face was lined with worry. His full mouth was drawn tight across his teeth. Tanon nearly recoiled at the anguish plaguing his gaze.

"What troubles you so? You leave to meet your king today, and your solemn mood frightens me. Has something happened involving my people?"

"Not the Normans." He averted his gaze from her questioning one. "It's my own people who threaten the peace here. My uncle has heard rumor that Prince Dafydd is planning an attack in Llandeilo."

Tanon drew in a sharp breath. The fear of losing him burned in her eyes. "Are you going to fight?"

He lowered his ax to his side. "If I do, I will win. Don't fret."

She couldn't stay away from him another instant, but when she moved to go to him, he held up his palm to stop her.

"I fear," he said, looking into her stricken gaze with eyes that ached with longing to hold her, "that if I touch you, I will not be able to go."

"If you don't touch me, I will not let you leave."

Gareth exhaled a deep breath and angled his head as if to see her from a different position. Mayhap one that didn't make his heart crash so in his chest. "Tanon, you've brought peace and innocence to my life where there was always bloodshed and violence. And in return I've laid you bare at the altar, like a sacrifice to the wolves."

She smiled tenderly and took another step toward him, closer to those strong, safe arms.

"What do you mean you have sacrificed me?" she asked him quietly, her smile deepening. "I daresay you've made my dreams real."

His scant smile was riddled with anguish. "You've dreamed of living in a hut, then? Tanon, you should be living in a fortress, safe and secure."

"Your arms are my fortress," she told him. "Everything I desire is right here with you."

He dropped the ax and closed the distance between them in two strides. He took her in his arms, locking her in an embrace of steel. Tunneling his fingers through the velvet curls at her temples, he drew her head back to meet her gaze. "I want to bury myself deep inside you." His voice was a hoarse whisper against her mouth. "And make you forget . . ."

His tight groan sent a scalding tongue of flame down

Tanon's back, and she pressed her swelling breasts to his bare chest.

"Forget everything but the feel of our bodies lost in each other." Bending his knees, he slipped his hands under her and carried her inside the cottage.

They fell to the bed, pulling at each other's laces, urgent to share a few moments of sweet intimacy, as if they might never enjoy them again. Gareth spread her beneath him and, with one powerful, sensuous grunt, impaled her to his hilt.

When they were both spent, he clutched her tightly to his body. "Forgive me, Tanon," he whispered, closing his eyes and holding her as if she were even more vital to him than the people he had sworn to protect.

~

Two hours later, Gareth's deadly *Teulu* were saddled and ready to leave.

Standing with Rebecca and Adara outside the village tavern, Tanon watched her husband share a few words with Ioan before he turned to Hereward next. He wore a tunic of deep scarlet, as did the rest of his men, announcing them warriors of the king's elite.

Tomas kissed his wife and babe and then backed away toward his horse. "Be vigilant. Keep safe until I return," he charged his wife before he leaped into his saddle, joining the other men.

A harsh realization settled over Tanon, chilling her to her marrow. In the midst of so many enemies, this village was vulnerable without its warriors. Any moment could find them facing deadly enemies from any number of regions. She hugged her arms around herself. The people of this village were not defenseless, thanks to Gareth. She said a silent prayer to God that everyone here knew how to fight.

When Gareth turned and motioned to her, she went without haste into his arms.

"I will return to you shortly." His lips moved against her ear, sending warmth and yearning coursing through her veins. He withdrew from her embrace and cupped her face in his palms. "Madoc has fallen ill and will not be joining me. Tanon," he said, his gaze fastened on hers, "I trust him to keep you safe."

"Hereward is here as well," she reminded him, wanting to ease the disquiet in his eyes. "I am not afraid. I will do as they say, and I will pray for you every eve until you return to me."

Gareth looked at her and swallowed. He ground his teeth as if he wanted to say something more, but chose against it. He dipped his mouth to hers instead, his lips needful, his breath ragged. "Would that I was in bed with you now. A peasant with no other care but to please you."

"You are a prince who pleases me well," she told him, kissing him again. "Godspeed, husband." She pushed him away before she surrendered to the need quaking her heart and clung to him.

Before he mounted, Gareth spread his gaze over the many faces staring back at him. "If any stranger enters this village, kill him. Entertain no one. As always, be watchful day and night. Carry your daggers with you at all times, and remember what you have learned in the practice circles." He vaulted to his horse and set his sapphire eyes on Tanon. "All will be well."

He flicked his reins and rode out of the village with Alwyn, Tomas, and the rest of his men at his side.

A deep sense of foreboding swept over Tanon while she watched them go. She turned, scanned the crowd, and then called out, "Has anyone seen Cian?"

~

"Are you going to go back to Winchester when Gareth returns?" Tanon asked Hereward later that day as she set a trencher on the table in front of him. She cut a quick glance to Rebecca, snipping the stems from the lilies she'd gathered by the stream.

"That depends." Hereward broke off a piece of bread and dipped it into his stew.

"Oh?" Tanon raised a curious brow at him. "On what?"

He shrugged his broad shoulders but smiled slightly at Rebecca.

Tanon looked toward her nurse, who was pretending not to pay attention to the conversation. "It depends on the lilies, then?" she asked innocently, quirking a teasing brow back at Hereward.

"Oh, stop it!" Rebecca snapped and swatted Tanon with a flower. "You can just cease this confounded scheme of yours to see us together. Hereward has already asked me to marry him."

Tanon almost leaped into Rebecca's arms. "Oh, I'm so—"

"I haven't given him my answer yet."

There came a knock at the door. "Come!" Tanon called out, then scowled back at her nurse. "And why not?"

"Good day, Madoc." Rebecca ignored Tanon and smiled

at the sable-haired warrior when he entered the cottage. "You're looking much better. Your illness has passed?"

"Bore da," Madoc returned her greeting with a slight nod. "Aye, and I have your honey and chamomile brew to thank." He glanced at Hereward, his expression unreadable. "Take a moment from your meal to escort me to the stable. There is something I would like you to take a look at."

"Of course." Hereward rose from the table and excused himself. "Something worrisome?"

"Let's hope not." Madoc slashed him a smile, then followed him out the door.

"He is worrisome." Tanon frowned after they left and began clearing the table. "Something happened between him and Gareth that made them both brooding and sour."

"Mayhap Gareth discovered how much his friend cares for you," Rebecca said with certainty.

"Madoc?" Tanon stopped to laugh at her nurse. "That's absurd. He cares for no one."

"He conceals his heart well because of his affection and loyalty to Gareth."

Tanon stared at her without saying a word, but she didn't have to. Rebecca knew what she was thinking. She sighed deeply, then finally admitted what Tanon had known for years. "I was coming down the stairs one day shortly after your father arrived at Avarloch. He smiled at me. That was all he did, but from that moment on, he has held my heart."

Tanon listened without judgment, understanding love because she had grown up enveloped in it, and because she wanted it so badly with Gareth. "I cannot fathom how difficult it has been for you. But now you have a chance to have your love returned. I think Hereward has cared for you for a long time."

Rebecca laughed. "Aye, the poor fool."

"I think he came here to be rid of you."

"He had no idea that I was coming with you."

They laughed together, and then Rebecca left her seat and drew Tanon's hands to her cheek. "I thought you would hate me if you knew how I felt about your father."

"I've known for years." Tanon decided not to tell her that everyone who ever saw her look at her father knew. "I could never hate you. Now, tell me." Her green eyes gleamed with an impish twinkle. "How does Hereward kiss? Do your knees grow weak?"

Rebecca blushed and then giggled like a girl half her age. "He's only kissed me once, but it was quite nice."

The door opened again, and Madoc stepped back inside.

"Where is Hereward?" Tanon looked behind him. "Is everything all right?"

"Aye. There was a crack in the stable door, but it turns out that Llwyd's horse caused it. The beast got free of its stall. Naught to fret over." His gaze softened as he strode toward Tanon. "Hereward went to the tavern to speak with Padrig about repairing the damage."

Tanon offered him a faint smile. Did he truly care for her? Heavens, she hoped not. He was quite a handsome man with his loose, sooty curls drooping over those deep obsidian eyes. His warrior's body was lean and honed to perfection beneath a black tunic and matching breeches. She would have to find him a wife soon so that he could be happy. She certainly didn't want another Rebecca on her hands.

"There's a field not far from here where the amaryllis

grows wild and jasmine scents the air," he told her, bowing ever so slowly.

"I've seen it." Tanon was tempted to take a step back as he moved closer. "We passed it on our way here."

"Aye, we did. Let me take you there." He stopped and plucked a lily from the table. "These are wilting already."

Tanon shot a helpless look at Rebecca. The nurse shrugged her petite shoulders in return. "I have much to do here," Tanon said. "Mayhap when Gareth returns—"

"My lady." He reached for her hand before she could pull it away. "I'm not the cruel beast you saw at the campsite before we arrived here. You must not fear me."

She laughed, and her eyes sparked with pride. "I don't fear you." It wasn't really a lie. She remembered all too well the cold, lethal warrior who had saved her by killing a man not two feet from her face, but she'd been able to put that out of her mind. "It's just that I . . ." Her voice trailed off when he lowered his eyes, shielding them beneath long, inky lashes.

"Gareth trusts me with you. I would never betray that."

Tanon chewed her lower lip. Something in the deep pitch of his voice, the sagging of his usually arrogant shoulders, convinced her that he was sincere. Gareth had told her that Madoc would keep her safe. Besides, if he did fancy her, this was the perfect time to speak to him about it.

"All right." She allowed him to pull her forward. "But we cannot stay too long. I promised Adara I would visit her today." She cast Rebecca a reassuring smile even though her nurse didn't look concerned at all.

Tanon was surprised to find two horses saddled and waiting right outside the cottage. Madoc hadn't expected her to refuse him. She placed her hand on her hip and was about to have her talk with him right then and there, when he flashed her a rakish grin.

"There's a road beyond the stream that will take us to our destination faster. I was careful not to trample Gareth's wheat when I brought the horses to the door. There's no need to scowl at me so."

He gained his saddle and reached over to clasp Tanon's reins. They left the glen just as afternoon practice began and lute, harp, and tabor drums filled the air.

Chapter Twenty-Two

REBECCA STRODE INTO THE tavern and looked around. Her brow furrowed above her powdery blue eyes. She had no use for such places. A few men sat at wooden tables stained with small white rings left by years of moist goblets. The sweet smell of *Bragawd* and ale filled her lungs and churned her stomach. She hoped Hereward wasn't here getting drunk so early in the day. Brand never touched a flagon until supper, and . . . She stopped herself. Would it be so difficult to stop thinking of him? Aye, she answered herself. She had loved Brand for a pair of decades. It was going to take some time getting used to loving someone else.

She scanned the tavern again. Hereward was not in it. Relief spread over her as she left.

Her heart had been held captive for so many years. But the binds were being broken, smashed to pieces by a strong Saxon warrior. She had given Hereward a moment, and he made her want another, until a moment without him stretched on for hours. Spending these last few days with him, she'd learned that he was a proud man, an arrogant warrior, someone who reminded her of her language and her heritage. He could frighten a dozen knights and their captain with little more than his name, but he made her laugh. He made her think, and he made her feel.

"Good day, Padrig," she greeted when she spotted him leaving his carpentry shop. "I am looking for Hereward. Is he inside?"

"Hereward?" Padrig squinted at her. "Haven't seen him, m'lady."

Rebecca paused at the shop's entrance and peered inside. "Forgive me. Madoc said Hereward was having a word with you."

Padrig shrugged before hefting a large slab of pine to his shoulder and carrying it to the door. "Mayhap he is with Lady Tanon."

Rebecca shook her head. "Lady Tanon left to pick flowers with Madoc."

Now Padrig stopped and cast her a look that said she was the worst liar in all of Cymru. "Picking *what* with Madoc?"

"Never mind," Rebecca said, looking past his shoulder at Ioan approaching the stable. "If you see Hereward, please tell him that I am looking for him." She swept past the carpenter without waiting for his reply and headed for the stable. She wanted to ask Ioan if he'd seen Hereward before he stepped inside.

Something about the way Ioan peered left and then right before he disappeared within the doors troubled her. Slowing her pace when she reached the entrance, she pushed open a door and peeked inside. A horse snorted in its stall, but other than that, no sound came from inside.

"Ioan?" she called out softly and entered. She left the door ajar behind her, allowing sunlight to puddle inside. "Ioan?" Louder this time.

At the far end of the stable, in an empty stall close to the last, Ioan's head appeared just above the enclosure.

"A moment, please, Rebecca." He held up his palm to keep her from coming any closer.

A fist, too large to belong to anyone but her giant Saxon, swung with a bone-crushing echo.

Rebecca halted in her tracks, her mouth hanging agape as blood spurted from Ioan's nose seconds before he crumbled, disappearing from her vision. She rushed forward and pushed the stall door open.

"Hereward!" She rushed to his side and helped him push Ioan off his chest.

With a muttered curse, Hereward sat up slowly. Droplets of blood from Ioan's nose speckled Hereward's tunic, but the crimson ribbon trickling from his forehead down to his jaw was his own.

"What happened?" Rebecca pulled a small napkin from a pocket in her gown and began wiping his wound. "Did Ioan do this to you?"

"Nay, 'twas Madoc." His eyes, usually so gentle on her, burned with fury.

Rebecca fell back on her rump as if he had just pushed her. "Madoc?" Her face paled in the dimness of the stable. "Madoc did this to you?" When he nodded, her mind refused to believe it. "He couldn't have. Why? Why would he harm you?"

"Woman, he did it," Hereward growled. "He led me here and then struck me with something." He rose to his feet, pulling Rebecca up by the hand. He looked around the stable, toward the doors. "Whether he meant to kill me, I don't know, but I want you and Tanon to stay inside the cottage and bolt the door until I figure out what is going on."

"Hereward." The fear in Rebecca's voice dragged his gaze to her. "He—" Her vocal cords stiffened. Speaking it made it real, and the thought of never seeing Tanon again was too heavy a sorrow to bear. "Madoc has already taken Tanon away."

"I think we must be lost." Tanon looked around the wooded landscape. They'd been riding for over an hour with no sign of a field in sight.

"We are not lost. We will be there shortly."

"I didn't realize it was so far." Tanon let one hand release the reins and rubbed her arm as a chill settled over her. "It will be getting dark by the time we head home. We should return now and come back another day."

Madoc didn't answer her. His eyes moved slowly, cautiously scanning the trees as if he were looking for something.

"Madoc?"

"Hush, Tanon."

She looked around. A stab of fear twisted her insides. Did he sense something amiss? She wished Gareth were here. Or even Hereward. She shouldn't have left without Hereward. The forest frightened her. Anyone could be lurking just behind a tree. Or in one. She was about to demand that they return, when she heard the approach of horses to her right. She whirled her mount around and choked on a harsh cry. A group of about twenty mounted men galloped toward her, looking even more savage to her than Gareth and his men had when she'd first seen them in the great hall.

"Madoc," she breathed, her gaze fixed on the troop coming closer. "We should run." Without waiting for his consent, she kicked her mount's flanks. Madoc grasped her reins and yanked her back.

"What . . .?"

"Keep silent!" Madoc commanded in a harsh whisper.

Tanon's heart pounded so hard it made her feel ill. She pulled on her reins, trying to free them from Madoc's fist as the sound of the horses grew closer. "They look about to run us down! You cannot fight them all!" she argued with him, panic making her voice rise to a near screech. Madoc remained silent.

She watched, stricken with terror as the lead rider pulled to a halt directly in front of her. Something about him seemed so familiar when he raked his dark blue eyes over her. His slow grin sent an icy tremor along her spine.

He resembled Gareth. He was slightly older, with thick, arrow-straight chestnut hair tied at his nape. He circled her and Madoc while his men waited a few feet away.

"My God, you are lovely," he said, reining in closer to her. He plucked her hand free from clenching her reins. When he pulled her knuckles to his mouth, Tanon noted that he was missing a finger. She turned her frightened gaze on Madoc, but he looked away.

"I am Prince Cedric ab Owain," the rider introduced himself, releasing her hand. "Your true husband."

Tanon snapped her hand back. Cedric! God's blood, it was Gareth's brother! And his cold, meaningless smile hadn't changed. What was the exiled prince doing in Wales? Had he come back for her?

"My true husband is Gareth, and this is his first in command," she said, mustering all the strength she possessed not to recoil when his gaze penetrated hers. "I give you fair warning to leave us in peace, or this mighty warrior shall be forced to kill you and your men."

Cedric laughed right in her face. "This man, you say?" He rode his mount around her and stopped in front of Madoc. "Why, it is he who has delivered you to me."

Tanon's eyes darted to Madoc. She would never have believed such a terrible lie if he had not, in that moment, lifted his gaze to meet hers squarely, boldly.

"Non." She could barely form a whisper. "I don't understand."

"Peace"—Cedric's taunting voice made her blink, but she could not tear her stricken gaze from Madoc's—"is an ideal that will cost my brother his life. Cymru has no place for cowards like Gareth."

She was only half listening. The rogue prince had to be lying. "Madoc, how could you?" Her voice and her hands shook. It couldn't be. Madoc would never betray Gareth.

"He is helping reclaim Cymru from your people." Cedric trotted beside her and pinched her chin between his fingers, forcing her to look at him. "As will you." He flashed her a grin that was devoid of anything but self-importance. He called over his shoulder to a large, rough-looking brute with hair as dark as Tanon's and a beard to match. "Dafydd, ride with the lady. I have matters to discuss with Madoc."

"You betrayed him." Tanon's eyes seared into Madoc's as he rode past her. "Bastard." He did not respond, nor did he look at her again.

Chapter Twenty-Three

THEY RODE SOUTHWEST, following the winding river Tywi across the rolling ranges of Deheubarth. After his talk with Cedric, Madoc returned to Tanon's side. She would have preferred not to look at him, but he rode his horse close to hers. She glared at him twice when his knee rubbed against her leg. She tried to concentrate on a way to escape, but even if she succeeded in getting away from the men, she had no idea which way to go. Her thoughts returned to Gareth's first in command.

He was good at deceit, that one. Why, no one would ever believe him capable of betraying Gareth. He was always at Gareth's side, guarding him from danger—at the tourney, at the wedding feast with Roger, at the campsite. How was it possible that Madoc could turn traitor on his childhood friend?

Gareth was clever. How could he not have known? He was Wyfyrn, the warrior who'd eluded William's marcher lords and then found a way to kill them in their beds. He had calculated and countered Bleddyn's next move that first night at the campsite. Tanon's heart began to pound in her ears. How did he know about Prince Dafydd's planned attack on the king? Unless Madoc told him. Was that why Gareth had been in such a sour mood before he left the village? *Non*, Tanon's heart rejected what her mind told her. If Madoc didn't betray Gareth, then that meant Gareth knew about her abduction, mayhap even staged it himself, careless of what befell her while in Cedric's company.

She laughed at herself, fighting the sickening knot tightening her belly. He didn't know. Gareth wouldn't risk her life. At the campsite, he had known Bleddyn's men would come to him. But he had been there all along. He hadn't left her, and he barely knew her then. *Non,* Tanon convinced herself. He didn't know about Madoc. He couldn't. She trusted her heart with him. He didn't know.

~

When the moon broke through the wispy clouds and bathed the land in a silver fog, they made camp within a stand of tall ash trees. Madoc returned to Tanon's side while Cedric's men spread out their pallets and built a small fire. Crouching beside her, Madoc offered her a hunk of stale bread and a cup of water. She refused both.

"Eat."

"Rot in hell."

"Madoc, slap the teeth from her mouth," Dafydd commanded on his way toward the fire. "The saucy bitch needs discipline."

Tanon glared up at him. Her fingers rolled into fists at her sides. She was afraid of them, but she never could tolerate bullies, and her temper got the better of her. "Did you discipline your daughter after she helped Gareth escape your dungeon?"

Dafydd pivoted on his heel and glared at her. "Lying bitch!" He was upon her instantly, his large hand pulled back over his shoulder to strike her.

Madoc reacted even faster. Curling his arm around Dafydd's calf, he yanked hard, bringing the northern prince to his knees, and then flat on his back. Madoc's eyes smoldered with murderous intent while he held a short dagger to Dafydd's throat.

"Touch her, and I'll cut off your hands, one finger at a time."

"Madoc, remove yourself from the prince," Cedric called out blandly as he strode toward them. "Dafydd, you will do well to remember that the wench belongs to me."

"You're deranged," Tanon flung at him. When he squatted before her, she met his level gaze directly. "My father and King William will—"

"Bring war to Cymru. Aye, I know." He studied her with a long, calculating gaze that made Tanon want to run for her life. "Does my brother tolerate such cheek from this woman, Madoc?"

"She's frightened, Cedric. She means no—"

"Because I will not tolerate it. Give me your knife." He held his hand out to Madoc.

"I said she is frightened," Madoc repeated, rising to his feet and pushing Dafydd away from him.

"And *I* said, give me your knife."

"I will not."

Cedric looked up at him with a deadly smirk spreading across his face. He stood up, facing Madoc. "I've never known you to be gallant. What? Do you care for her? Do you recite poetry to her, or have you skipped the wooing and gone straight to fucking her?"

Madoc tightened his jaw and dipped his gaze briefly to Tanon's. She looked away. "I have not touched her. Nor will you." He moved closer to Cedric as he spoke, his voice flat and lethal. "If you lay a finger on her, you will face Gareth alone. I vow I will not help you, and though you may be able to kill the king, you cannot fight Gareth without me. For while you spent your royal years fighting your petty wars with the north and coupling with every woman who was afraid to refuse you, your brother practiced day and night, preparing himself for his true enemy. He moves faster than your eyes could follow and strikes with the precision of a serpent. Cedric, without me, you will die before you have time to shit your breeches."

Cedric stared at him. The challenge in his gaze was unmistakable. "You care for her. A Norman. Would you defend my enemy to my face?" He narrowed his eyes on Madoc as if trying to read his thoughts. "Has Gareth taught you his ways, then?"

Madoc glared at him, his teeth clamped down and making the scar along his jaw twitch. "You may ask me that again while I carry his head to the battlement walls. But when he is dead, I want her." He heard Tanon's sharp intake of breath, but he didn't look at her. "I will seize Gareth," he promised Cedric. "I will hold him still while you cut his throat. But only if she becomes mine when he is dead."

Cedric chuckled at him as if Madoc had gone completely mad. "And I'm to give up my war because you've gone soft over a Norman?"

"Nay. You'll have your war when you break peace. You'll have your throne when you kill the king's heirs and his regent. You don't need her for it. Refuse me, and you fight Gareth alone . . . and lose."

Cedric eyed him, still unsure if he should trust any man who cared for a Norman. He had no choice, he realized an instant later. He needed Madoc. For now. "You're still the most arrogant bastard I know, Madoc ap Bleiddian." He pounded Madoc on the arm and then walked away, calling over his shoulder as he went. "Help me kill him and she's yours."

"Aye," Madoc agreed in a low voice. He turned to look down at Tanon. She scooted away from him, dragging the hem of her gown along with her. A ribbon of moonlight fell on her face.

"You speak so easily about killing him." Tanon eyed him narrowly. "I will hate you for as long as I have breath."

"So be it," Madoc said, glancing away from her contempt. "I intend to keep you alive regardless."

Tanon opened her eyes just before dawn. She pushed herself up on her elbows and looked around. The fire still burned, but the men were all asleep. She guessed Cedric had left Madoc to watch her while she pretended to sleep. She had no idea where she was. She was afraid, but she knew she had to find her way back to the village and warn Hereward. Holding her breath, she slipped away from Madoc's side.

His hand shot out and shackled her wrist.

Tanon's heart jolted to her throat. *Merde,* but she hated him. "I have to relieve myself."

"I will come with you."

Her wide green eyes sparked with challenge. "You most certainly will not!"

In the dim dawn light, she saw his lips tighten around his teeth. "Then you will not relieve yourself."

"Fine," she relented with a scathing glare. "But you will turn away."

He nodded and followed her for a short distance to the trees, then waited while she crouched behind a thick currant bush.

Tanon eyed him from over the bush. When he turned to look toward the campsite, she crawled away another yard before she lifted her skirts and sprinted toward the denser woods in front of her.

She felt Madoc's hands close around her waist before she even heard him moving. But she was prepared when he spun her around. Removing the dagger from where she'd kept it tied to her thigh (thanking Gareth silently for telling her to keep it with her always), she sliced the blade across Madoc's face.

He released her with shock and numb amazement animating his features. He brought his fingers to his face. She had cut him deep, just below his left ear and almost down to his jaw. He pulled his hand back and gaped at the blood staining his fingers.

"Tanon . . ." He lifted his eyes to her. "You—"

"Now you wear the mark of your betrayal so you may never forget it." She backed away, pointing her shaking dagger at him. She felt tears streaming down her face but didn't dare move her fingers to wipe them away. He was too quick and would have her dagger before she had time to blink.

"Get away!" Her teeth clattered, and her heart drummed hard and fast with fear. She took another step back and darted her gaze left and right. Defeat settled over her. She could never outrun him. God help her, she would not be able to hold him off. But she had to try. "I warn you, Madoc. You cannot win. No matter what you do to me, my father will find you."

"Tanon, give me the knife." As he spoke, he moved toward her, cautiously, his arms outstretched at his sides. She swung and missed.

"Madoc!" Cedric's voice boomed through the thick columns of trees. He stepped out from behind one, his eyes blazing at Tanon. "What the hell is going on?"

"She is frightened, Cedric. I've got her," Madoc called back without turning his sharp eyes from Tanon's. They gleamed like smoldering coals an instant before he came at her in a rush of speed that stalled her breath. Before she even had time to react, he sprang to his left and leaped behind her. Coiling one arm around her waist, he snatched the dagger from her fingers with his free hand.

"Non!" Tanon screamed. She struggled against his vise-like hold, but to no avail. Her back was pressed firmly to his chest. "Madoc, *non!*" She began to sob and wilted in his arms. "How could you do this? How could you do this to Gareth?"

Madoc's eyes seared into Cedric's from over Tanon's shoulder, but when he whispered close to her ear, his voice was cool and steady. "You're a lady. Do not tempt him to strike you."

When they reached Gareth's brother, Cedric's hand snaked around Madoc's arm to stop his advance into the camp. "You're bleeding." The look of astonishment on his face matched Madoc's when he'd first felt the sting of his wound. Cedric raised a questioning brow. "No one has ever touched a blade to your flesh but Gareth."

"She caught me unawares. I didn't know she carried a dagger," Madoc answered grimly.

"Nay, she weakens you." Cedric pulled him closer. His low snarl grated against Madoc's ear. "How will you fight Gareth if you cannot even fight his wife?"

Madoc shoved him away with a menacing scowl. "Worry about your part in this, Cedric. I know what needs to be done, and I will do it." He tightened his grip on Tanon and dragged her away.

Tanon didn't speak to him for the rest of the day. When he trotted his horse next to hers, she moved her mount away, preferring to ride near Dafydd's men. At least their hatred for Gareth was open and honest.

When they finally made camp for the night, Madoc spread his pallet close to hers. They both remained silent, staring up at the pinpoint lights strewn across the sky.

"The wound is close to your neck." Tanon finally spoke. "Does it pain you?"

"Nay," Madoc told her, folding his arms behind his head.

"Pity," she sighed and turned over onto her side, away from him. "Next time I will aim lower."

Christ, Madoc thought to himself as he lay in the darkness, Gareth was a fortunate bastard.

Chapter Twenty-Four

⸻

WATCHING THE ADVANCING troop from a well-hidden position within a stand of giant oak, Hereward surveyed the armed soldiers surrounding Tanon as they made their way toward Llandeilo the next morning. Calculating their number to be about twenty strong, he cursed his meager bow. He could take out Cedric and Dafydd easily enough, but not without giving away his position. He could probably kill another five or six men before they reached him, ten if he wasn't so weary from riding for the last few days without sleep. His eyes narrowed on Madoc. Would the commander try to stop him? Hereward ground his teeth together. He'd kill the bastard if he did. And then he would kill Gareth as well and deliver his head to Tanon's father.

At least Tanon appeared unharmed. Hereward said a silent prayer of thanks for that, and for Rebecca, who had revived Ioan by dousing him with a bucket of cold water. It hadn't taken much, just a few threats to skin the steward alive, to get Ioan to talk. What he had told Hereward had turned the Saxon's blood cold.

The tension on Hereward's bow increased as he drew back, ready to let his arrow fly. Something immensely hard slammed into his side, knocking him off balance. The arrow was snatched from his bow as it was released. Momentarily stunned, Hereward looked up at Alwyn, and then at Gareth clutching the arrow in his hand.

"You! You bastard!" Scrambling to his feet, Hereward balled up his fist and swung.

Gareth ducked and stepped backward, easily avoiding the bone-breaking blow. "Cease, Hereward!" he implored, holding up his palms, his fingers still curled around Hereward's arrow. "Hear me!"

"Nay." The burly Saxon came at him again. Gareth sidestepped and looked at Alwyn for aid. Only Alwyn was large enough to keep Hereward still, but when he tried, Hereward knocked him aside as if he weighed nothing at all.

"What would you have me hear, you rogue bastard?" Hereward demanded. "That you put Tanon in jeopardy to stop a war? Aye." He nodded when Gareth cast him a surprised look. "I know everything. Ioan told me what you have done before I put my fists to him a second time." Hereward moved closer to Gareth. "'Twas clever of you to send Madoc to your brother pretending to be his ally after you learned that Cedric had returned to Wales."

Gareth kept sharp, watchful eyes on Hereward as the Saxon began to circle him. "It was the only way to discover Cedric and Dafydd's intentions," he hastily explained. "Dafydd's daughter told me that Cedric had been seen with her father. I had one chance, Hereward. One. To find out what they were planning. If this does not proceed as I've arranged it, I will not know when the next attempt will be on the king's life."

"And if Madoc truly does betray you—"

"He will not."

When Hereward reached for his sword, Gareth shook his head. "Don't make me fight you. Please, my friend."

Hereward lunged at him, lifting his mighty sword over his head. He brought it down with a chopping blow. Gareth sprang to his right. The blade sent dirt flying as it landed in the earth. Gareth spun around and kicked the sword out of Hereward's grasp.

"King William does not want a war, and neither do I." Gareth spoke quickly, praying that Hereward would listen. "If the other princes join forces with Dafydd and Cedric, thousands of lives will be lost."

"Has simply killing Cedric and stopping the attempt on the king's life not occurred to you?"

"Aye, many times." Gareth took a chancy step toward his heaving opponent. "For God's sake, hear me. My brother does not ride alone. King Rhys cannot accuse Dafydd of treachery without proof. To do so would bring the princes of Gwynedd and Powys against him, along with King Gruffydd of the north. We have to bring the proof to my uncle."

"You did not have to bring her!"

"I didn't want to," Gareth insisted, his voice lowering to an anguished whisper. "I had no choice. Cedric believes I know nothing. He must continue believing that until the time is right. She will not be harmed, Hereward. Cedric will do nothing to her until I am dead. And my death is not part of this plan."

Hereward would have laughed at Gareth's arrogance if the young prince didn't sound so convincing. "What's to stop him from killing her and carrying her dead body straight to Rhys's throne and dropping her at his feet?"

"I am," Gareth answered.

"You are here!" Hereward pointed out with a frustrated shout. "A hundred yards away from her. You cannot stop a dagger from here, you fool."

"Cedric wants the throne. To have it, he must kill the king, the king's children, and me," Gareth argued. "He wants that even more than his war. But he knows he cannot fight me without Madoc at his side. He knows it, Hereward. He will not risk losing Madoc's allegiance." When Hereward still didn't look convinced, Gareth continued. "Madoc has my command to kill Cedric if he touches her. We will kill them all if we must. But I set my course to stop Cedric once and for all many months ago, and only if she is harmed will I alter it." Gareth's eyes grew hard with unshakable resolve. "You must not try to stop what Madoc and I have begun. We must bring proof of Prince Dafydd's intent against my uncle. We must stop them from killing the king and his family. If my brother succeeds, he will have the armies of the north behind him and he will decimate the Norman marcher lords first. But war with William will not be fought in England. The Normans will come here, and *my* people will die. I cannot allow that to happen."

"So you risk her life for the people," Hereward threw at him, his voice riddled with resignation to the truth and with disgust.

"I did not want her to be a part of this, Hereward. But she is, and now, even more than before, I cannot steer from my course. I want to give her a future without bloodshed and sorrow, famine and death."

The fierce determination in Gareth's voice was unmovable. Hereward knew he would have to kill him to rescue Tanon. Lowering his head, he muttered a low oath. He really didn't want to kill Gareth. He was fond of the bastard. He also understood all too well the horrors of war. The Normans had killed his brother, a simple farmer, when they had first come to England, setting him on a path of destruction that lasted over a decade. The Risandes' young sister Katherine had also been killed by the Saxons. Innocents died when kings battled. And battle seemed inevitable here, unless Gareth could stop Cedric and Dafydd.

Hereward studied the man in front of him, a prince of the south, who would do anything to keep his people safe from war, even wed a Norman. But he was also the famed Wyfyrn, a warlord who, as of yet, had never lost a single battle. If anyone could stop an army bent on killing a king, it was Gareth. Leave it to a cunning serpent to outwit a jackal.

"Very well." Hereward dusted off his breeches and retrieved his sword. "I'll not stand in your way. Damn me, but you make perfect sense." He drew in a tight breath, knowing he had to be daft to go along with this madness. "Your reputation for finesse does not exceed you. One more question before I place my neck on Lord Risande's chopping block by allowing this. Does she know that Madoc has not deceived you?"

"Nay," Gareth answered, his eyes shadowed with deep regret. "She knows nothing. It's safer for her."

"Aye, it is." Hereward ran his hand over the dark auburn bristles on his chin. A pensive frown creased his thick brows. "Ioan told me that Cedric's attempted assassination would occur when you and your uncle were together. How will that happen if you are here?"

Gareth cast Hereward an impatient look. "You said one question."

"I am not known for being all that truthful," Hereward said with a shrug of his broad shoulders. "I am curious to know why you are hiding in the woods while your king awaits your protection."

Without saying a word, Gareth turned his gaze toward Tanon growing smaller in the distance.

"I see." Hereward sighed. "I was wrong, then. She has come to mean more to you than the peace you seek. Come, then." The Saxon pushed him toward their horses, his beard not quite concealing his faint smile when Gareth nodded. "Let us watch over her together, and when the time comes, I will help you impale some heads on pikes to decorate your courtyard. And may God have mercy on us both if her father ever finds out about this."

Chapter Twenty-Five

A VEIL OF CHARCOAL CLOUDS rolled across the vast swath of sky, dulling the light of a pale crescent moon and darkening the rising hilltop, where Tanon stood with Cedric and the others, with shifting shadows.

"Soon I will rule all of Deheubarth, and then I will defeat the Normans and cross Offa's Dyke."

Tanon looked up at the man standing beside her. Cedric stared at the distant fortress bathed in the illuminating incandescence of thousands of torches. His dark eyes reflected the flickering lights, so that an unholy fire seemed to burn from within them. A tight grin, mirroring his macabre thoughts, snaked over his lips.

"You think to kill King William next and take over England?" Tanon found it difficult to mask her mocking expression. "You forget William's elite commanders, as well as the king's own sons. Rufus is especially unkind to his enemies."

Cedric turned to her and angled his head, his mouth

carved in amused disdain. "Woman, I, too, can be quite unkind, as you will no doubt discover."

She ached to tell him that she already knew he was an uncouth, unkind, brazen barbarian, but she doubted Madoc could stop him again if he tried to strike her. She looked away from his wry smirk instead and returned her gaze to the fortress.

The grand structure was built upon a motte at least thirty feet in height. A wooden tower jutted upward at the fortress's right, both overlooking the high ramparts constructed of wood and sandstone boulders that encircled an enormous bailey below. A palisade of timber planks with sharpened points was hammered into the top of the motte around its perimeter, and another tall timber wall encircled the bailey. Tanon could make out tiny figures moving about along the causeway that gave access to the bailey from the motte, and more men patrolling the land from the walkways behind the palisades.

"However do you hope to get past the king's guards?" Tanon asked.

"They don't expect us." Cedric's smile was laced with arrogance. "They will not even realize we have breached the walls until it is too late. Tomorrow we will dress ourselves as musicians and gain entrance into the town without lifting a sword. My uncle has an affinity for music. If the gods look favorably upon me, we will be taken directly to the king and his regent, kill them and any soldiers who are with them, and leave in the same fashion we entered without anyone knowing we were there. Those *Teulu* we kill will be named heroes for defending their king and losing their lives to the king's assassin."

"And who is the king's assassin?" Tanon asked, staring up at Cedric's strong profile, so much like Gareth's.

He looked at her from the corner of his eye. "Why, Gareth, of course."

Tanon's lips tightened into a thin line. She knew he had told her too much to let her live. He had to know she would never allow Gareth to be blamed for killing King Rhys. She would probably never leave those walls alive once she entered them. Cedric wanted to go to war with the Normans. Killing her would ensure that. Her mind told her that Cedric was a fool for believing he could even strike a blow to her husband. But Cedric had Madoc at his side, and Prince Dafydd. Did all Welsh princes move in battle like Gareth? How skillful was the prince of the north? He'd managed to capture Gareth and imprison him in his dungeon. Could Dafydd fight Gareth and win?

She almost wished her nagging suspicions were correct. If Gareth was aware of this heinous plot, he would be prepared for it. Killing him would be that much more difficult. Of course, if he knew, it would mean that he also knew that Madoc had brought her to Cedric and that Cedric planned to kill her. *Non,* she told herself for the hundredth time. Gareth wouldn't be so willing to let her die. He would never have left her alone with his enemy for almost a se'nnight, not knowing, not caring what became of her. Would he?

"You will not kill him," Tanon said quietly. "And even if you do, King William will never believe that Gareth killed his uncle."

Cedric laughed. "I don't care what William believes. I need the Cymry on my side. When they learn that their beloved prince has murdered their king, they will accept me back into their arms."

"You're mad." Tanon glared up at him.

"Come, it's late." Madoc appeared at her side. He cupped her elbow and pulled her toward him. "I will walk you to your pallet."

Cedric chuckled as they left, then sauntered to Dafydd, who was sharing a drink with two of his men.

"After Madoc gives his testimony to the people that Gareth has killed the king, put your sword to him. He'll not stop me another day from taking that mouthy wench to my bed."

~

"You've been oddly quiet these last few hours." Madoc slowed his steps when they were out of Cedric's earshot.

"I've been busy praying for your death."

Cloaked in darkness, Tanon could not see the rueful smile creasing Madoc's mouth.

"This will soon be over," he promised her softly.

Tanon remained silent, yanking her arm free of his when they reached her pallet. She lay down and closed her eyes, letting him know that she didn't wish to speak with him further.

She thought of her parents, and a pang of need sliced through her while she listened to Madoc settle down for the night next to her. She missed her family desperately. She wished she could have told her mother of the happiness she had found living in this untamed land with its vivid emerald moors. How sad her parents would be when they were told of her death. Her mother's eyes flashed in her mind. Brynna Risande would not be lying here considering her death. She would be thinking of a way to save her husband. Tanon could almost hear her father's strong voice telling her what she needed to do. She was the daughter of a warrior whose name alone brought fear to the hearts of men.

True, he had kept her cocooned within the thick walls of Avarloch, shielded from danger and men, and their wars. But Brand's passion ran deep in her blood. How could she let some foul-mannered exiled prince drag her before the man she loved so she could watch him die? *Non,* she had Risande and Dumont blood flowing through her veins. And she had a husband to protect.

~

Tanon waited until Madoc's snoring grew deep. The muffled roar of thunder in the distance warned of a coming storm. Nervously, she eyed the slumbering traitor, hoping the sound hadn't roused him. She considered hitting him on the head with a good-sized rock, but her strength was such that she'd probably have to strike him more than once, and no matter how much she hated Madoc, she was not about to bludgeon a man in his sleep.

One of Dafydd's soldiers was still awake, but he'd stopped looking in her direction hours ago. He sat across the bonfire with his back to her, probably reveling in the idea of pillaging King Rhys's homestead, Tanon thought angrily.

Inching her way closer to the edge of the surrounding forest, she closed her fingers around a rock, just in case Madoc woke up. She wouldn't strike him while he slept, but if he tried to stop her this time, she would have no choice but to give him a decent crack in the skull. She prayed fervently for him to remain asleep. Without a sound, she crawled into the shadowless web of trees. And then she stood up and ran.

Chapter Twenty-Six

THE AIR TURNED CRISP and damp as the storm drew nearer. Darkness, as complete as the stillness within it, eroded Tanon's fortitude. She shouldn't have left the camp. But only certain death awaited if she'd remained— hers, Gareth's, the villagers', and mayhap ultimately, her family's. If Cedric's campaign succeeded and he brought war to their countries, her father would certainly be called to fight. She couldn't stop. She had to make it to the king's holding and warn him of Cedric's return. She wove her way through the labyrinth of trees, twice banging her knee and scraping her cheekbone on the crusty trunks. She didn't let her bruises stop her, though she paused and clung to a tree when a wolf howled from a direction she could not pinpoint.

Fear robbed her of her breath, but she had to continue. She ran west, toward the trembling torchlight still burning at the fortress.

His arms.

She summoned the memory of Gareth's unyielding

embrace to keep her mind off the terror of being alone in the pitch-black woods. The need in him that tightened his muscles when he drew her in. The longing for her that softened his expression. She had allowed her old fears to make her doubt him, but he cared for her. She was almost certain of it. She had captured his heart without using a single feminine wile. He was everything she had ever dreamed of. He gave her all that her heart desired.

She had to save him.

A crack of lightning sizzled the air and lit her way as the clouds finally tore open above her. Heavy droplets battered the canopy of leaves until at last they gave way and surrendered her to nature's fury.

Swiping the rain and her sopping curls from her eyes, Tanon kept Gareth's face vivid in her mind. She imagined his eyes, painted like a warm indigo sunset ever on her, bathing her in amusement, anger, interest, and affection—all of them raw, unguarded emotions he could not control.

She must save Gareth.

An arrow of light pierced the darkness. His face appeared in front of her seconds before she would have crashed headlong into him.

Her scream shattered in her throat as Gareth's arms came around her.

"Tanon, be still. Don't be afraid." His voice, a rapid whisper laden with remorse, swept across her ear.

"It can't be . . ." Without even thinking about what he was doing here, Tanon lifted her fingers to his wet face and then flung her arms around his neck, convincing herself that he was real. She was safe. They were all safe. "Gareth." She pulled back and looked over her shoulder into the darkness. "Madoc, he . . ." She couldn't bear to tell him how his loyal friend had deceived him. "Cedric rides with Prince Dafydd and they—"

"I know." He wiped her dripping hair from her eyes. "Come, we must leave the forest." His voice rang in her ears, but she heard nothing after his first words.

He knew. He . . . knew.

"Gareth." She recognized Alwyn's voice from the shadows. "We cannot bring her back with us. Let's be off now. Madoc knows his duty. He'll not let harm come to her."

Tanon took a step back as her value to Gareth and to Wales came flooding back to her. She blinked back the stinging tears clouding her vision. She had known why he married her. Fool! She was a fool to have believed she would ever mean anything more to him than a way to secure peace. Still, the blow cut deep.

"I see." It took her a moment to speak, for the relief of finding Gareth here, the joy at being safe in his arms again, was difficult to extinguish.

She didn't protest when he pulled her forward, ignoring Alwyn's muffled oath, and led her toward the fortress.

She did not speak, even after they entered his stronghold and he lifted her in his arms and carried her to the chambers above stairs. She told herself that he hadn't truly betrayed her. She had known her worth to him from the beginning. But the way he had looked at her, the way he kissed her, touched her . . . was none of it real? How easily he had tricked her. But then, he was Wyfyrn, after all. The serpent, whose finesse and stealth—great enough to breach any stronghold, including Winchester, and her father's protection—were known throughout England. The dragon, whose mouth breathed a fire that had consumed her whole. He'd seduced her, mind, body, and heart. How skillfully he'd caressed the part of her she had forgotten existed. The girl who didn't care about the rules of proper etiquette while she played in the pigpen with Petunia. The woman who wanted to love as fiercely as her mother loved her father and who had given up that hope before it became too empty to bear.

She remained still while he kissed her head, whispering across her forehead, her cheekbone, words of thanks that all had not been lost. It seemed, she thought coldly, there was yet a purpose for her to serve. When he left her, at the insistence of Alwyn and Tomas to make haste, for there was much to be done before morn, he did not leave her alone.

Seeing Hereward the Wake was all the betrayal Tanon could endure. She turned her gaze away from his and wept.

Chapter Twenty-Seven

MORNING FOUND TANON slumped in her chair, her ebony curls dotted with grass swept to the floor. Poor girl, Hereward thought, regarding her from across the room. What could he tell her that her heart didn't already know beneath all those layers of pain and anger? Aye, he knew why her sobs lingered on into the morn. Her husband and her friends had joined in a dangerous scheme to outwit their enemy, even at the cost of her life. He sighed at the weight of her sorrow. He was one of her friends.

A knock at the door ushered Hereward to his feet. He looked at Tanon one more time before he allowed entry to one of the king's guards.

"Let no one enter," he charged as he left the room. He would help her understand later. Right now, he had more pressing concerns to tend to.

The troubadours were coming, a bit less confident mayhap now that they no longer possessed the Norman king's promise of peace, but still just as dangerous. Perhaps even more so.

He threaded his way toward the great hall, passing beneath canopied corridors, draped in sheer wool. The fortress was ominously quiet. The vassals who had scurried about at their duties last eve had been sent back to their homes. Guardsmen had been ordered to desert their positions throughout the fortress and stay out of sight unless they were needed.

Hereward peered over the second landing and spotted Gareth sitting at a long trestle table of polished oak, speaking quietly with the king of South Wales.

The Saxon grunted. He didn't care how the Welsh conducted their affairs. He thought it mad that a king would allow himself to appear so vulnerable. Were he Cedric or Dafydd, the absence of the king's royal guard would alert him to danger. But Alwyn had assured him that Rhys often met his vassals in private. He was well loved in the south. That might well have been, but men from the north were coming today.

Scanning the hall from above, Hereward noted the slight flutter of curtains sectioning off two long corridors beneath him. Gareth's *Teulu* were here hidden, waiting.

Would they be enough to stop Cedric and Dafydd's men? Hereward drew his long sword from its sheath and stepped into the shadows. They would have to be.

Moments passed into quarters while Gareth and Rhys's voices drifted up to Hereward's ears. They spoke of Rhys's children, Nest and Gruffydd, safely hidden leagues away. They discussed Tanon, and peace with the Normans, without a thread of anticipation marring the casualty in their tones.

The angered screech of the fortress doors heralded the entry of King Rhys's chief steward, Baddon. Dry rushes cracked beneath his feet as he turned to the two men sitting at the table.

"A traveling band of bards and jugglers begs audience with you, Your Majesty."

"How many?"

"Twenty."

"Send them in."

Hereward flexed his fingers around the hilt of his sword and readied himself for a fight.

~

Gareth watched the entertainers file into the great hall. His brain signaled him to inhale. Breathe, and stop thinking of Tanon. When he'd left her upstairs, he'd accredited her trembling to the elements. She was wet and cold, probably terrified. But the expressionless shield that dulled her eyes alarmed him. She hadn't spoken a word to him. She hadn't looked at him.

He fought the urge to race up the stairs and speak to her, comfort her. Assure her that she was safe now. That she had been safe all along.

Christ, he wanted to hold her so badly.

He inhaled. He had to focus on the situation at hand.

His eyes immediately found and surveyed the three men who concealed their faces beneath hooded mantles. Cedric, Madoc, and Dafydd. The only three he would be able to identify.

Marking their positions, he stood up and stepped around the table.

"Tinkers." His eyes narrowed slightly and snaked his lips into a thin smile. "You have audience with the king, as you desired." He stretched his arms out slightly at his sides as he walked toward them. "Do you need to practice before you can give us a showing of your skill?"

The bard to the far right raised a shaky hand to the hood shadowing his features. Cedric was surprised to find his heart drumming hard in his chest. He'd been certain he could kill his brother without facing the king's army. But now, standing here before him, Rhys at his right side as if he were the prince and Gareth the king, gave Cedric a moment of doubt. It was the gleam of intelligence in Gareth's eyes that slashed through Cedric's self-assurance and compelled him to look toward the doors.

Nay, he could not falter now. It was time for Cymru to make a stand. Peace was earned through war, Cedric reminded himself. Begging a conqueror for it only made Cymru easier to consume.

Summoning his resolve, Cedric pulled the hood back from his face. "*Bore da,* brother."

He wished the Norman bitch hadn't escaped. What satisfaction he could have enjoyed when Gareth saw her with a dagger to her throat. No matter, seeing him would have to be shock enough for Gareth. He watched for the helpless disbelief in his brother's face, but he saw a shadow slip across Gareth's expression instead. Disappointment. Regret. Cedric looked away and flicked his gaze to King Rhys.

"Your reign is over. The new king of Cymru will cower to no one."

"You mean the new king of the *south,* nay?" Gareth quirked his brow and brushed his gaze over Dafydd. "A slip of the tongue, mayhap?"

"You allied yourself with our enemy," Cedric charged his brother before Dafydd had time to consider the insinuation. "Men who now rule our entire eastern border. A privilege won through the massacre of our people. Do you think the Normans will ever truly withdraw from their campaign to conquer us when we've made it so easy for them?"

"Nay, they won't," Gareth answered solemnly, sincerely. "Cymru is divided by its own rulers. A warrior as tactically proficient as King William recognized our weakness long ago. If, as you say, peace, even for a time, can never be found with them, then tell me, where are they now?"

"They will come eventually. Why wait like sheep to the slaughter?" Cedric demanded.

"Why be so eager to stain our soil with more of our people's blood?"

"We must be aggressive in our campaign to wipe them out," Cedric erupted. "We can beat them!"

"We cannot." Gareth shook his head, his eyes fired from his impassioned heart. "The warring between our rulers has weakened us. King William's army is as vast as the sea that divides his two thrones in England and Normandy. But a third of its men were enough to gain the land of the Celts in Sicily. They fight upon horses, Cedric. We do not. They build defenses of stone, impermeable to our meager weapons. We can continue to hold them off until every man in Cymru has died defending his land, leaving the women and children truly at the mercy of the invaders. Or we can hold them off in another way and use this time to teach our people how to avoid becoming their serfs."

"You teach them how to surrender before the fight has even begun, Gareth." Cedric spat as he advanced on his brother. One of the other two hooded men moved forward with him. "You betray every life lost in the war to stop the Normans by making one of them your wife."

"An alliance I made for those who still live, that they might enjoy a better life than one wrought in sorrow and loss," Gareth answered calmly.

"Peace at the price of our people's dignity is cowardly."

Gareth exhaled deeply. "Peace has no price, Cedric."

"It does today." Cedric stepped forward. "You are a usurper, Gareth, an imposter. You cannot lead Cymru, because you are afraid. You always have been. Even when you fight, you run," Cedric accused with a wry smile. "But you will not run today." He gestured to Madoc to reveal himself and seize Gareth. "The rest of my men are just beyond these doors. No one will enter and no one will leave until this is over. Dafydd's army surrounds the entire fortress at this very moment."

Without looking at him, Gareth lifted a finger to Madoc, halting his approach.

"Your men are already dead," he told Cedric. "Prince Dafydd"—he turned and looked directly at the man in the third hooded mantle—"you should know, before your men share the same fate, that the king's army surrounds yours—at this very moment," he added, his expression marked with arrogance. "But we will let them live if you surrender to me now."

Dafydd yanked back his hood and cursed Gareth to the farthest pits of hell.

Cedric felt as if the floor had caved in beneath him. Impossible! His uncle had no time to ready his army. Gareth was bluffing. He and the king would have had to know of his plan all along. Nay, it wasn't possible. His brother couldn't be that clever. How? How could he have known? His gaze shifted to Madoc's dark, inviolable eyes.

Christ, nay!

"Madoc," he commanded, hoping he was wrong, "show this coward what you've come here to do."

With a seemingly effortless tug, Madoc slid his left blade free of its scabbard and swiped it across the belly of one of Dafydd's men. His eyes returned to Cedric, sparked with condescension.

Traitor. Cedric's mouth twisted with fury. His gaze darted around the hall as the rest of Gareth's *Teulu* appeared from behind the curtained walls.

The odds were not in Cedric's favor. He smiled through the choking realization that his plan had failed.

"Brother," he began, supplying himself with time to form a plan that might get him out of this alive. "There need not be any blood spilled here. You never did fancy unnecessary bloodshed, preferring to use your wits, as you've proven here today. Let us sit down at the table and discuss our positions of the welfare of Cymru in a civilized manner."

Now King Rhys stepped around Gareth and spoke directly to Cedric.

The strapping warrior Cedric remembered from his youth had been gone for years now, but the potency in King Rhys's dark gaze remained. The courage of a thousand warriors still etched his countenance.

"Cedric, you plotted to murder my children," the king accused through tightly clenched teeth. "There is nothing civilized in you. And you, prince of the north." His unmerciful gaze raked over Dafydd. "You will be brought before your father, King Gruffydd, with charges of treachery, proven by Prince Gareth."

Dafydd's mouth twitched an instant before he lunged for the king. An instant was all the time Gareth needed.

Tearing two daggers from the belt at his hip, Gareth spun on his feet in a blur that severed four of Dafydd's fingers, two on each hand.

The northern prince gaped at his bloody hands, then blinked at Gareth and let out a wail that echoed off the walls.

The shadow of a behemoth moved down the stairs, sword gripped in both hands.

Hereward the Wake hurled his sword like a javelin halfway across the great hall. It landed with a thud and a twang at Dafydd's feet.

For the space of a breath, no one moved while Hereward's hilt swayed before Dafydd's nose. Cedric used the moment to regain the element of surprise by drawing his dagger and plunging it into the man beside him.

Madoc crumpled forward, and blood spurted from his wound as Cedric withdrew his blade.

Instantly, two of Gareth's men leaped toward the exiled prince. Cedric held them off long enough to hear his brother's stricken curse as he caught Madoc in his arms.

"Gareth, Tanon . . . she . . ." Madoc pressed his hand to the wound in his side.

"She's here, my friend. Safe above stairs," Gareth reassured him as a small battle erupted around them between the two sides. "You've done well."

Cedric's eyes darted to the stairs an instant before he hurled his fist into the man closest to him. He spun on his heel before his brother looked up. He sprinted toward the stairs, avoiding the other fighters. He had to find her. His course was clear, his steps determined. All hope was not lost. The treaty could still be undone. The Normans could still face them in an all-out war. He simply had to kill her.

He made it to the second landing and didn't stop to look behind him. He kicked open every door, his eyes wild with fear and purpose as they scanned each room.

~

Gareth sliced his dagger cleanly across the throat of a colorfully clad troubadour. He looked up to search the melee even before his victim's body sank to the floor. When he didn't find Cedric, his skin paled as he tilted his face to the second landing. He took the stairs two at a time, his hands clenched around the hilts of his daggers.

When he reached Tanon's room, he stopped in midstride, avoiding the dead body of the guard who'd been sent to watch over her. He looked into the room and saw his wife clutched beneath Cedric's arm, the bloody dagger he'd used to stab Madoc positioned at her throat.

"Cedric, nay. Please." Gareth dropped his daggers to the ground and held up his palms.

"The only way to stop the Normans is to kill them." Cedric angled his head and pressed his lips to Tanon's cheek. "Your death will serve a great purpose."

Without a sound—indeed, it appeared with no movement at all—Gareth was upon them. He did not pause to calculate the time it would take Cedric to slice Tanon's throat. He acted instinctively, instantaneously, snatching the dagger from his brother's fingers and ramming it into Cedric's throat a hair's breadth from Tanon's face.

When she felt the splash of blood across her jaw, Tanon looked up into Gareth's eyes, and then she fainted.

Chapter Twenty-Eight

TANON WOKE UP SOMETIME later in a bed only slightly larger than the one in the cottage. This one was far softer, stuffed no doubt with fine goose down instead of straw. She sat up and looked around. When she saw Hereward sitting in a chair across from her, she thought she might have dreamed of Cedric's death. Mayhap she dreamed this entire nightmare.

She drew her hand to her cheek.

"Gareth cleaned you."

Tanon turned away from the pale green eyes she'd known most of her life. "I want to go home."

Hereward regarded her gently. "You speak of Avarloch," he said, knowing where she meant. When she nodded, he continued, "Your home is with Gareth."

"*Non,* it is not." Tanon turned her frosty gaze on him. "Just as your home is no longer in England."

Leaning back in his chair, Hereward folded his arms across his chest and met the betrayal that glazed her eyes head-on. "If that is what William decrees, I will be forever in his debt, as I expect nothing less than his sword."

"Why, Hereward?" Tanon finally confronted him. "Why did you allow me to be—"

"For the same reason he allowed it," the Saxon warrior told her. "For peace. You've never lived in the middle of a war, Tanon. Gareth wants it to remain that way."

"Gareth didn't do this for me!" she argued softly with him, sweeping her fingers across her eyes. "He did it for his people. Just as he married me for them. *Oui*, Hereward, I know his cause is noble indeed, but where is the honor in breaking someone's heart?"

He paused, and then a faint smile drifted across his face. "Mine has been broken many times. But my love for her always granted her my forgiveness."

Tears spilled down Tanon's face upon her hearing of such love—she was happy that Rebecca finally found it. She thought she had found it as well. She could forgive Gareth for putting her in danger. She could not forgive him for betraying the thing she had longed for her whole life. He had lured her out into the open, stripped her of her defenses, and exposed her heart to his thoughtless seduction. But the elusive Wyfyrn had remained untouched. She was cursed to live the same existence Rebecca had suffered for almost twenty years.

A sob drew her shoulders upward before she spoke. "I will never grow accustomed to such an accursed lifestyle, Hereward. I will no longer settle for less than what Gareth is able to give me."

Gareth stepped away from the doorway of the chamber, his heart caught between pounding and stopping. Every muscle in him jolted with the need to go to her, to tell her that he had never loved anyone before her and would never love any woman after her. To plead with her not to go. He would do anything to make her happy.

But she would never grow accustomed to this accursed lifestyle.

Christ, she was right, it was accursed. Cymru was a warring country. It had been so for centuries. Her life would always be difficult here. All he had offered her since he took her from her father was danger. She deserved so much more. And he would see that she got it, even if it meant giving up the peace she brought to his soul.

Clearing his throat, he stepped into his room. He was certain that meeting her gaze would be more difficult than meeting his greatest enemy on the battlefield.

"Gareth!" Alwyn plunged into the chamber directly after him, one beefy arm slung under Madoc's shoulder. Tomas supported his wounded brother on the other side.

"The king has dispatched missives to King Gruffydd. Dafydd will be returned to his father alive, although he will never again wield a sword."

"War has been avoided." Tomas grinned and gave Madoc's shoulder a hefty pat, earning him a death glare from his brother for his effort.

"How do you fare?" Gareth asked his best friend.

Madoc shrugged slightly. "It's a flesh wound. I will live."

Tanon watched the men turn to gather Cian under their arms. She sighed softly with relief at the sight of the young poet. She'd been so worried about him. His errand, it seemed, was to ride here to warn the king. The plan had been so carefully executed.

She felt Gareth's eyes on her like a sorcerer's spell tempting her to look at him. She resisted, fearing that if she did, she would run straight into his arms. She turned her gaze on King Rhys entering the chambers instead.

Up close, the lines creasing the king's skin were deeper, the air of authority around him thicker. Like Tanon's own beloved King William, this man did not need the ornately carved golden torc above his snowy brow or the flaming red mantle draping his shoulders to proclaim his sovereignty.

Tanon dipped her knees and bowed her head before him.

"Lady Tanon, I understand your mother to be a great beauty." His gravelly voice seemed sweet in her ears. "You must share her likeness."

Another snake, Tanon thought. She remembered when the biblical Eve had first recognized one—after she had been seduced by the serpent. King Rhys hadn't simply taught Gareth to dance, then.

"My mother's beauty is unmatched, Your Majesty."

King Rhys smiled at her guileless brow as she straightened. "I understand now why my nephew defied me and wouldn't leave your side these past several nights. No harm came to you, aye?"

Tanon finally slipped her gaze to Gareth. What did the king mean about Gareth not leaving her side?

"Uncle." Gareth's eyes stilled her breath. When he spoke, the controlled determination in his voice warred with the anguish in his gaze. "I request you allow my wife be returned to her family. I intend to travel into the north and bleed out the rest of your enemies. If I live, I will return for her in a few years."

Tanon stared at him as if he had just driven his sword through her chest. She shouldn't have been surprised that he was sending her away. Her use to him was over, and he couldn't wait to be rid of her. She didn't want to care. She didn't want to live with him another day without his love. She had told Hereward that she wanted to go home. But hearing Gareth discard her so easily nearly rocked her to her knees. She fought not to cry. But she wasn't prepared for the pain, and her eyes gleamed with tears.

"What of the peace agreement?" The king's voice echoed in her ears.

"I will remain her husband. Our pact with the Normans will stand as long as she is alive. I wish her to live a long life in England."

The peace agreement. Her worth was no more than a blend of parchment and scribe's ink.

Tanon wanted to scream at his back as he turned and walked out of the room, out of her life without even a farewell. Arrangements were quickly made for her departure from Wales. She could leave as early as tonight, escorted by Hereward and one hundred of King Rhys's own men. When they reached the marches, Hereward would request a Norman escort the rest of the way. The king's men could be back here in time to return home with him.

So simple.

She was going home, just as she wished. A fortnight ago she would have rejoiced. Now she wanted to sink to the floor and weep until the last breath left her body. Either that, or storm after her husband and tell him what a heartless, unfeeling bastard he was.

Never one to let her circumstances defeat her, no matter how terrible they were, Tanon chose the latter.

Chapter Twenty-Nine

WITH CIAN HOT ON HIS HEELS, Gareth strode toward the fortress doors and pushed through them like a plague being set loose upon the earth. Outside, the bailey swarmed with his and King Rhys's men seeing to Dafydd's assembled army. His eyes found their prince, a man twice Gareth's age and twice as thirsty for war. The sight of him sizzled Gareth's blood. He knew he should deny himself the pleasure of killing the bastard, but whatever was left of his control had been vanquished when he asked Rhys to send Tanon home. If Prince Dafydd desired war so badly, Gareth was going to give it to him.

His stride was long, deliberate, as he cut through Dafydd's men and his own, including Alwyn and Tomas. His eyes blazed like twin flames beneath the virulent dip of his brow. He reached his destination and without word or pause in his steps, he clamped his fingers around Dafydd's throat.

"Oh, Christ." Cian unsheathed his blade and set his

back against Gareth's, prepared to keep any of Dafydd's men from attacking his lord from behind.

Almost knocking Dafydd off his feet didn't stop Gareth from dragging him a few more inches. "Is it blood you want?" Gareth bent and growled into Dafydd's face, tightening his grip and cutting off the prince's air.

"Kill me," Dafydd challenged with a choking gasp, "and my father will bring war to the south."

Gareth regarded him with a blood-chilling smile that had evoked the prayers of marcher lords and the men of their garrison before they perished at his hands. "You came here to kill King Rhys. We've proven it. Your father cannot declare war now," Gareth said. "It is only by my uncle's mercy that you live. Though I have made certain your threat of war is over for good, I find the idea of you breathing another day on this earth offensive."

"Pardon me."

Tanon's voice behind him restored something more civilized to Gareth's deadly glare. He blinked and angled his head around to see her. His blood quickened at the sight of her. Christ, how was he ever going to live his life without her in it? Without looking into those clear green eyes and being reminded of innocence in a world of greed, betrayal, and blood?

"I would like a moment of your time." She scowled at him and cast a scolding glance at Dafydd clutched in his hand.

"Right now?" Gareth asked her.

"*Oui.*" She folded her arms across her chest and turned her chin up a notch. "I wish to tell you a few things before I go."

Gareth unclenched his fist, dropping Dafydd to the ground like a sack of wheat. "You have my ear."

The instant he was free, Dafydd tried to scramble away, but Gareth stopped him with a shove from his foot that sent the northern prince reeling back on his rump. "Move again and I'll kill you." He swept his gaze over the men beginning to form a circle around him. "Alwyn, watch him."

Goodness, but her husband looked lethal, Tanon thought. His body was ready to spring as he began to pace before her. Even now, after he'd proven what an unfeeling lout he truly was, his appearance heated her blood.

"I think Cedric was correct about you," she forged ahead. There was no use in recalling how he made her feel so alive. It was all a lie. "You are a coward."

Cian made a sound to her right like someone had just jabbed a blade into his back. Alwyn narrowed his eyes on her and tossed her a disapproving glare.

Gareth halted in his spot. The look on his face made Tanon lift her fingers to her throat and take a step back. He ground his jaw, ready to say something she might not like hearing, so she cut him off. "You're afraid of being touched, of getting caught. You've spent your whole life learning how to avoid it. It controls you," she said with certainty, as though she'd been studying him for years.

"Does it?" he asked her quietly. He had the insane urge to laugh at how wrong she was. It would have been the first time he did the like in a se'nnight.

"*Oui.* It is why you could lie so easily to me."

A long raven curl swept across Tanon's slightly mocking smile. She hooked her pinkie around the strand and pulled it away. She moved so delicately, so femininely.

Gareth's muscles flexed with the very *uncontrollable* need to take her in his arms.

He hadn't told her about Cedric that day when he'd left her at the village because it was safer for her not to know. He hadn't wanted to lie to her. She wasn't supposed to have anything to do with this. "I would not have let harm come to you, Tanon. I lied to keep you safe."

Tanon quirked her brow at him. She wasn't talking about the danger he had put her in. But now that he brought it up . . . "How do you know if I was safe or not, Gareth? You left me alone with—"

"Nay, I didn't. I never left you. I watched over you every day and every night. If my brother had tried to touch you with anything more than his eyes, Madoc would have ended his life. The rest of us were close enough to take Dafydd and his men."

"You were there the whole time, you bastard?" Dafydd accused, listening to the entire conversation. He reached out and gave Gareth a shove with his bloody, bandaged hand.

Gareth pivoted slowly. His stunned expression would have been comical if not for the murderous gleam in his eyes.

"You could have killed us at any time." Dafydd threw his head back and laughed. "You're an even bigger fool than I suspected."

Cian bristled. "Killing you without proof of your intentions to murder King Rhys would have sparked the war we did all this to avoid."

"But"—Tanon's voice dragged Gareth's attention back to her—"you just said that Madoc would have killed

Cedric had he touched me. You and your men would have taken Dafydd. If you had killed them—"

"Aye." Gareth nodded at her, confirming what she was just beginning to understand.

A breeze blew his scent toward her, that wild, musky fragrance that contended with the golden torc of royalty around his neck.

"You would have risked a war for me?" Her voice was soft, her eyes misted with tears. When he nodded, she took a step toward him. "But why?"

Gareth thought it odd that she would ask him such a question. His mouth hooked into a tender smile that warmed his gaze. "Because your value to me goes infinitely beyond peace, Tanon. I would rather live each day at war with you by my side than endure one day of peace without you. But I will not ask it of you."

"And why not?" Tanon practically stomped her foot at him. How dare he convince her of his love and then refuse to let her enjoy it?

He looked around him at the warriors filling his bailey. "Cymru is not where you should live. You deserve a better life than this."

Tanon stared at him. She had always done what others thought was best for her. Every request she granted William and her parents stemmed from love for her, a desire for her well-being. But no one had seen to her well-being the way Gareth had. He had returned to Winchester not as a savage, but as her champion, to save her from marrying Roger and living a meaningless life.

"This is exactly where I should live, Gareth," she told him with conviction strengthening her words. "To the unfamiliar eye, Cymru appears fragile, but she has been loved and nurtured by remarkable people, dedicated men. She will never collapse under any weight. Nor will I." She turned on her heel and began to walk away from him. His hand on her arm stopped her.

"Where do you think you're going?"

"Home." Tanon gazed up into the wonderful emotion in his eyes, the love she had desired her whole life. "I have a wedding to plan with Adara before Hereward changes his mind."

Gareth smiled and hauled her into his arms for a kiss he'd been waiting all week to give her.

Chapter Thirty

LADY ANDREA RISANDE opened her mouth and produced a wail that resonated throughout the halls of Avarloch. Holding her, King William smiled at her pink cheeks and pouting mouth. "A day old and already you sound like your mother." He looked up at the man standing beside him. "You are blessed, *mon ami.*"

Brand took his swaddled daughter from the king's arms and placed a tender kiss atop her cap of wispy auburn hair. "Tell that to my heart, William. Another daughter will surely be the death of me. I'm considering putting Ellie and Anne in a nunnery." He motioned for Elsbeth, who waited by the entrance of his private solar, to come take the babe. "Tell Brynna I'll be in to see her shortly."

"And send for Lady Tanon," William added, moving toward the window. "I've been here an hour already and she has yet to visit me."

When Elsbeth left, Brand turned to have a look at the king. Sunlight puddled around his dusty boots. He folded his hands behind his back and watched the men practicing outside.

"What troubles you?" Brand came to stand at his side.

"*Merde,* am I that easy to read?" William shook his head with mock disdain. "We've been friends for too damn long."

"Much too long," Brand agreed, and then smiled when William glowered at him.

An instant later, the king's features softened. "You are closer to me than my own sons."

"I know."

"It pains me to have to question your daughter."

Now Brand turned to him fully, his smile faded into concern. "About what?"

William stepped away from the window and poured himself a drink. "I received a missive from Chester. Lord Geoffrey Fitzpatrick governs the marches there."

"What does this have to do with Tanon?"

William raised his gaze from his cup before he drank. "He informs me that Prince Dafydd has Gwynedd abuzz with rumors that he lost his fingers to Wyfyrn."

Brand took a step away from the window. He wasn't at all certain he wanted to hear what William was about to tell him. Still, he couldn't help but ask, "So? I put the question to you again. What does this have to do with Tanon?"

"Well." William cast him a dismal look. *Enfer,* he hated having to tell Brand, but he wanted to find out the truth. "If you recall that skirmish Hereward told us about a few months ago . . . the one in Llandeilo when Cedric returned to—"

"To kill King Rhys. *Oui,* I remember," Brand finished for him.

"Hereward told me that Gareth killed Cedric and disabled Dafydd."

Brand's face went pale at the same time his daughter plunged into the solar.

"Do forgive me, William. I was with Mother." Tanon curtsied without pausing on her way to his outstretched arms. Or rather, she attempted a curtsey. Her protruding belly prevented her from bending overmuch.

William almost didn't recognize her. Her long ebony curls tumbled free around her shoulders. Her cheeks were lightly bronzed from the sun. But it wasn't her healthy appearance that struck the king, or even her sure, unhurried steps. Her smile gleamed with a confidence he hadn't seen in her before. Something in the way she angled her head that revealed the inner strength she'd always possessed but concealed behind her dutiful gaze.

She accepted the king's offered hand and rose up on the tips of her bare toes to plant a kiss on his bristly cheek. "Mother insists on getting out of bed. I know this birth was the easiest for her yet, but really, who ever heard of a woman walking about after such a trauma to her body?"

While she spoke, William gazed at her, his heart gone soft with love long ago.

"How do you fare, *ma précieuse?*"

"Oh, wonderfully," she replied with a cheerful smile that made her dimple twinkle. "I've barely been ill at all."

"You're staying here until after the child is born, *oui?*" William asked her.

"*Oui,* but I fear Madoc may end up killing one of Father's knights before then." She slanted her teasing smile to her father and winked at him. "I jest. You know Madoc is as sweet as a newly born lamb."

Brand flicked his gaze back to the window and winced as Madoc flipped one of his guardsmen completely over his shoulder. "*Oui*, a lamb."

"Sit down, *mon amour*." William swept his arm toward the nearest chair. "There's something I need to ask you."

Tanon eyed him curiously, taking the seat he offered.

William paced before her with his hands folded behind his back. Tanon cast her father a bewildered glance, and something in the gentle concern of his gaze made her feel like she was six years old again.

"Tanon."

Her eyes shifted back to William.

He stopped pacing and spread his gray gaze over her. "Do you know the identity of Wyfyrn?"

Her shoulders straightened. She had anticipated this day, worried what she would tell him if he ever asked her. But she wasn't a child anymore. She would not lie to protect what she loved. She would stand up for it in the face of any threat. "*Oui*, I do. He is a man who has sworn to defend his people. As you have."

William's eyes narrowed on her. She didn't blink under his scrutiny but met the power in his gaze with the courage that declared her a Risande. The king smiled.

"I do not involve myself in what takes place on the marches," William reminded her. "I made a peace agreement with Rhys, but I've left the governing of the borderlands to the lords who rule them. I ask you this for the satisfaction of my curiosity only."

Someone knocked at the door. Brand called out for whoever it was to enter.

When Tanon saw her husband, she rose to her feet and went to stand by his side.

"William." She turned back to him after Gareth greeted him with a formal bow. "You told me once that you considered it a noble thing to protect something you love, *oui?*"

"*Oui*, I did."

"Then I ask you now to leave Cymru's champion to his duty of protecting Cymru, and let this matter be ended."

The king studied the couple for a moment that, in Tanon's estimation, lasted an eternity. He glanced at Brand and nodded. "Very well. You may both go."

Sighing a breath of relief, Tanon offered him her most heartfelt smile, then grasped Gareth's hand and turned for the door.

"Gareth," William called out before they left. The Welsh prince stopped and turned to face him. "Prince Dafydd has a loose tongue. You should have killed him instead of just cutting off his fingers."

"Aye," Gareth agreed. "My mercy was wasted on a fool." He smiled with genuine affection for the shrewd Norman king. "Yours, I vow to you, is not."

William watched them leave and then turned to Brand. "Wyfyrn or not, I like that Welshman. Mayhap King Rhys would agree to a union between your babe, Andrea, and his young son, Prince Gruffydd."

Brand tossed him an angelic grin. "I'd kill you first."

William's hearty laughter drifted to the hall outside the solar, where Cian and Madoc stood watching Gareth as he bent to kiss his wife's swollen belly.

> *"The dragon's breath he did impart*
> *Upon the maiden's unsullied heart.*

Whate'er he sought by peace to gain,
The beast the lady's love has slain."

Madoc turned to his younger brother and tossed his arm over his shoulder. "That was quite good," he said, leading Cian toward the great hall for a drink.

"My thanks. I am easily inspired." Cian grinned at him. "I love them both."

Madoc looked over his shoulder and nodded. "Aye, little brother, so do I."

About the Author

PAULA QUINN has been married to her childhood sweetheart for seventeen years. They have three children, a dog, and too many reptiles to count. She lives in New York City and is currently at work on her next novel. Write to her at paula@paulaquinn.com.

"Quinn tells a passionate
and exciting tale."

—RomanceReviewsMag.com

Don't miss her next novel!

Turn the page
for a preview of

Laird of the Mist

AVAILABLE IN MASS MARKET
Fall 2007.

Chapter One

GLENCOE, SCOTLAND, 1658

CALLUM MACGREGOR, clan chieftain of the MacGregors, reined in his mount atop the crest of a hill and watched the small battle taking place in the vale below. His dark brows creased over his eyes as he scanned the men engaged in the melee around the small Campbell holding and those lying dead in the grass. Duncan Campbell was not among them.

"Looks like we've stumbled upon a raid by the McColls," said one of the four men flanking him. "There will be fewer Campbells for us."

"Ya said the Earl of Argyll would be here, Graham." The chieftain cut his gaze to his first in command.

"He's here, Callum," Graham Grant, commander of the Chieftains men, assured him. After pretending to be one of their kin from Breadalbane and living in Kildun Castle for the last three months, Graham knew all there was to know about the Glenorchy Campbells, and the tenth Earl of Argyll. "This is his brother's homestead. Duncan knew naught about it until a few months ago when his nephew, Roderick, appeared in his courtyard. I heard with my own ears the duke preparing to travel here. Look." Graham pointed into the vale at the soldiers. "Campbell's men are here. Mayhap Argyll's hiding in the manor house. I told ya he lacks courage."

"Save fer when he's brandin' MacGregor women," another man said, popping the cork off a leather pouch dangling from his belt.

"Can ya no' go anywhere without yer poison, Angus?"

Angus took a swig, belched, and then swiped his beefy knuckles across his mouth. "Ya know I like killin' Campbells with a bit of old Braden's brew in me, Brodie." He grinned at his cousin stationed beside him. "It fires up me innards."

Callum shook his head when Angus slapped the pouch of brew against his arm, offering his laird to take part. Callum didn't need whiskey to fire his innards. Hating the Campbells was enough. They had taken much from his clan. They had taken everything from him.

"If Argyll is there, the McColls might get to him before we do," Jamie MacGregor, the youngest of Callum's men, pointed out.

"There's a lass fightin' among the men!"

"That's no' a lass, Brodie." Angus guzzled another swig of whiskey. "'Tis a Campbell with mighty long hair."

Brodie flashed his much larger cousin an incredulous scowl. "'Tis a lass, ya dull-witted bastard."

Callum heard the side of Angus's sword smack against Brodie's head, and Brodie's subsequent oaths, before he pounded his fist into Angus's chest. The chieftain ignored his kinsmen and observed the object of their disagreement. The warrior certainly looked like a lass. He'd never seen a lass fight before, though many times he'd wished he had. Glynnis MacGregor's screams still haunted his sleep. He was a lad when Duncan Campbell's father raided his village and his men raped and branded the women. But here was a woman who had the spirit to actually fight to save her life.

" 'Tis a lass," he said, more to himself than to his men, when her mount turned in his direction.

"Aye." Graham nodded, watching lush chestnut curls swing around her shoulders while she deflected another mighty blow. "She tires against the McColls. I know she's a Campbell," he said with a hint of quiet admiration lacing his words, "but it looks like a good enough fight. Shall we aid her, Callum?"

Graham smiled at his friend's slight nod, and then he flicked his reins and took off a moment after Callum kicked his stallion's flanks and raced toward the battle.

Callum cut a straight path to the girl, swiping his claymore through any Campbell in his way. His men fanned out around him, killing the rest. The closer he came to her, the harder he rode. Her arms were weary. She could barely lift her blade to parry the flurry of strikes hammering down on her. He told himself, while he hacked at a McColl riding up behind her, that he was rushing to her aid to keep her alive so that she could tell him Duncan Campbell's whereabouts.

She whirled on him just as he reached her. Callum felt something in his gut jolt at the sight of her. Her skin was smooth alabaster against a spray of dark tightly coiled curls, dampened by exhaustion. Her eyes were as beautiful as black satin, and when she looked up at him, they told Callum she had just lost hope in surviving this day. He didn't expect her to swing at him, looking as defeated as she did. So for an instant, Callum merely gaped at the blood soaking his thigh, and then his eyes smoldered with fury. He lifted his claymore over his head and brought it down hard on another McColl. The lass turned away from the force of his deathblow, but a moment later she returned her gaze to his. Callum responded to the great relief in her expression by wheeling his mount around and calling out to his men to guard her on every side. They shielded her until the only men left in the yard besides them were dead ones.

When Callum turned his mount around to face her again, her sword slipped from her fingers. He glanced at it, then lifted his eyes to hers. "Are ya injured?"

She blinked at him as if coming out of a daze. Her breath still came heavy enough to part her lips.

"Are ya hurt?" he demanded again.

She shook her head nay. "Are you?" She slipped her attention to his thigh, looking remorseful. "My deepest apologies for wounding you. I didn't know who you were, or—"

"Are ya Duncan Campbell's niece?" he interrupted. When she nodded, his eyes hardened on her. "Where is he?"

She looked around at the fallen. "I had hoped he was here. But he must have run off with one of my sheep."

A faint suggestion of amusement swept across Callum's expression before he barked out another order to the four men around her. "Brodie, check the manor house with Angus. If there are any others inside, take care of them, but bring the Campbell out to me."

"Who are you that I may properly thank you for aiding me?"

Callum's gaze swung back to her. She was a delicate creature for all her fire; with petite features, save her huge, wide eyes. Or mayhap 'twas just the reverence she paid him that made them appear so big. Gratitude from a Campbell! As he had never saved the life of one before, he had no idea how to react to her awe. He shifted again, feeling damned uncomfortable and blaming her for it.

"I am Callum MacGregor." Best to get it over with sooner rather than later, though a part of him regretted having to watch that veneration turn to hatred. Her face paled to such a milky white, he thought she might faint dead away and tumble from her horse.

His eyes were usually very quick, and on any other day he would never have missed an enemy reaching for a weapon. But for an instant her beauty made him forget about fighting and hatred, and blood. An instant was all it took for her to slip her hand beneath her belt and retrieve a small dagger she had hidden there.

The glimmer of surprise that sparked his eyes belied his cold, impassive voice. "Ya have courage to point yer dagger at me." He moved in a blur of speed, yanking her from her horse to his. Pressing her to his chest, he closed his arms around her, pinning her dagger securely behind her back. "Ya insult the laird of the clan MacGregor with such a meager weapon, lass."

"Let me go, vermin!" she hurled at him, and spent the remainder of her energy kicking and wriggling, trying to free herself. "Let me go if you be a man, and let me fight you with my sword."

Callum glanced at Graham, mirroring the commander's expression of admiration at her furious promise. She was a fiery, braw lass, something all Highlanders valued. But she was a Campbell, Callum reminded himself, grinding his jaw.

"Is Argyll in the house?" he asked her, barely straining a muscle against her attempts to be free of him.

"I don't know where he is, but when you find him, take him to hell with you!"

Aye, now this was more like the reaction he expected from a Campbell. "Graham, get me some rope. The wench tires me."

Her fight came to an abrupt halt. She glared up at him. "Will you rape me, then?"

"Would ya like me to?" he offered in a quiet voice. His gaze fell to her lips for a brief instant, then drifted over the rest of her body in a leisurely inspection of her feminine aspects.

"I would cut off your—"

Callum saw one of her uncle's men exit from behind the house, cocked bow in hand. He had no time to shield her as the arrow whistled toward them and penetrated her right shoulder, just above her breast. Though it happened within the space of a breath, he watched it pierce her perfect form, watched the breathtaking spark of life grow dull in her eyes. As Graham raced toward the guardsman, Callum's eyes met hers again when she realized she'd been hit.

"Oh, hell." Her breath was a ragged whisper, sweet against his chin. "I think that was meant for you."

THE DISH

Where authors give you the inside scoop!

♥ ♥ ♥ ♥ ♥ ♥ ♥ ♥ ♥ ♥ ♥

*From the desks of Shari Anton
and Paula Quinn*

Dear Readers:

From intimate visions to dancing warriors to King Arthur, Shari Anton and Paula Quinn dish in this author-to-author interview.

Shari Anton: Paula, how nice to see your **LORD OF SEDUCTION** (on sale now) on the bookstore shelves with my **TWILIGHT MAGIC** (on sale now) this December! Double the medieval fun! You really must tell me about your story.

Paula Quinn: Well, Shari, Tanon Risande is a prim and proper lady of the realm. Her predictable little world is turned upside down with the arrival of a fierce Welsh prince, Gareth ab Owain, who has come to claim her as his bride. Tanon has no intention of submitting to such a rough warrior, but Gareth is determined to prove to her that he is no savage. He will use far more persuasive methods to lure this lady willingly into his arms . . . and into his bed.

Is your couple as seemingly mismatched as mine?

Shari Anton: Of course! Lady Emma de Leon is about to present a petition to King Stephen when Darian of Bruges is accused of murder. She recognizes Darian as the man she once saw in a very intimate vision, so she's compelled to save him by giving him an alibi, claiming they spent the previous night together. The king then insists they marry. Emma had planned on the bedding, but not the wedding, especially to an ungrateful Flemish mercenary who wants no wife! The last thing Darian wants is to be the man of Emma's dreams, but ignoring Emma's charms and rebuffing her advances prove futile.

Prince Gareth sounds like a true **LORD OF SEDUCTION**! What aspect of him will intrigue readers most?

Paula Quinn: My favorite thing about Gareth is that he learned to fight by dancing. Yes, this warrior dances like nobody's business! I also love that he goes barefoot and wears torcs. There's something very feral about it. He's extremely confident without being arrogant (although Tanon would disagree).

You've added a paranormal element to **TWILIGHT MAGIC**. How fascinating that Emma has visions!

Shari Anton: Poor Emma doesn't like having them. Lucky for my story Emma saw Darian in a vision before she learned how to halt them! And scattered throughout my Magic trilogy is the legend of King Arthur.

So between us we have Norman ladies, a Welsh prince, a Flemish mercenary, torcs and dancing, visions and intrigue. Wow! I'd say Warner Forever readers are in for a real treat this month.

Paula Quinn: Agreed!

Sincerely,

Shari Anton   *Paula Quinn*

TWILIGHT MAGIC   LORD OF SEDUCTION
www.sharianton.com   www.paulaquinn.com